A Killer for the Chairman

Other books by Mark Hebden

THE EYEWITNESS

THE ERRANT KNIGHTS

GRAVE JOURNEY

MASK OF VIOLENCE

MARK HEBDEN

A Killer for the Chairman

Harcourt Brace Jovanovich, Inc., New York

First American edition
ISBN 0-15-146985-7
Library of Congress Catalog Card Number: 78-174510
Printed in the United States of America

One

I

Esmond's place was in one of the less expensive areas of Hong Kong, in an old set of offices which still, in spite of the influx of concrete and air-conditioning, maintained a shabby Edwardian façade, even to the creaking lift with clashing grilles, rosewood panelling and slow-moving fans in every room.

In spite of its age, however, it had been built for comfort, and Esmond's room was light and airy and there was a balcony which gave him a panoramic view of the roof-tops of Wanchai and the skyscrapers of Hong Kong and the Peak. Across the blue water of the harbour, which was covered with ships of every kind, was the waterfront of Kowloon with a view of the bare hills of the mainland, stretching across like the backdrop from a film with colours worked by Gauguin.

I'd always thought Hong Kong staggeringly beautiful, with its mountains running down to the water and the green coves full of sand. The junks—poops and prows like pagodas and ancient sails like dragonfly wings—and the myths of the 'perfumed isle' were only part of the picture, though; because there were radar masts on the heights, too, and not just for the airliners coming in from the West, either.

All that breath-taking beauty was just a colourful curtain that hid the menace that lay on the other side. Any time they wished, the Chinese could descend from the mainland and snatch Hong Kong back. Any time at all.

As it was, however, it suited them to allow it to remain in being: a strange foreign colony on their doorstep, where everything about it was Chinese, even its background and customs, despite all the Westernisation that generations of British had stuffed into the place.

It was a useful little outlet for Chinese goods—frozen rabbits and things of that sort that cost nothing to produce but brought in a fair amount of Western currency to build up the new and noble China—and it was also a useful little channel for trade in gold, the narcotics that had begun to trouble the West so much, strategic materials, rumours, information—and agents. I'd often wondered how many of the new Chinese restaurants that had spread like a rash across England contained young men who'd received their instructions in Peking and had passed through Hong Kong, arriving at the border as refugees, whimpering to be let in, and weeping, singing, laughing, dancing when they were. I often wondered how many of those who appeared out of the darkness in sampans they said they'd stolen had been provided with them by the Party, together with a story that would hold up under the scrutiny of the interrogators in Hong Kong.

Nobody in the colony kidded themselves that they were there with anything else but the full permission of the Chinese on the mainland. And somehow, while it didn't exactly stop you sleeping at nights, didn't stop you eating, drinking and making a pass at someone else's wife, it never quite left you, either. It was a bit like the Bomb. It was always there. You didn't think of it most of the time but, when you did, it was enough to give you the heebie-jeebies just considering the possibilities.

Perhaps it was as well that Esmond could see it all the time. It helped to keep him on his toes.

The old soldier outside the door didn't know me. He'd been in Hong Kong when it had fallen to the Japanese and since he had no love for Asiatics, he didn't much like the look of my face. Thanks to the Manchu girl who'd left Peking in a hurry with my grandfather seventy-odd years before, it had the look of a high-bred Chinese about it if you searched for it. My eyes weren't slanted or anything like that but my skin was pale and ivory and my hair was as black as any Party comrade's. It was enough to make the soldier officious.

'You have an appointment, sir?' he asked.

'I don't suppose so,' I said.

His manner changed abruptly. 'You can't go in there then, son,' he said firmly. There was condescension in his tone but it didn't put me off.

'I think I can,' I retorted, equally firmly and equally condescendingly. 'And don't call me "son." '

He looked a little uncertain. 'He's too busy to see anybody.'

'I don't think he'll be too busy to see me, sweetheart.'

His frown deepened with suspicion, but he was obviously a little put out by my confidence and aggressive cheerfulness. 'Okay,' he said grudgingly. 'I'll try if you like.'

'You don't have to,' I said. 'It's not necessary.'

He tried another tack. 'Who shall I say's calling?'

'I shouldn't bother to say anything. No one ever does. I'll go straight in. But, if it'll set your mind at rest, the name's Dempsey.'

His expression changed at once. 'Well, fancy.' He grinned. 'First time I've met you. Heard of you, of course. Always thought you were older, though. Bigger, and more meat on you.'

'It's the late nights,' I said.

As I opened the door it pushed against someone on the other side and I realised it was Esmond who'd been leaning against it.

He moved his eyes in a sidelong warning glance and I saw his desk was occupied. It was Dwight. Large as life and looking as though he'd just stepped out of the pages of Debrett. I'd thought he was in England, but Dwight never surprised me when he appeared unexpectedly like this. It was a habit of his.

The message I'd received had made no mention of him but it had obviously been urgent. I guessed now that Dwight had been somewhere in the area and had showed up unexpectedly to take over whatever it was that had gone wrong.

He was sitting in Esmond's chair—almost at attention, I thought—listening to the telephone and reading a bulky file. He looked up as I appeared and, without speaking, tossed a packet of cigarettes across and motioned me to a chair at the other side of the desk. Esmond hooked it forward with his foot, saying nothing, and there was something about his face—a taut strained look—which warned me that Dwight was making one of his periodical checks. For some time, Dwight went on reading and holding the telephone to his ear, then at last—probably half a cigarette later—he nodded.

'You've been at it long enough,' he said into the telephone. There was a pause while whoever it was at the other end made his excuses for whatever it was he'd taken too long to do, and Dwight stared at the instrument for a second as though something white and ugly with half a dozen legs had crawled out of it.

Then he jammed it to his ear again and spoke in those icy tones he kept specially for inquisitive politicians, rude cabdrivers and inefficient subordinates. 'You've been at it for nearly twenty-four hours,' he snapped. He listened again. 'And don't keep calling me "Esmond." This is Dwight speaking.'

That seemed to bring the speaker to his senses sharply and for a long time Dwight merely listened without comment, as though he were suddenly beginning to receive the report loud and clear.

'Lucas,' Esmond breathed into my ear.

'Poor bastard,' I breathed back. Lucas was not a smooth operator and the very presence of Dwight in Hong Kong would be enough to give him the willies.

Clearly he was already nervous. Dwight always made everyone nervous with that chilly, precise manner of his. Everyone except me. I was too young to get nervous and I knew I could do the job better than anyone else.

You had nothing to worry about so long as you made sure your escape route was always open. Always look for the exit before you settle down, then, when things get sticky, do a bunk. Quick. In the meantime, enjoy yourself. When the drink was there at someone else's expense—particularly the government's—don't stop at one, have two or three. When they were paying for the cigars, don't take one, fill your pocket. When there was a willing girl involved, don't shy at her like a frightened stag, indulge in a little gracious fornicating. So long as there was a thick carpet and a canopied bed and a bucketful of champagne in the fireplace. The perks were the only things that made the job worthwhile. It was a cynical middle-aged attitude for a man my age but I'd developed a cynical middle-aged attitude. It went with the job, somehow.

'What the hell's going on?' I asked, and Esmond was just opening his mouth to tell me when Dwight looked up and his face froze.

'How long have they given her?' he asked into the telephone.

The voice at the other end clattered away and Dwight's eyes narrowed. 'As close as that?' he said unemotionally. 'Very well then, listen to anything she might say and let me know. And next time, don't mess around. Use your imagination. It's creaking like an old pair of corsets.'

Good old Dwight, I thought. If you've anything unpleasant to say, say it unpleasantly.

Dwight put down the receiver and stared at the desk. 'That man,' he said coldly, 'is as coy with me as an unmarried mother. I'll have to do something about him.'

That's it for Lucas, I thought. He'd got the skids under him.

Dwight closed the file he'd been reading and sat for a moment with his fingers entwined, staring blankly into space. Nobody said a word.

At last, life seemed to come into his pale blue eyes and he stared directly at me. Click. He was switched on. Dwight always liked a second or two to clear his mind so that he could rid it of all the cluttering details.

'Dempsey,' he said. 'It took you long enough to get here.' It seemed we were all a bit slow that morning.

'I was at Kowloon,' I said. 'I wasn't on duty.'

'Pity you couldn't let us know where you'd be.'

'It isn't always convenient.'

He stared at me for a second, and his brows came down, so that he looked exactly the ex-Guardee he was: smooth-faced, eyes like blue marbles, immaculate in a white shirt and a linen suit that had not been made in Hong Kong. For a second there seemed to be interest in his eyes.

'What was her name *this* time?' he asked dryly.

I ignored the question and he pushed the file about on the desk a little. Then he looked at Esmond.

'What's the latest from your end?'

'They were too late to stop him,' Esmond said, and I wondered again what the hell was going on. 'He'd already passed through the barrier. Nothing we can do about it now.'

'Isn't there?' Dwight said. 'Isn't there indeed?' His gaze swung to me and he stared at the shabby suit I wore. 'I'd have thought you'd need something lighter than that out here,' he commented, apropos of nothing. 'You only need a trench coat and you'd look like an I.R.A. officer. Or one of these woolly do-gooders that arrive here in droves to make sure we aren't forgetting that the wogs are more equal than we are.'

Good old Dwight, I thought. Never one to mince words.

'Maybe if they paid me more,' I said, 'I might dress better. Even a bowler, umbrella and striped pants. London rig.'

He looked down his long nose at me. 'I manage to conform,' he said icily. 'Without being *too* conventional.'

I smiled back at him. Though I'd never have dared to tell him so, I had a curious affection for Dwight. He was a genuine eccentric. Expert rose-grower. Japanese print-collector. Writer of scholarly histories. God knows how he'd managed to rise in the closed-shop, upper-crust atmosphere of the Guards. But he had. *And* collected a D.S.O. and an M.C. and, into the bargain, somehow managed to look as though he had. I liked him as much as anyone my age could like anyone his age. He fitted the part perfectly. What was more, he never slipped, so that people tended to class him with all the other officers who'd been his friends, men who'd now retired after unsuccessful army careers to equally unsuccessful business careers. There were dozens of them in Hong Kong, and nobody ever took Dwight seriously. Which was just as well, considering the business he conducted in his suite of shabby offices in London.

He looked up, languid and bored, his face still blank.

'How are you, Dempsey? Keeping fit?'

'Not very,' I said. I was as fit as I could be but I could never resist tormenting him. He wasn't blessed with a marked sense of humour.

He frowned slightly, knowing I was trying to be funny and not very pleased about it. He always disapproved of flippancy.

'You should be,' he said. 'It's necessary in this job.'

I shrugged. 'I'm not so sure. Take Armour, for instance. He worries so much about keeping fit, he gives himself stomach ulcers. It isn't the job that gets him down, it's keeping fit for it.'

'Armour's a good man.'

'Not as good as me.'

Dwight allowed himself the faint chilly smile that was his version of a friendly grin. 'No,' he agreed. 'Not as good as you. All the same, if you ever felt like it, you could use the gymnasium at Esmond's club. Chap your age oughtn't to let himself get soft. Esmond would arrange it for you, I'm sure.'

'Did *you* ever use a gymnasium? At my age?'

Dwight stared at his fingernails for a moment. 'No,' he said.

I sat back and knocked the ash off my cigarette. 'You always seemed to get by all right from what I've heard.'

For a second Dwight was silent, and I crushed out the cigarette. 'You've got a job for me, haven't you?' I asked. I knew the drill.

Dwight looked up, as though he was startled that I'd guessed. 'Yes, I have. Nothing much.'

I frowned. I'd come across Dwight's 'nothing much' on previous occasions.

'I've only just got back,' I said.

'Saigon, wasn't it?'

'Yes.'

'Hm.' He permitted himself a little smile. 'Just the man I want. The way you look. Everything. Your Manchu blood.'

He never called it simply 'Chinese.' Dwight was high-class himself and he liked the things that surrounded him to be high-class. He'd have liked my grandfather. He'd been as big a snob as Dwight was. Not for him one of the little tarts he could have picked up so easily on the Shanghai waterfront. Not even the daughter of a wealthy merchant. My grandmother had to be the youngest and most beautiful daughter of a noble from the court of the Empress, so important they'd had to dash for the shelter of a British gunboat with a whole horde of pigtailed soldiers after them flourishing swords and muzzle-loading rifles. For all I knew, the incident probably helped to start the Boxer Rebellion.

She'd died twelve years before and I could remember her only as a little old woman with grey hair, delicate hands and a joyous sense of humour. But my grandfather had adored her and she had made my background high-class enough for there never to be any trouble for me, not even in the snotty white clubs they ran in Hong Kong. Although I could have passed for a Latin any time—and often did—I didn't really have to bother because it seemed to be common knowledge in Hong Kong who my grandmother had been.

'It's nice,' I said sarcastically, 'to know that I don't look like something you pick up cheap at Marks & Spencers.'

I was feeling a bit resentful by this time. Actually, I'd not been with a girl when the telephone had rung. But it was a story I always liked to let them believe. It was always a good excuse for deliberate dilatoriness or for unexpected disappearances when people were expecting you. Always keep your exit clear. Even with Dwight. I wasn't a desk operator like Esmond and I liked to feel free. As a matter of fact, I'd been doing nothing more than cooking and singing to the dog in the kitchen of my flat when the telephone had rung. If a dog could look disgusted, my dog was looking disgusted at that moment, because I was no singer and what I lacked in skill I liked to make up in noise. But I was glad to be home and feeling gay. I was enjoying the singing even if the dog wasn't.

The ringing of the bell had jarred, and I had stared at the door towards the hall where the telephone was situated, all desire to sing suddenly gone. I'd known exactly who it would be. Nobody else knew I was there. Nobody else knew I was home, except the kennel where I always left the dog.

The telephone had rung first in the early hours and I'd ignored it, and it had gone on ringing at intervals throughout the morning. This time I'd known I'd have to answer it.

'God damn,' I'd said with bitter feeling. 'Another job.'

I hadn't enjoyed the last one in Saigon. I hadn't enjoyed working with the Americans. Not because of them personally—mainly I liked them—but simply because they always had more than I had and it made me faintly humiliated. It was simply bloody-minded resentment, that was all. What was more, it hadn't been just the Americans who'd had me worried. The opposition had caught on to me. Which was why I was back in Hong Kong early and expecting to take a rest. I'd been looking forward to a few weeks on my own, getting over it.

And here was the bloody telephone going already!

I'd waited a while, hoping it would stop. But it hadn't. They knew I was home. Probably the janitor worked for them. He was a nasty old bastard and I spent all my time dodging him, just in case, but I expect he had his own ways of finding out whether I was in or not: probably listening from the flat below or watching the electricity or something. Big Brother always knew in the end when I was home, and when Big Brother knew he didn't ring off in a hurry. If I hadn't answered the phone, Big Brother would have sent someone like Esmond or Lucas round to fetch me.

Finally I'd gone into the hall and picked up the receiver. The man at the other end of the line had been Esmond. I'd expected that.

'Better come over,' he'd said simply.

'Do I have to?' I'd asked, making the resentment in my voice clear.

'Yes,' he'd said. 'You do.'

I'd frowned. I knew I'd turn up. I'd always turned up. They'd always been in the position merely to crook their little fingers at me and make me.

'Right,' I said. 'When?'

'Now!'

'Christ, man!'

But Esmond had rung off without saying goodbye and I'd put the telephone down slowly, pausing for a while with my hand on the receiver. Then I'd walked back into the kitchen, and the dog had looked up at me, grinning.

'Sorry, cock,' I'd said. 'Back to the kennel.'

The dog's rear end had wagged and I'd sighed. I was very fond of the little blighter and it always hurt me to see him disappear. Fortunately, he was happy enough and, in fact, regarded the kennel as his second home. Yeh Yang didn't stick him in a cage like the others, but let him live with his family in the house. They knew I was often away for long periods and it was a special concession.

They thought I was a newspaperman—chiefly because Esmond's office had *Far Eastern News Agency* on the door.

I stared back at Dwight now, still not quite over my resentment. 'Okay,' I said. 'What's it all about? Am I going to China, for God's sake?'

I was being sarcastic, but Dwight didn't turn a hair.

'Looks like it,' he said.

It shook me. 'I *am*? Jesus! Why?'

He leaned back in his chair, fiddling with his pipe and looking like the aide-de-camp to end all aides-de-camp to the governor-general to end all governors-general. It was a habit of Dwight's when he was giving his instructions. I don't know how he did it. He just seemed to stiffen all over, and his face became blanker than ever. At that moment he was the Great Unapproachable. Sea-Green Incorruptible. Three tiers higher in the social scale than everybody else—even me, to whose impeccable background he occasionally dropped on one knee.

'Remember Mitchill?' he asked.

'Yes, I remember Mitchill. Nice chap. I—er—took his daughter around for a while. He had a rough time when Mao's crowd kicked out Chiang Kai-shek.'

Dwight's eyes were expressionless. 'What else do you know about him?'

I lit a cigarette and considered. 'Charles Edward Macey Mitchill,' I said. 'Fifty-two. Seven foot high and built like a cart horse.'

'Don't be stupid,' Dwight snapped.

I grinned. 'Six-foot-two. Heavyweight. Married a daughter of Brigadier Hollis. One son still at school. One daughter, Amy—of blessed memory—now married to a doctor in Manchester.'

Dwight tapped with his finger on the desk. 'It's Mitchill I want. Not his relations.'

I stared back at him, irritated in spite of the fact that I knew it was only Dwight's mind trying to keep things uncluttered. He always said he had a lot of things to think about and liked to avoid unnecessary details. All the same, I couldn't help wondering what it was all about. Ten to one he had all the information he needed on Mitchill in his bulky files. We were *all* there—everybody who'd ever worked for him.

'Sinologist,' I said. 'Adviser to the Foreign Office. In an unofficial under-the-counter capacity. One of his jobs was to make sure all our agents were evacuated when the People's Liberation Army came through and pushed Chiang Kai-shek over to Formosa. He was beaten up by Red soldiers. I think the bastards must have disliked him because he was so big and they worked him over—but good. There was a lot of misery at the time and I gather Mitchill let it get him down more than it ought. At least, more than *I* think it ought. It was his job *not* to be upset by things like that.'

'You were in Hanoi during the bombing,' Dwight said. 'Were *you* upset?'

'I suppose so.'

'I never saw you weep much.'

'I don't weep.'

'I saw Mitchill weeping in Shanghai.'

'I suppose, big as he is, he's a bit more emotional than me.'

'We haven't room for emotion.'

'I suppose not.'

Dwight studied his fingers for a moment, then he spoke bluntly. 'He's unbalanced,' he said.

I sat up. 'Mitchill? Unbalanced?'

I glanced at Esmond but he refused to meet my eyes and went on standing by the door, trying to look uninvolved.

Dwight shrugged. 'I've been wondering about him for some time. But you know how it is. This dim civil service mind we have to get round. Mustn't act without good reason. Mustn't get rid of a chap who's due for a pension. I was thinking about bringing him to London, where he'd be safe, but nobody would listen to me. They said I was talking through my hat. They left him where he was. Hong Kong. Singapore. Burma. Indo-China. He knows that part of the world, they told me. He knows all our people. He's a good man.'

'He certainly knew his stuff,' I said.

'In this game knowing your stuff isn't enough. I've been working for some time to get him home. The excuse had to be good, though, and I had to waste a lot of time looking for it. The office in London was all for Mitchill. Thank God I put in my objection.'

'Why?'

Dwight shrugged again. 'I told you, he's unbalanced.'

'And has he toppled over or something?'

Dwight nodded. 'Tell him, Esmond.'

'He attacked his wife,' Esmond said automatically.

I was still feeling a bit flippant. 'He's not the first to feel a bit stroppy with the missus. Especially out here. I think it's the heat.'

Dwight glanced at Esmond again and Esmond frowned. 'It wasn't that kind of attack,' he said. 'He went for her with a gun.'

'A service revolver to be exact. He shot her with it. Several times.'

The remarks Dwight had been making on the telephone were beginning to make sense. I indicated the instrument. 'Is that what you were on about on that thing?'

Dwight nodded.

'But, hell, I got the impression from what you said that she was . . . well, you said "How long have they given her?" It sounded as though she were dying.'

'She is.'

'Good God! He must have gone round the bend.'

Dwight looked irritated. 'That's what I've been trying to tell you ever since you came in,' he snapped.

I gestured at the telephone again. 'But you were speaking to Lucas,' I said. 'Lucas is here in Hong Kong. Is Mitchill in Hong Kong?'

Dwight nodded again. 'He *was*.'

'I never knew.'

Dwight's face stiffened. 'You don't have to know everything,' he said. 'Officially, he was back here as a tourist. His wife was with him.'

'Why did he do it?'

'She was born in Hong Kong. One of you. About one-sixteenth Chinese.'

'I never knew. She didn't look it and Amy's got green eyes and fair hair.'

'Not many people did know,' Dwight said. 'But *I* knew. I found out.'

'Is that why he attacked her? Because she was part Chinese?'

'So she says. She's in hospital now. They've given her two or three hours to live. That's all. As you said, he's gone round the bend.'

'Christ!' I whistled. 'What direction has he taken?'

'It seems he dislikes the Chinese so much he just wants to destroy them.'

'But—but I thought China was his life's work! He was an expert on it.'

'That's so.' Dwight's face was smooth.

I looked at Esmond. There seemed to be more to it than appeared on the surface. 'Did you expect something like this?'

Esmond spoke quickly in self-defence. 'Why should we have?' he said. 'He seemed all right. And his wife never told us anything about what he felt. She didn't know herself. Not properly. She just thought he was what he appeared to be. A China specialist at the Foreign Office.' He looked in appeal at Dwight. '*I* didn't know,' he said.

'Of course not,' Dwight said. 'Nobody did. I was having him screened.'

'Did you find anything?' I asked.

'Quite a lot.'

'What, for instance?'

Dwight blinked at me. 'Well, for a start, he didn't like you.'

I tried to be flippant again, though I wasn't feeling like

it any more. I'd known Mitchill's wife well in the days when I'd chased Amy.

'That's nothing to hold against a man. Not many people do.'

'I'm quite aware of that,' Dwight said. 'But it was the reason that was interesting.'

'Amy?'

'No. It was your grandmother he objected to.'

'My grandmother!'

'She was a Manchu. Chinese.'

'Didn't he ever like the Chinese?'

'It seems not. I dug up a story about him beating up a boy at school. Chap called Kay. Imagine my surprise when I found Kay's name wasn't John Willie Kay or Clarence Kay or Thomas James Kay but Kay Huai Chung. The son of a Chinese merchant banker sent to England to be educated.'

'It's beginning to jell.'

'I thought it might. Kay. His wife. You. His father, too.'

'His father?'

'He was a China specialist, also. Seems he neglected Mitchill a bit as a child. Always in China. Mitchill resented it. Must have built up something against the Chinese.'

'Why the hell did he make China his own work then?'

'Why do doctors' sons become doctors? And dentists' sons dentists? Because it's the easiest thing to do. They grow up with it. They know what they're talking about before they even start studying. I expect it was the same with Mitchill. Might even have thought that he could use his knowledge to pay a few scores back.'

I thought for a moment, then I looked up at Dwight again.

'Is this all?'

Dwight pursed his lips. 'Not really. He seems to have been rather prone to fighting at school. I got a report from his old housemaster. One foot in the grave now but he remembered Mitchill all right. Quick-tempered, he said. Uncontrollable. Bit of a bully. During the war he was severely reprimanded and lost six months' seniority as an officer for striking a sergeant.'

'Quite a history of fisticuffs. Didn't we know about this?'

'No. He kept it pretty well in control most of the time, it seems, and until we dug up Kay, the sergeant, and now his wife, it didn't matter much.' Dwight frowned. 'Except that those fools in London should have guessed he was too bloody quick on the draw for this department.'

I was trying to work it all out. Even now it didn't seem enough.

'There's still nothing to pick on, though,' I said. 'Nothing to suggest that he's completely crazy.'

Dwight tapped the desk. 'No. I quite agree. There wasn't anything really. Not until a few days ago. Then I found something and I was on my way here to make sure he didn't do anything stupid.' He indicated a telegram on the desk in front of him. 'We found out his grandfather died in a mental home. This is the confirmation. Unfortunately it came too late, and I arrived after it was all over.'

I glanced at Esmond and again he tried to look as though it were nothing to do with him.

Dwight looked at the file on the desk and I saw now that it had Mitchill's name on it.

'Naturally, I was keeping my enquiries to myself,' he went on. 'His daughter doesn't know. Neither does his son. No need to let them start worrying. No need to give 'em sleepless nights in case they think they're going nuts, too. They probably aren't. Mitchill's father was normal enough —if you accept his obsession with China. But that's how heredity works, isn't it? Sometimes it misses a generation. We found out about it from an ancient great-aunt of his who lives in Brighton. Old dear with a face like a horse. I had someone persuade her to talk. She knew about his grandfather because she once had to fight him off herself. It was all hushed up, of course, and probably even Mitchill didn't know because the family seems to have kept it dark. But she knew, because she was involved.'

'Jesus!'

'Nice commentary on our screening system, isn't it?' Dwight observed. 'I never did think we went back far enough. Is he a queer? Is he in debt? Does he go with women? Ever belonged to the Communist Party? Never did seem enough to me. There are more things that cause a man to deviate than just those. Here's one—a grandfather who had a habit of chasing his relations with a poker.'

I frowned. 'And Mitchill? Did he ever set about his relations before?—as well as these kids at school?'

'So we learn now.'

'From his wife?'

'Yes. Now there's nothing to be lost by admitting it, she's willing to talk about it. It seems this isn't the first time it's happened.'

Now that we'd mentioned it, I, too, could also remember times when I'd called for Amy and she'd appeared on the verge of tears but had resolutely refused to say what was troubling her, and times when her mother had been said to be in bed with some sort of nebulous illness. I realised now that Amy had probably been crying because of one of these unholy flare-ups I was hearing about, and her mother had probably been in the habit of taking to her bed to hide her bruises from visitors. A lot of things suddenly began to click together and make sense.

'Why did it start now?' I asked. 'This anti-Chinese feeling, I mean. Why didn't it manifest itself before?'

Dwight shrugged. 'It seems to have. In various ways. But not so violently. But eccentricities develop as we grow older. From what were once youthful aberrations. In the same way that paranoia springs from youthful obsessions. He's just growing older, that's all.'

I nodded. 'Where is he now?'

Dwight stared at me with those blue eyes of his. 'Last time we spotted him,' he said, 'he'd crossed the border and was taking a train north—we suspect to Peking.'

'You've had him tailed?'

'No. One of our men saw him. That's all. He had plenty of time. It's two days since he shot his wife. She's only just recovered consciousness.'

'Can he give much away?'

'Under normal circumstances, nothing we need worry about. His wife says it's his idea to pretend to want to write a book on Red China. To explain them to the world. She expects he'll be welcomed with open arms.' Dwight frowned. 'So do I. They've got a film star obsession about publicity just now. They love it so long as it's good. And he's made plenty of contacts over the years. I expect he's using 'em now.'

'Isn't he a bit dangerous there? I mean, with this phobia thing he's started.'

Dwight nodded. 'Yes,' he said. 'He's dangerous all right. Damn dangerous. That's why *you're* here.'

'I thought there was some reason.'

'Yes.' Dwight smiled slightly. 'You might have to kill him.'

II

For a long time I sat still, staring at Dwight.

'You have to be joking, of course,' I said.

Dwight looked as impassive as a Buddha. 'Never been more serious in my life.'

'But, Jesus ... !'

He leaned forward. 'You never raised any objections when you had to get rid of Volkov.'

'That was different. Volkov was trying to strangle me.'

'Slatin then.'

'Man, Slatin was dangerous!'

Dwight fished in his pocket and produced a monocle which he stuck in his eye. When everybody else in the world had stopped using monocles, Dwight would still be wearing one. He made his own rules. There was only one Dwight.

'All the others then?'

I scowled. 'They were working against us. They were enemies. For God's sake, Mitchill's English! Amy and I . . .' I stopped lamely because I could hardly say that, unknown to her father, we'd been rather good in bed together until she'd opted out of the affair to marry her doctor. 'I've known Mitchill a year or two,' I ended. 'He's part of this department.'

Dwight moved restlessly in his chair, as though I were raising troublesome and unnecessary objections.

'Not any more.'

'Well, Christ, you don't want me to go and fetch him out of Red China just because he shot his wife!'

'I didn't say I wanted you to fetch him out.'

'Well, kill him then. Look, I've got this correct, haven't I?'

'I expect so. You usually do get things correct.'

'But why? For Christ's sake, why?'

'Because if we don't stop him, he'll kill the Chairman of the Chinese Communist Party.'

I stopped dead.

'Who?' I said.

'The Party Chairman. The Oracle. The Great Pan ... jandrum. The Wizard of Oz himself.'

It took some time before I got the implications of the thing. It took my breath away.

'Is that why he's gone to Peking?'

Dwight looked cool and unperturbed. It's easy to be cool and unperturbed when you don't ever stick your neck in a noose. I'd often thought that when it became my turn to take over Dwight's job, I'd always be cool and unperturbed, too.

'Well, *is* it?' I demanded.

'So his wife insists,' he said. 'She told the police a great deal, and by the grace of God, there was one among them who hadn't got a brain like a pudding. He decided it wasn't the ravings of a seriously injured woman. He told Esmond. Esmond contacted me. I was in Macao, as it happened.'

I still found it hard to believe him. 'How are we with Peking at the moment?' I asked.

Dwight held up two fingers tightly closed up. 'Like that,' he said. 'Since they released all those people, everything's been all sweetness and light. People are beginning to recognise the régime at last and they're looking for friends again now that they can't settle their quarrel with the Russians. They need friends. They're even allowing our people in there. Non-deviationist people, of course. People who belong to the Party or write for the Nancy Left. In the hope that they'll convert us to their way of thinking, shouldn't wonder. We've no quarrel. In spite of what other people would like. Although we're all on the same side, when it comes to our line of business we all row our own boat. We recognise Peking, not Formosa. We trade with them. The last thing I heard, we were even selling them a five-million-pound plastics factory to be erected at Tiengfeng. The fact that they'll probably convert it to explosives which will be used against us in twenty years' time is just by the way. At the moment, it's important for us to sell. We need the money.'

'And if someone with Mitchill's diplomatic background bumps off the Dearly Beloved,' I said, 'they'll think it's official—or at least, under-the-counter official?'

'Exactly.'

I had to consider it for a moment before I went on. 'When he gets to Peking, will he be free to move about as he likes?'

Dwight glanced at Esmond, who nodded. 'Anywhere he wishes. With or without interpreters. That's what we hear. You know the set-up. Anybody who's writing them up can get a visa to travel anywhere—even if the Chinese themselves can't. They want people to come back here and tell the West how they're doing. Either because they're proud or because they're trying to scare us. One or the other. After all, they claim they've already passed Britain in steel output. They'll welcome Mitchill. Especially as he'll tell 'em he's seen the light and wants to jump on the bandwaggon.'

'Are you *sure* he's after the Big Boy?'

'He's got a gun,' Dwight said. 'At least, the gun he shot his wife with wasn't found.'

'He can't get far with a pistol.'

'He doesn't need to. Just trying would be disaster enough. She told us this was what was in his mind. This was what started the final trouble between them. When she tried to dissuade him, he thought she was trying to defend the Chinese.' Dwight lit his pipe and puffed at it. 'The silly thing is, it had actually been suggested we should help him into China. By Esmond here.'

Esmond looked hurt and Dwight glanced at him.

'All right, Esmond,' he said sharply. 'You needn't look like a sick stag. It was quite official. It's even linked with the C.I.A. It was a good scheme. It was the fault of those

Esmond's been on it all day. If they clai
Dempsey you've only to produce your pape
enquiries, of course, but we'll see that t
necessary reports. They'll be satisfied.'

'What about my dog?' I asked.

'He doesn't talk, does he? I expect you'll
him back when you come home.'

'What about my friends?'

'You've got no friends. Nobody in this
friends.'

'I have some girl friends.'

'They'll be very upset,' he said, quite
course, you'll have to leave your flat. You c

'There are things in that flat I want.'

'We'll see that you get them. The small
things'll have to be sold, just as they woul
way. Armour'll take care of it. You'll b
though, if I remember'—his nose wrink
'there isn't much in your flat that has any

'It has to me. Nothing intrinsic. The o
The odd lingering whiff of perfume.'

The sarcasm didn't touch him. 'You'll
said.

'Suppose I don't want to do this?'

'Unfortunately, once you work for this
not easy to get out of it.'

I sighed. 'Okay. How do I set about it?'

Dwight glanced at a piece of paper on t
of him. 'You can't do it from here, of c
'They'd be on to you at once. You'll have
fly out from London. These reports will a
time you arrive in England—after you've
That way they'll lose you. Armour'll give
you need. Just one last bit of advice—' his
to mine—'try to keep your nose clean. You

bloody fools in London who sent him to you.' He turned to me. 'Esmond didn't know his background history. He was all for encouraging the idea of him being a defector. It had been going on for some time—pamphlets, lectures, meetings—to make it easier for him.'

'Why?'

'We wanted information. The plastics factory. What they're doing with it. Its exact location. He was supposed to be finding out.'

'But, instead of that, this happens.'

'Precisely.'

'And now he's changed his mind?'

'He has indeed.'

'And I'm to stop him—sharpish?'

'You have it exactly.'

'There's just one snag.'

'What's that?'

'I'm already *persona non grata* in China. After that affair in Canton, when I had to get General Ling out. Boy, did they want General Ling! They had a tail on me. One of their best boys—a chap called Tai Tso Hua. He damn nearly got me, too. I had no idea. I'd even been out drinking with him.'

Dwight said nothing and I went on quickly. 'Tai would know me. They'd never let me go back. I ought to have killed him.'

'Probably you ought.'

'And if I did go back,' I continued, beginning to think by this time that perhaps the dog might not have to go to the kennel after all, 'they'd never let me stay. In fact,' I ended, 'they might conceivably do something about me. I know they boast that they don't chop off heads any more—only make 'em a different shape in those corrective prisons of theirs—but there'd be nothing you could do for me if they did get me.'

'They won't get you,' Dwight said.
'They might. They've picked up a f
the West. And Tai was good. They *mi*
'It wouldn't matter,' Dwight said.
that. You've been around too long anyw
for you to die.'
'What!'
He pushed across the file. 'Open it,' I
I did so, slowly, as though it might
thing that caught my eye was a typed
in Northampton after a pile-up on the
'You've got a bloody nerve.'
'Think of all the girls you have tro
smiled. 'Think of all the difficulties you
of all those debts you won't have to pa
'I don't have debts.'
'My information's different.'
'You're a cool bastard,' I said.
'So I'm told.'
'How're you going to do it?'
'It's all fixed. Death certificates. Cor
paper cuttings of the inquest in the *Neu*
London Advertiser. That's where you
it? Nice tidy burial. Copy of the ur
Photograph of the wrecked car. Photc
and the sorrowing mourners.'
'Who am I now, then?'
'Eugene Patrick Nolan.'
'Man, you do think 'em up! What
Smith?'
He didn't seem amused. 'It suits you
new wave of young writers. Anxious to
a fair crack of the whip.'
'You think of everything, don't you?
'You should be grateful. We had a

a too youthful, too frivolous approach.' He closed the file. 'I don't need to tell you, of course, that you're on your own if anything goes wrong. We don't want to know you.'

'That's what I always enjoy about these jobs,' I said. 'One feels so secure.'

'You're young enough to cope. They thought in London you were too young when I took you on. They seem to think all agents have to be middle-aged men with dandruff and hangovers. I think you present a nice new image. People even trust their daughters with such pleasant, clean-limbed, open-faced youngsters as you. Most people, that is,' he added. 'I wouldn't.'

I thought for a moment. 'Why can't we just pass the information about Mitchill on to the Chinese police? Or leak it, if you like? And let *them* deal with him?'

Dwight gave me the sort of look which indicated that I wasn't even worth his trouble.

'They might put pressure on him,' he said. 'And he knows too much if they do. He knows every man we have on the mainland. And I'm not having that. Old Wen in Shanghai's worth all the rest of the Far Eastern branch put together.'

I saw Esmond wince. Dwight had an unfortunate habit from time to time of letting you know just what your rating was.

I paused, thinking. 'Do I *have* to kill the poor old bastard?' I asked eventually.

'Not if you can stop him some other way,' Dwight said. 'But somehow I don't think you can.'

III

Peking hadn't changed much. When I blew in on the jet from India, there they all were, just the same as last time, crisp and efficient as hell in blue Sun Yat-sen boiler suits with tunics buttoned to the neck. There were a few lounge suits among them, of course, and a few of the women wore *cheongsams* or Western-style dresses, but they were mostly Party officials, guides and ministry workers trying to impress the tourists, and on the whole the boiler suit was still the most popular. China had a long way to go and boiler suits were easy to produce and blue was a cheap dye when you were making a lot of it. They still looked a bit priggish in their self-righteousness, however, as though in their belief that all men were equal, they'd discovered a great truth that had completely escaped the rest of the world.

The Western belief that the Chinese face presents an impassive mask has always been way off beam. Westerners are much cleverer at hiding their feelings. I'd never found the Chinese slow to enjoy a good joke, and I disliked Communism all the more for what it had done to the happy giggling coolie who could roll on the floor in gales of laughter at seeing some pompous individual taken down a peg or two.

Armour had been efficient in London during the few days I'd spent there and I had no fear of being caught out on documents or clothes. My luggage was just sufficiently shabby to indicate a well-brought-up well-bred leftist who wouldn't worry about a thing like that. My clothes were also just the right mixture of well-cut colourful shabbiness. There were even a couple of books in my luggage, *Russia and America: The Question* and *The New Asia*, both by

Eugene Patrick Nolan. Armour had had them rushed through by the printing department while I was in London, and I'd made a point of reading them carefully to find out just what I was supposed to believe. They were enthusiastic for socialism but vaguely non-committal and produced just the right image of a young author that the Chinese might want to win over to their side. I supposed Armour had had them all ready in the basement for just such an event as this, just waiting for the jacket and the title page.

There was only one man in Peking I needed to worry about, and that was Tai Tso Hua. As far as I knew he was the only one in the whole bag of tricks who knew what I looked like. I'd heard he'd caught it in the neck because he'd let me escape. It was my sincere hope that the worry of it all had left him a burnt-out has-been relegated to something important like assistant ticket collector at the booth outside the Forbidden City.

As we left the plane, an officer entered it and methodically began to pump a spray gun which gave out a sickening antiseptic odour, and as we went into the airport rooms the same smell was there, coming this time from a gun worked by a gauze-masked girl, who carried a fly swatter strung from her belt. Eventually, I decided, the whole world would have the astringent hygiene of a hospital, and I wondered what would happen then to Naples and Sicily and all those lovely scruffy places in the south of France.

Perhaps it was in my blood, but I'd always thought Peking was one of the most beautiful cities in the world with its pagodas, towers and pavilions, and its acres of woods and lakes. But all the new buildings they were putting up now had flat roofs, and it was already on the way towards losing a lot of its charm. Town planners in the new China had no time for the belief my grandmother had once tried to slap out of the legion of servants who'd danced attendance on her: that there were demons who flew at a height of a hundred feet and needed plenty of clearance. Nobody believed these days that demons dwelt on roofs and that therefore eaves had to be curved so that when they slid down to attack you they'd be caught smartly in the groin by the gutter. There was no room for sentimentality in the creation of a modern state and they were being ruthless in clearing away the old.

The Hsinchiao Hotel was new, functional and coldly efficient—just the sort of place where a bright modern young writer would stay. The Ching Chiang still had all its old furniture from the days of the Americans and the English, when it was the Cathay Mansions, but it was neither Chinese nor Western now and I suspected it was regarded as decadent. I had decided on the Hsinchiao.

It had a bas-relief depicting the team spirit of the workers—the sort of thing that normally gets erected outside a trade-union headquarters or in Switzerland outside a new tunnel through the mountains to indicate the effort that goes into industry; and the bookstall seemed to feature nothing much but Chinese Party publications and the jolly thoughts of Mao Tse-tung in English, Russian, French, German and Chinese. I decided not to bother, and pushed my way towards the desk through what seemed to be a team of Manchurian football players—at least they all seemed to be carrying a football.

A girl was standing near the desk, her face half hidden behind a newspaper, and when I gave my name to the clerk, she folded the paper up with a quick deliberation and turned towards me.

'Mr. Nolan?' she asked. 'Mr. Eugene Patrick Nolan?'

'That's me,' I said. Trust Dwight to pick a name like that. He always believed in finding names to fit the character and he'd felt that a young left-wing writer wealthy enough to go to China off his own bat would have a good background and would have been to the right school. There were even overtones of Ireland and Roman Catholicism in it, too.

It seemed to impress the girl. 'My name is Han Tsiu Lin,' she said shyly. 'I am a student of English.'

'Hello,' I said. 'It's nice to meet you.' It was, too. Under any conditions, Han Tsiu Lin was a joy to behold. She was tall for a Chinese, with good legs and a nice before and a nice behind. She was wearing a well-fitting black suit and a white blouse so that she looked a little like an air hostess. I guessed immediately she'd been appointed by Intourist to wait for me and was agreeably surprised, because you could have marched with her into a Hilton hotel anywhere in the world and passed her off as a new film star. Her skin was pale ivory and her high cheekbones gave the impression that her eyes were more slanted than they were, particularly when she smiled. She wore her long black hair in a soft curve round the top of her head, and underneath,her face was a neat oval topping a slender neck. She was attractive enough, in fact, to make me cautious, because too many of these guides also had connections with security. All the same, though, I wondered if the rules for behaviour in the new China would permit me to take her out to dinner and whether seeing her to her door would be considered decadent and bourgeois.

She was staring at me with interest, and once again I had occasion to be thankful that my grandfather had chosen a wife with a few good looks. It had worked wonders in the past.

'You are younger than we expected,' she said with a smile. 'Most successful writers are much older.'

'I'm very clever, Miss Han.'

'You may call me Tsiu Lin if you wish,' she offered. 'We are encouraged to use familiar names. It does away with the old bourgeois idea of servant and master.'

'Okay, then. You'd better start off by calling me Gene. Or Pat. Whatever you like.'

'Nolan is best,' she decided. 'It sounds familiar to Chinese ears. No Lan. It might almost be a Chinese name. In fact, you yourself . . .' She stared at me curiously, her eyes on the contours of my face, and I shook my head quickly.

'No,' I said firmly. 'I'm not. My grandmother was Spanish. That's where the black eyes and the black hair come from.'

She nodded briskly, accepting the story unquestioningly. 'I have been ordered by the Information Department of the Ministry of Foreign Affairs to meet you here in case you need help,' she said.

'I certainly do need help,' I admitted.

She made a note on a small pad in her hand. 'You have an appointment to meet Minister Cheng?'

'No, but I'd like one.'

She made another note. 'It can be arranged. We shall be pleased to supply you with information.'

'Fine,' I said. 'I've never been to China before and I'm going to make it a story with a difference. I want to know how it all works and what's happening. I suppose *you* could help me there?'

'I am an Intourist guide. That's what I'm here for.'

'Good. Well, I want to see all I can. Am I free to travel anywhere?'

'It can be arranged. For you. Anywhere except the Fukien front.'

'Fukien?'

'The coast at Tsinkiang. There is activity going on there against Quemoy and Formosa.'

'Ah!'

'You understand, of course, that we are still at war with Chiang Kai-shek. The American capitalists still do not deny that his is the true and only government of China, although it is obvious to everybody that it can't be, concentrated as it is on one island off the coast. Only when he is gone will they be forced to accept *our* China, the true China.'

'Right,' I said enthusiastically. 'I understand. I'll not ask questions about that. But I'd like to see your celebrities, of course. For instance, are there to be any occasions when the Chairman will appear in public? I've heard a lot about him and, in addition to writing his story, I'd like to see him. I want to go back to London after this trip and be able to tell them there that I know what he looks like.'

'The Chairman is to open a new drainage system at Chengsha in the Tiengfeng area in two weeks' time. I'm sure you could be given a place where you could see him. The Ministry likes to encourage foreigners. Undoubtedly there will be journalists. I could arrange it.'

'I'd like that. Will you be there? I'll need an interpreter.'

'I can arrange that, too. We are eager to show you the blueprints for our nuclear-powered ships, and we want to destroy the lie put out by the capitalist jackals in the West that our back-street blast furnaces are not turning out pig iron in vast quantities. Even our Party officials and waiters work at it in their spare time. We have already passed the output of the decadent English.'

She gave me a smile that was warm and friendly and quite unmarred by the out-dated propaganda that poured from her lips.

'You must not be insulted by what I say, of course. My words are directed against governments, not individuals, and I am more than eager to show you around.'

'It's a date,' I said. From under all the froth, I had at least found out where the dearly beloved Chairman was going to appear next in public. Undoubtedly that would be where Mitchill would appear, too, and I'd got to stop him and convince him he was making a mistake before then.

'I'll look forward to having you show me around, Tsiu Lin,' I said, laying it on a bit to encourage the belief that I didn't know my way about. 'I'll look forward to your company.' This time I meant it, because Han Tsiu Lin would have decorated any occasion, even one with the bigwigs of the Party present, when the atmosphere, to say the least, would be a little turgid with politics.

She gave me that shy friendly smile of hers.

'I am entirely at your service, No Lan.'

That sounded encouraging. 'Well, let's start by having lunch somewhere,' I said. 'Is that permitted?'

She looked dubious for a moment, then she nodded.

'If you wish it. Under the circumstances that exist in China nowadays—'

'Good.' I interrupted before I got another flow of Party propaganda, and rubbed my hands briskly as though I couldn't wait to learn the number of tractors in the province of Hupeh or how they'd harnessed the kids' seesaws to the pumps of the irrigation ditches in Honan. 'I'll just wash and change and meet you here in half an hour. How's that?'

There was no key to the hotel door and when I offered a tip to the porter who carried my bags up, he frowned and refused it.

'It is as decadent and bourgeois to receive gratuities,' he said solemnly, 'as it is to offer them. Mao Tse-tung said it humiliates a man.' I didn't argue.

As I unpacked, I paused for a moment over the plastic-wrapped Biretta. I wondered for a moment whether to leave it; then I remembered that no one ever locked doors and that though it was considered decadent to steal, someone might still be curious enough to investigate, and ardent young left-wing writers don't normally carry automatic pistols around with them. I shrugged and stuffed it into my pocket.

Han Tsiu Lin was waiting for me in the lounge, sitting between a plump Indian and a man who, judging by his flat grey face and the long overcoat he wore despite the heat, was probably a defecting Russian. She was reading a paper and was sitting with her legs crossed. They were nice legs, too, and it occurred to me how much prettier still she could have looked if it hadn't been considered decadent in China to wear make-up.

She got up when she saw me and came towards me, her head high, tendrils of loose hair about her small ears. She lowered her gaze shyly.

'They tell me,' I said, 'that duck's a speciality here in Peking and that it's raised on a diet of millet and kept tethered to make it tender.'

She smiled. 'That is correct. It helps it to grow in the right proportions. In the new China we have a belief that all things should be in the right proportions.'

'They've done all right with you,' I said, feeling well in character because even young left-wing writers weren't against eyeing pretty girls.

I half expected her to give me a lecture on puritanism, because I'd found that, even when courted, a good Party member in China still preached Communism. But she blushed and said nothing.

'I expect you know the right restaurant,' I said.

'Yes, I know it.'

'How about a taxi? Or do we take a pedicab?'

'We are doing away with rickshaws and pedicabs. We consider them humiliating. A man isn't born to be used as a horse.'

'Of course not,' I agreed, not reminding her that it was the old enemy, Chiang Kai-shek, who'd first thought that one out. 'I'm sure you're right. But they're a lot of fun, aren't they?'

She didn't answer and we found a taxi in silence.

The streets were festooned with posters, some of them simply anti-American, some of them handling campaigns against flies, mosquitoes, rats and even sparrows. Some of them, which Tsiu Lin explained as being good for hygiene, were trying to persuade the Chinese out of the ancient tradition of spitting on the pavement, while others advocated contraception in no uncertain terms. 'It is in the interest of women's health, home life and national prosperity,' they claimed, and the displays left little to the imagination as to how the contraceptives should be used. Tsiu Lin made no comment on these and even, I noticed, managed to avoid looking at them.

The restaurant was neither small nor intimate but the duck was certainly good and when we'd finished I ordered a Chinese brandy. It had a kick like a horse and I felt sure that a lot of it might have a devastating effect on morality and decadence. It certainly seemed to start Han Tsiu Lin talking.

'We hope that when you go home you will tell them the truth about us,' she said earnestly. 'We don't expect sympathetic reporting, but we do expect the truth. Our only objection is when people go back to the West and say everything here is bad and ugly.'

'You're certainly not ugly, ducky.'

She looked a little worried. 'This "ducky"?' she asked.

'A term of affection,' I said.

'Endearment?'

'Not really. Just friendly. All young men in the West call their girls things like that. Ducky. Sweetheart. Love. Especially if they look like you.'

She didn't know quite how to react.

'Young men should not say things like that,' she said

sternly. 'I should have stopped you before. It is frowned on. Compliments should only be paid for endeavour and skill. Beauty is nothing.'

'It means a lot to most young men,' I pointed out.

'Even our buildings are no longer built for beauty,' she said. 'We build them to be functional. We are creating a modern China that will be able to take its place beside the most advanced nations of the Western world.'

'And are all the Chinese people behind the Chairman in this struggle to create a new state?'

'Of course. We are united against the imperialist American aggressors.'

I made a few pencil scratchings in a notebook as though I were doing an interview, then I looked up.

'Why is it then that refugees continue to flood into Hong Kong? At one time they came at the rate of ten thousand a month!' I couldn't resist it, and it would make me seem an earnest seeker after truth—even if a bit dim and difficult.

'That, of course, is a lie.' Tsiu Lin's face seemed to close up and become blank and disbelieving. 'That is a deliberate untruth put out by the capitalist jackals across the frontier.'

I studied her for a moment. I knew how many Chinese found their way across the border. They came from all parts of China—from Kwantung and Fukien on the shores of the China Sea, and from Jehol and Hsing-n'gan on the marches of Siberia—some taking years and great cunning to flee from the Communist paradise to the good old capitalist hell of Hong Kong. Some nights the smugglers carried as many as two hundred of them—called 'coiled serpents' for safety—packed at the bottom of a junk; and more waves of them rolled into Macao, Quemoy, Matsu, Formosa, Burma, and northeast Pakistan. If they hadn't had to have the internal passes that made every Chinese province a prison cell, there'd have been even more.

'I've seen them, Tsiu Lin,' I said earnestly. 'There are refugee camps at Rennie's Hill, Hong Kong, Kowloon, Ma An Shan and Chian Wan.'

'Concentration camps,' she insisted.

'With kindergarten schools? And temples and churches for every denomination from Taoist to Christian Catholic? The people in them are free to go into the city, if they wish. They're free to return to your new China. But none of them do.'

'Because they are afraid of the punishment they would receive as discontented deviationists.'

'In a free world, Tsiu Lin, a man has a right to be everything he wishes to be—even a discontented deviationist.'

I was putting on an act of self-righteous honesty but she began to look a little desperate and I formed the opinion she had either not been very well briefed or that she was not entirely convinced. I decided to be merciful because I could see she was retreating inside her shell of beliefs and she was much more interesting when her eyes were alight and there was a smile on her lips.

I began to ask her questions about China's achievements and she seemed much happier as she listed what had been done: the increase in steel from the backyard blast furnaces that was greater now than in Britain; the tremendous leap forward in agriculture; the fact that China was producing bicycles more cheaply even than Japan. Gradually she thawed out again and, when I teased her, she began to laugh in her soft gentle way, the sound like small tinkling bells as delicately fashioned as herself. I started to enjoy myself once more.

'We are putting up buildings in great numbers,' she said. 'Factories are operating with the machines inside as soon as the roof is on. We have learned to do everything faster than anywhere else in the world. The student organisations have turned out dictionaries in three weeks, and invented fertilizers in ten days. Two hundred of us built a new earth dam at Wuchang in twenty days.'

'Did it stay built?' I asked. 'When you put the water in?'

She blushed again and the bright eager artificial light of a revivalist disappeared from her face.

'No,' she admitted. 'It fell down.'

I gave a hoot of laughter and, for a second, I was afraid that she'd get up and leave me in disgust. But I hadn't been laughing because the dam had fallen down, but at the wry expression on her face when she'd honestly admitted it. The infection of it must have touched her—because the laughter was honest and not scornful—and she managed a smile and finally laughed with me.

'That's better, ducky,' I said. 'Now you've started to be honest. Let's go on like that. You don't have to convince me with a lot of statistics that China's making a great leap forward. It's obvious everywhere. I've nothing but admiration for a nation that's jumping out of the Middle Ages into the twentieth century in one bound, that does twenty years' work in one day. But you admit your faults, and I'll admit ours. I'm trying to write an honest story and we'll get along better that way. I promise you the Information Department of the Ministry of Foreign Affairs will never know.'

I'd tried to put on a show as a half-baked earnest young researcher and she seemed to accept it.

'Very well,' she said.

'Surely it's easier,' I insisted.

She looked at me with a long steady gaze, as though she were wondering if she could trust me. She obviously decided she could.

'Perhaps it's a great relief,' she said.

IV

I saw Tsiu Lin every day for the next week.

I'd been extraordinarily lucky to have drawn someone like her. I might easily have got a frozen-faced Chinese dolly with a brainbox full of propaganda. Tsiu Lin's head was stuffed as full of political clichés as the next person's was, but the difference lay in the fact that clearly she didn't wholly believe them all. What was more, she had a marked sense of humour—or, at least, it hadn't been entirely crushed out of her—and she was pretty enough even for my taste, cheerful and more than willing to help. She was always full of enthusiasm, despite her shyness, and was pleased with the magazines I'd brought with me and which I gave to her as a sort of bribe. She stared delightedly at the fashion advertisements and crowed over the pictures of lingerie with all the joy of an out-and-out deviationist.

'Do they really wear such things?' she asked in a breathless whisper.

'Of course.'

'They're so brief, so flimsy. They look very decadent. They must be criminally enticing.'

'That's the idea. Their boy friends like them like that.'

She looked shocked but, I noticed, more than interested.

Sometimes she wore the black suit and sometimes slacks and a lightweight flowered tunic, and once a *cheongsam* which took my breath away. It made her look quite different, as the spray of blossom printed on the silk wound round her tiny waist and across her bosom in a summery garland. She had small high breasts, a willowy figure with the compact oval hips that always looked best in a *cheong-*

sam, and slight sloping shoulders that were called *meijen-chien*—shoulders of beauty.

We visited all the usual places: the Echo Wall inside the Tien Ten Park where you can hear a whisper at any other point along its surface, and the Summer Palace, with its two hundred acres of woods and lakes and its scores of pagodas, towers and pavilions. The Hall of Benevolence and Longevity and the Hall of Delight in Longevity were being used for exhibitions depicting the advance of culture in China, and the Hall of Virtuous Harmony had become a rest home for workers, who rightly felt they were entitled to it after producing from nothing their penicillin and television and tools. She showed me the Broad Avenue leading past Tien An Men Square, which is a bit like Moscow's Red Square, and the great vermilion doors and renovated tower of the Hsin Hua Men gate leading to the Forbidden City, where the ministries were, and which you could visit for a small fee. The fact that once inside all you saw were workers doing massed exercises and that the atmosphere was as sterile as a gymnasium didn't spoil the charm of the place at all.

Despite the stifling atmosphere of priggishness and propaganda, the traditional politeness of the Chinese still existed, and though the loudspeakers brayed on every street corner and casual conversation was never much more than a series of clichés based on the news items, there was still an immense amount of warmth. And nothing could destroy the excitement of Han Tsiu Lin's company. It was a case of like returning to like, I suppose. She reminded me all the time of my grandmother—her sense of humour, her eyes, the way she moved—and her fragile shyness appealed to me far more than the hearty companionship of the English and American girls I knew.

I took her out several times to meals. Once we went to a communal eating place where the wireless blared out a mixture of martial music and propaganda until we both collapsed into laughter trying to talk above it, once to the bleak-looking restaurant where we'd eaten the duck, and finally to a smaller, more intimate, place she knew, that was hung with Chinese lanterns and banners daubed with the delicate brush strokes of Chinese words. It was quietly lit and we were able to talk there in peace.

She chattered happily to me and it was only when I felt that I had to make a show of being Eugene Patrick Nolan, political writer, that I made the effort to question her about China. Most of the time, she was occupied in asking about the women of the Western world, the things they did, the homes they lived in, the dishes they cooked, the way they pleased their husbands.

'Do they really rule the home in the West, No Lan?' she asked in awed tones.

'Not really, old love,' I said. 'That's just a fallacy that's grown up. They like to think they do and the intelligent men let their wives believe it, but, in any world, a man's more fitted to run the show because he's not emotional. In some cases, in fact, he's plain ox-like.'

She laughed.

'And what does the woman do then, to make sure that her husband stays with her? If she thinks she rules, she must surely give something in return?'

'You said it yourself when I met you,' I pointed out gently. '"I am entirely at your servicc." A good wife considers herself in that way towards her husband.'

She stared at me, blushed, and quickly, as though she thought I was making suggestions, began to talk about the advances that had been made in China.

'Ours is a young people's country now,' she said. 'Some communes are directed by seventeen-year-old girls—people even younger than I am. They take care of food and shelter for the old, medical care and education. They direct the blast furnaces, the soil and how to handle a rifle. The Russian revolution was a revolution of city workers. The Chinese revolution is a revolution of peasants.'

I was growing a little tired by now of statistics and achievements and I began to pull her leg a little, suggesting all sorts of clandestine meetings. I was only fooling—though I could easily have been serious—and she laughed with me. Eventually, however—perhaps because she thought we were laughing too much in a country where laughter was at a premium—she became serious.

'You mustn't talk to me like this, No Lan,' she said.

'Why not?'

'Because Chung Yen Siang would be offended.'

'Who's Chung Yen Siang?'

'He is my lover.'

'Your what?'

'What do you call him? A promised one?'

'Boy friend. Fiancé.'

'Yes. He is a student, too.'

'And is he as honest as you are?'

'Of course.'

'And thinks for himself?'

'Of course. Sometimes, in fact, I'm very afraid for him. He says it is our duty to be honest. He says it is the duty of all intellectuals to make a stand—to die if necessary—for truth.'

Chung Yen Siang sounded a bit of a drip. Anybody who had the nerve to class himself as an intellectual needed watching, I'd always felt. But at least he seemed to have encouraged Tsiu Lin to think for herself, if nothing else. To see anyone as beautiful as she was repeating the parrot handouts of the Ministry of Information—and believing them—would have been too much.

'Have you known him long?' I asked.

'Six months,' she said proudly. 'We were in the Young

Pioneers at the time. He was a leader. Our job was to collect scrap metal. We searched in the street for nails and things like that.'

'I've heard you even pinched the rear springs off buses.'

She gave a little laugh that made her seem like a schoolgirl. 'Not quite,' she said. 'But sometimes when there was someone we didn't like, we used to take their railings. They never dared to object. Yen Siang said they must be deviationists, anyway, to have railings. He was joking, of course, because he doesn't believe in it much. He says all the posters are propaganda.'

I leaned forward and spoke more quietly. 'Does he ever say this to anyone but you?'

'No. Never. We have to be very careful. But he says that if the occasion ever arises I must be prepared to suffer for the sake of truth.' She glanced at me and smiled. 'That was why I admitted that our dam fell down. Yen Siang always insists that to be an intellectual requires courage.'

Yen Siang seemed to have a blown-up idea of his own importance.

'Courage is one thing, old duck,' I warned her, feeling like a grandfather. 'Cunning's another. It's a cruel world, Tsiu Lin, and the first object in life is survival. Don't be courageous just to please Yen Siang. Take it easy. Remember you've only known him six months.'

'That's quite long enough.'

'I wonder,' I said, thinking about Mitchill. I'd known Mitchill for quite a while through Amy, and it was only when Dwight had told me that I'd realised that there was a lot I didn't know about him. I hadn't even begun to know Dwight and I'd worked with him for years.

I felt it was time to change the subject because, for some reason that I couldn't explain, I didn't like Chung Yen Siang and had even begun to wonder if he were a *hanchou*, one of the agents the government used to encourage the incautious to be too honest.

'Where did you learn to speak English so well, Tsiu Lin?' I asked.

She hesitated for a moment before answering, almost as if she suspected my dislike for Chung Yen Siang, as though she'd been able to read my thoughts. I could see she was wondering what to say, then she lifted her small head, pale and proud, the cheeks smooth and delicate and touched with colour.

'In Canton. I am a Cantonese. Until our armies drove out the Kuomintang in 1949 my family lived there. My father worked with the British businessmen there. I learned to speak English from my parents. I have never forgotten.'

'Where are your parents now?'

Her expression clouded, a suggestion of doubt in her eyes. 'They are dead. My father was killed after the occupation of Canton. My mother died later. She was a reactionary.'

I didn't take my eyes off her face.

'Was or was considered to be?' I asked.

I got a fluttering look of doubt. 'My duties,' she said softly, 'are to show you the ways of the new China, to assist you in finding out facts about our achievements, to present what we are doing in a way that will be acceptable to the Western world.'

'How can I present your country to my country and to other countries, ducky,' I asked, 'if I have a guide who I believe is telling me only half-truths and more-than-truths?'

'You can always ask for another guide.'

'And then you'll be punished for not being competent at your job.'

'I must accept that.'

'I don't want another guide.'

She raised her eyes. 'Why not, No Lan?' she asked shyly. 'Because you are afraid that I shall get into trouble?'

'No,' I said frankly. 'Because I prefer you. Because I enjoy your company and because, until now, I'd begun to feel I'd met someone who was being honest with me. I talked to the head of your section the day after I came here. He was a nice old boy. He shoved a lot of drinks at me and offered me all the help in the world. But he wasn't telling me the truth. Like you, he also tried to tell me that all Chinese are happy, and I know they're not because I've seen the refugees in Hong Kong.' It was a good speech—the sort of bold 'death rather than dishonour' stuff that Eugene Patrick Nolan would be adept at. Then I became more honest. 'He also asked me,' I said, 'if I was satisfied with my guide. I told him I was more than satisfied.'

Her eyes dropped. 'But you're not. You've just said so.'

'I am when you're honest with me.'

She looked up at me again, faintly startled and curiously fragile-looking with her pale skin and soft black hair. For a moment she stared at me, her lips apart, as though trying to sum me up, almost as though she felt my questions and my persistence were too much for her. Then she lowered her eyes once more.

'Very well, I will try to be honest.'

'Always? It doesn't matter, really, old love, that I might disagree with you. When I leave we shall never meet again.'

Suddenly I found myself wishing I was to be there longer than I'd planned.

'Now,' I said, 'tell me: Your mother—was she, or was she just *considered to be*, a reactionary?'

'Was considered to be,' she said in a low voice.

'Did you consider her to be a reactionary?'

'I didn't consider her as anything but my mother.'

All of this had nothing to do with my quest to find

Mitchill but that was something that couldn't be rushed too much. I had to establish myself first. In a way, I didn't like deluding her, especially when I was asking her to be honest with me, but that was one of the hardest parts of the job. You had to get people to be themselves with you while you were busy being someone else.

My concern with Mitchill was due to start at any time. I'd been accepted for what I appeared to be—even by the man in charge of the Information Section—and I'd got permission to go where I wanted, even without a guide. When the time came to act and Tsiu Lin found out who I really was—if, in fact, she ever did find out—she would be just one more disillusioned commy who'd thought she had made contact with a promising young representative of the West. I wasn't looking forward to that part of the affair but there was nothing I could do about it, so I shoved it to the back of my mind.

'What happened to you?' I asked. 'What happened to you when your parents disappeared?'

She moved an empty rice bowl on the table and answered without looking at me, and I'd got to know her well enough by this time to be aware that I was about to be treated to another propaganda handout.

'I was sent to boarding school to be re-educated. I saw the error of my ways and the mistakes my parents had made and I am now completely cured of any reactionary instincts that might have remained.'

'Phooey!'

She looked surprised.

'Phooey!' I said again.

'You do not believe me?'

'They might have stamped out a lot of instincts in your friends, ducky. But I bet they haven't in you. I'm not running your country down—or you—but they haven't changed you much.'

'You go too fast,' she said in a small breathless voice. 'You frighten me a little. You look young, yet somehow you are so old.'

That had always been one of Amy Mitchill's complaints, and she'd always claimed it was Grandma Dempsey's fault, a sort of hangover from Manchu gravity and Chinese patience. But it wasn't really. It was the job. It made you grow old—inside, where it didn't leave lines or crow's feet round the eyes.

'In all the time I've been doing this work no one has ever talked to me before like this,' Tsiu Lin went on.

'Perhaps all the others were old men who were afraid you'd report them and have them arrested,' I suggested.

'Aren't you afraid?'

I shrugged. I'd never had much reason to be afraid. Things had always gone right for me and I'd always found I could more than handle the poor fish they'd tried against me. And I had to behave like a cocksure young man who considered himself a fearless worker for truth, a man who'd been properly brought up and, in spite of his left-wing bow tie and socialist leanings, still believed that one Englishman equalled two Frenchmen, three Germans, four Italians and any number of wogs, whether they were yellow, red or brown.

'No,' I said. 'I'm not afraid. I'm just interested in your country. I don't agree with everything you're doing but I certainly agree with a lot of it, so I've no need to be afraid. That's fair enough, isn't it?'

'I suppose so.'

She began to reach for the shoulder bag in which she carried her maps and notepad and the sheets of information that she always had with her.

'Just one last thing before we go,' I said. 'There's a friend of mine here in Peking. An old cock by the name of Mitchill. Charles Mitchill. Used to be a government official of some sort, I think. Knew my family. He's a Far East authority. I gather he's also here preparing a book. Would you know where he is?'

She seemed glad to get back to familiar ground.

'We have a section of the department solely for the benefit of permanent and semi-permanent foreign residents,' she said briskly. 'We have several Americans, for instance, who have remained in China ever since they were captured during the capitalist wars in Korea and Vietnam. I expect they will know of him there.'

'Can you let me know?'

'I think so.'

'At the hotel?'

She nodded.

'Perhaps we could have another duck,' I suggested. 'But don't let the old boy know I'm here. I want to surprise him.'

'Very well. Do you know him well?'

'I very nearly married his daughter several years ago.'

She looked suddenly interested. 'And why didn't you?' she asked.

'She decided she preferred someone else.'

'And so you also went off and married someone else?'

I gave her a long look. She seemed to be fishing. 'No,' I said. 'I didn't. I'm still looking around. Are *you* free?'

She blushed again. 'Marriage is easily entered into. But it is hard to throw off.'

'Tsiu Lin,' I chided her gently, 'don't start disappearing inside your shell again. Do me the honour, old dear, of talking sense to me.'

She smiled, naturally and honestly. 'I'm sorry. It becomes a habit. I have never talked to anyone as I have to you and it's hard to do it normally. I mustn't let it become a habit.'

I stood up. 'I'll see you home,' I said.

'No.' She seemed suddenly scared. 'No. I have to report

to my office. Besides'—her voice dropped and her eyes failed to meet mine—'I have Yen Siang.'

'Yes, of course. Enjoy yourselves.' I handed her the sling bag. 'There's just one more thing, though.'

'What's that?'

'Tell him there's no shame in treading warily.'

She seemed unhappy. For a moment her eyes rested on my face, her brow wrinkled by a small worried frown, then she swung on her heel and hurried to the door. As she opened it, she turned and stared back at me, still frowning, then she was gone.

V

It wasn't easy to enjoy yourself in Peking. When I'd last been in Moscow, I'd been able to dance to jazz bands and pick up girls, and they were even managing to make jokes about their own system.

But not here. Not in China. They hadn't had their new régime long enough yet to be light-hearted about it and everybody was dead serious. There were no courting couples in the shadows in the evening, and to do a bit of necking in public was decadent and bourgeois. The 'street blossoms' who plied their wares for money everywhere else in the East had vanished in China, and frustrated foreign sailors in places like Shanghai had to make do with a bottle of beer instead in the Seamen's Club.

About Peking, like the rest of China, there was a stringent asexual quality. There was no cheek-to-cheek dancing, no one walked arm in arm, and life was too earnest for love. In this world of theirs, where adultery and promiscuity were crimes with prison sentences, God alone knew how the more passionate among them ever conducted their *affaires*. It must have been hard work taking a girl to bed only to find she'd brought the figures for blast-furnace production to read to you before getting down to the serious business of the evening.

I'd found Chinese girls in other parts of the world lively and interesting. The hollow shell the writing boys had foisted off on the world for generations as the typical Chinese woman, with nothing but tinkling childish gaiety and seductiveness, had only ever existed in the bawdy houses of Singapore, Hong Kong and the old Shanghai of the gunboat days. There the little harlots had developed their style to suit the trade of the wandering soldiers and nostalgic matelots looking for a bit of enticing crumpet in the melting-pot towns along the coast. In fact, those were probably the only Chinese girls they ever met. The ones I'd known were individualists who had brains and patience and courage, and still managed to find a little fun.

But these little dollies I saw around me in the hotel and in the streets with their sober faces and their earnest conversation had minds like adding machines and were just about as exciting. There wasn't a smile among the lot of them and they went about their business like Tory women workers during an election.

What a horrible thought, I felt, that there were six hundred and fifty million of these humourless blue ants, and, even worse, that there would be a thousand million by 1980. Somebody would have to step up world humour a lot to counteract the effect they'd have on it.

There were propaganda rallies everywhere, with youngsters beating gongs to call the faithful to prayer, using the old methods to produce new results. It was like a religious revival and even the tiny kids chanted Party dogma as they marched about the streets. It wasn't hard to see that ideas were being strangled and frank conversations were disappearing. The mood in Tien An Men Square was severe and stifling, and after a day's labour everyone seemed too footsore to want to go out looking for fun—even if there'd been somewhere to go. The theatre was presenting a stirring play on how the workers' co-operatives were formed and the cinemas all seemed to be showing a gripping drama about how to design a people's car, so it must have seemed wiser to go home.

I decided to stay in the hotel.

There was a restaurant on the sixth floor and I sat there alone, watching the Manchurian footballers as they ate together, chattering noisily at the next group of tables, discussing the food loudly and holding their bowls close to their mouths and shovelling away with the chopsticks.

Afterwards I had a Chinese brandy—a large one to brighten the mood I was in—and paused to consider what to do about Mitchill. Nobody seemed to stop me moving around, though I'd taken a great deal of trouble to make sure nobody followed me too closely. It was time, I decided, to act.

I was glad to get back to my room because the brandy had been as devastating as I had expected, but there was a radio in the street outside and I could hear it blaring music and slogans—'We must act or perish,' 'We will surpass Britain,' 'We work for socialism'—and in the end I grew sick of hearing it.

It was beginning to grow late and I was wondering how long it would be before Tsiu Lin let me know where Mitchill was. I'd been in Peking just over a week—long enough for people to be used to seeing me around—and I'd even been to a cocktail party at the Ministry of Information to meet a few condescending Party officials eager to put me right on my facts. Familiarity bred indifference and I was hoping that by now they'd even stopped bothering to be curious about me. I should do something soon.

I hadn't seen Tsiu Lin since lunchtime and I'd just begun to think I'd seen all I was going to see of her for that day when there was a knock on the door. I was standing by the window, staring down into the street, but, as I turned, she hurried inside without waiting for my call and stood beside the bed with her back against the wall. She looked scared and there was a taut, strained, miserable look behind her eyes.

For a moment, I was startled, because it seemed so out of character. Up to then, she'd always been more than discreet and I wondered if they'd put her up to something. I'd heard of girls getting themselves into the rooms of Western officials and romping on the bed while secret cameras clicked behind one-way mirrors, and I'd questioned more than one man who'd been compromised sufficiently to be willing to work for the Russians. Promiscuity had become a policy instrument for foreigners, part of the red carpet that could always suddenly roll up and engulf the victim if he were worth it.

Somehow, though, I couldn't imagine they'd ever have forced Tsiu Lin into that sort of work—not after spending over a week with her. I knew something about girls and she hadn't struck me as the type who'd do that kind of thing well. She was too shy and too fresh and there was no suggestion of sexiness about her. She was as feminine as they come, particularly when she dressed the part, but she hadn't the practised manner of a seducer. Stranger things had happened, however, and I'd had attempts made on me by more unlikely girls, so I was cautious at first.

'It's a good job I wasn't changing my trousers,' I said.

She flashed me a quick look out of the depths of her black eyes that made her look more fragile than ever, then her face set in the blank mask I kept seeing which indicated at once that she was in her best Intourist-guide-statistics-expert mood.

'It would make no difference,' she said automatically. 'Immorality is only a failing of the West.'

'Come off it, old love,' I said. 'I bet you have it here, too, in spite of everything.'

'Yes. We have it here, but the eyes of the people are snow-bright on the deviationists who pursue only pleasure.'

There was a curious toneless quality about her voice that seemed unnatural.

'Tsiu Lin!'

'We spurn the American obsession with sex. Our country and our people have a host of men and women who have toppled all the old idols....' She seemed to be reciting the words like a parrot, her face dead white and agonised, and I took her shoulders and shook her, gripping her so tightly that my fingers dug into her muscles.

She gave a little moan of anguish, then she seemed to come out of the trance and collapsed into my arms, weeping, the tears falling on my hands, her whole body racked with sobs.

'Tsiu Lin, for God's sake, what's happened? Have they been finding out all the things you've been telling me? Have you been punished?'

'No, it isn't that.'

'What is it then?'

'I shouldn't be here. It is frowned on to visit the rooms of visitors to the country. It is considered quite possible to pass on all information necessary in places of public access.'

'For God's sake, stop talking like a bloody pamphlet and tell me what's wrong!'

She lifted her head, her eyes moist, her mouth writhing in misery.

'No Lan, Yen Siang has been taken by the police.'

'Yen Siang? Oh, Jesus, not the boy friend?'

She nodded wretchedly. 'The police went to his home today and took him away. They tell me he has been sent to a corrective prison.'

'For talking too much?'

'For saying all the things he has said.'

For the first time in my life I felt helpless. There wasn't much I could do even if I wanted to. Nobody was going to take any notice of Eugene Patrick Nolan, even if he chose to protest. And Eugene Patrick Nolan didn't choose to protest, much as he wanted to. He wasn't in Peking to sort out the love life of an Intourist guide nominated by the Information Department of the Ministry of Foreign Affairs. It seemed hard and cold and tough on Tsiu Lin, but Eugene Patrick Nolan had to keep his eye on the ball, unpleasant as it might be for her.

'Hell, I'm sorry, Tsiu Lin,' I said. 'I hope it isn't anything I've done or said.'

'It was nothing to do with you, No Lan.' She lifted a tearful face, no longer a living example of the spirit of the new China, but just an ordinary girl who was in love and had lost her boy friend. 'I often warned him. He was always indiscreet. If I had not been blinded by his words, I might have reported him myself.'

'Oh, Christ, no, Tsiu Lin! Never that.'

'Other people do these things.'

'Other people might. But not *you*. What happened? Who gave him away?'

'People he called his comrades.'

'Bloody fine comrades,' I said.

'Now I have nobody.'

'But you must have relations?'

'Only in Hong Kong.'

'What about friends?'

'I only had Yen Siang. That's why I came to you. You were the only person I could think of.'

'Surely to God you've got neighbours?'

'I have found it harder than I thought to accept community living,' she said. 'I am not a good example of the new China. I ought not to be doing this job. I should benefit from my mistakes and from Yen Siang's mistakes and try to improve.'

This was the girl talking who had been taken away as a child to be educated in Party doctrine, pulled two ways all the time by all she'd been taught, by the Party dogmas that had been pumped into her and by the normal womanly instincts remembered from her mother which were lying dormant in her. For them to remain so strongly after so many years of brainwashing, her mother must have been quite a woman! She'd have got on well with my grandmother, and I wished to God I was free to help.

'Tsiu Lin, let's go out somewhere and have something to eat.'

'I have eaten,' she said, still in a flat voice.

'Something to drink, then.'

'It isn't easy to buy drinks.'

'Then let me get them to send up a brandy for you.'

She shook her head. 'I could be reported for being here. We must go downstairs. I must collect myself.'

It's never easy in a foreign country and certainly not in Red China, with everybody looking over your shoulder, to comfort a distraught girl, but in the end I calmed her down and made her sit quietly, at least until the misery had died out of her face and the lost look had faded a little from her eyes.

'I can lose myself in my work,' she said at last in a shaky voice. 'Perhaps that will take away the pain. I must remember what I am supposed to do. I have brought you the address of your friend, Mr. Mitchill.'

My heart leapt, and I looked at Tsiu Lin with affection. She seemed to be recovering a little now and had stopped crying. She was fishing busily in her shoulder bag, as though the effort might manage to take her mind off things, and after a while she produced a notebook.

'The New China Hotel,' she said. 'It's on the other side of the Tien An Men Square but it's not quite as new as it sounds. In fact, it's quite old.'

'He's probably doing it on the cheap,' I pointed out. 'After all, he's given up his job now and I expect he's trying to watch his cash. What else do you know about him?'

'He seems to spend his time between the hotel and the library. It's in what used to be the Hall of Enduring Industry. He's always there.'

'How do you know?' I asked. 'Do you keep watch on him?'

'To a certain degree,' she admitted. 'We keep watch on all foreigners.'

I stared at her. 'Even me?'

'Yes.'

'Who? You?'

She nodded miserably.

'Well,' I said. 'So long as we know. Thanks, anyway. I'll look him up.'

The New China Hotel was a shabby place with a long sign running down the front from the second floor to the door. It was painted in red letters on a yellow background and looked vaguely like the streamer for a circus.

It was in a narrow street where old buildings had been pulled down and replaced with blast furnaces. By the look of them I guessed the iron they produced was probably all right for household equipment and not much more. Grey walls stretched from end to end of the alley, broken here and there by bright red gates opening on to compounds that looked like the backyards of Manchester or Birmingham or Sheffield. The street was unpaved and there were hordes of children around; but there was remarkably little litter and there were no offensive smells. The scarred walls were covered with old posters showing a Chinese worker throttling the imperialist American dragon. I found myself wondering how you lived with that facing you all the time and whether, in fact, you just ignored it.

I stared at Tsiu Lin. 'You're sure this is it?'

'This is it.' She seemed to have recovered from her grief and was her old efficient self again. 'Would you like me to accompany you?'

'Only as far as the desk clerk,' I said. 'After that I'd prefer to see Mitchill alone.'

'The desk clerk speaks English.'

'Then I'll manage.' As I climbed out of the taxi, I looked back at her, sitting erect and quiet in the far corner of the seat. 'Take the taxi back,' I said. 'I'll pay for it. And, Tsiu Lin, I'm sorry about your troubles. I wish I could help, but of course I can't. I hope it all comes out all right.'

She looked at me, an impenetrable depth to her black eyes.

The clerk seemed almost to be expecting me and I guessed that Tsiu Lin had already spoken to him.

He gave me the number of Mitchill's room and indicated the stairs. There was no lift so I set off slowly, because it was a long way up and the stairs were steep.

As I went higher, they seemed to grow steeper and narrower. At one point I passed an elderly Chinese sitting on the steps, smoking, and later one of them asleep, his lolling head against the wall, his wispy white beard draped on his chest. On the second floor, I passed a girl coming down with a white face and vermilion lips. She was wearing a *cheongsam* and it looked very much to me as though the 'street blossoms' who were claimed to have disappeared from the corners, hadn't *all* vanished. If this girl, with her red lips and swaying hips and the arch look she gave me, wasn't a 'street blossom,' then I was a monkey's uncle. Perhaps, however, she put in her stint at the blast furnace during the day and did the other job in her spare time. I decided I'd have to remember her to quote at Tsiu Lin.

I came to Mitchill's door at last, right at the top of the building under the roof. The old boy had obviously not picked it for comfort or for publicity, but as you couldn't hear the loudspeakers he'd clearly been looking for somewhere quiet and private where he wouldn't be found.

I heard his voice as I knocked, and I went in.

The room had a shuttered window without glass that looked over the tumbled tiled roofs of the old town, and coming up through the windows you could hear the chatter of the back streets and somewhere a radio playing a tinkling gong tune that was flat and toneless. They'd built another blast furnace at the back of the hotel and I could hear them chattering round it. Above the din came the strident tones of a woman who, I supposed, was the community chairman.

There was nothing but a rush mat on the floor, and a shabby bed that was really only a string mattress fastened to a frame. There was one table, one chair and a curtained corner that did duty, I supposed, for a wardrobe. A heavy carafe full of water stood by the bed with a glass on top, just as you get in old-fashioned English hotels.

Mitchill seemed to be living out of his suitcase because it was on the bed with the lid open, and the floor was scattered with books and papers and clothes. He was writing at the table by the window, and as I closed the door behind me, he threw down his pen and turned quickly, a burly man with a thick red neck that bulged over his collar and a wide balding head on which the greying hairs stuck out awkwardly.

He was so busy thinking that he didn't really see me at first, then he recognised me and his expression changed. I saw in his face fear, anger, frustration, weariness—a whole host of changing emotions.

'Dempsey!'

'The very same,' I said. 'I've come to pay a call.'

He stood up hurriedly, and accidentally knocked the sheets of paper he'd been writing on to the floor.

I stooped to pick them up for him and, as I did so, I saw the last words he'd been writing.

I wish to be judged for what I have done by posterity. I wish to be judged by history, not by the present day....

Oh, Christ, I thought, the testament. The inevitable testament that was always left behind by the assassin or the suicide, the note that spoke out loud their need to be understood. It was not enough for them to do what they had to do, quietly and without publicity. They also had to be appreciated.

I put the papers on the table without comment and turned to Mitchill, who'd moved towards the small window and now stood with his back to it, his face twisted.

'What do you want?' he said.

'Just a few words. I thought we might be able to have a talk.'

'I've nothing to say to you, young man!'

'You might have. You never know.'

'You've been sent to find me. You didn't come on your own.'

'Jesus, no! What makes you think I'd chase you halfway across the world for fun?'

'You've come to take me back!'

'If you'll go back, that would be a good idea.' It would even be a damn good idea, I thought. Much better than blowing the poor old bastard's head off to stop him doing what he had in his mind.

'I'm not going,' he said shrilly.

'What the hell good are you doing here?' I asked him.

'I have a job to do.'

'So I heard.'

'I'm writing a book.'

'That's not my information.'

'You can check at the Ministry of Foreign Affairs. They know all about me.'

'Not quite all,' I said. 'It wasn't a book that brought you here, though I know you spend a lot of time at the library.'

'Who told you?'

'The Information Department of the Ministry of Foreign Affairs. They keep tabs on everybody.'

'On you, too?'

'On me, too. I'm writing a book as well.'

'I'm not going,' he repeated.

'Listen, Mitchill,' I said, as quietly as I could, 'I've known you a long time. I've worked with you. I've visited your house. I was once in love with your daughter. I knew your wife.'

'How is she?' he asked in a faint pathetic voice.

'Dead.'

He paused and I wondered if I'd touched a raw spot. Then he looked up. 'She was Chinese, you know,' he said quickly. 'She was on their side. She was like them. She sympathised. She thought their desire to rule the world was a right and proper one. She was watching me for them.'

I had a feeling I was backing a wrong horse, but I went on trying. 'I'm sure she wasn't,' I said.

He gestured vaguely. 'I had to do it. I couldn't let her pass on to them what I was going to do.'

'I hope you're *not* going to do it,' I said.

'Of course I am.'

'Look, Mitchill,' I said. 'You're a grandfather now. Amy has a baby. Wouldn't it be better if you went back to them?'

'She was Chinese.'

'Part Chinese. A very small part.'

His eyes flickered uncertainly. 'So was Amy. She just agreed with her. All the time. She thought she was right.'

'She was probably just sticking up for her mother.'

'No.' He shook his head. '*She* was Chinese, too.'

'*Part* Chinese. Less Chinese than your wife even, who wasn't much, God knows. So little, in fact, I didn't know until they told me.'

'Who did tell you?'

'Dwight told me.'

His eyes took on a chilly, baleful look. 'You see. They knew. Dwight knew. They must have been watching her. I expect they knew, too, that these people here pushed her in my direction. They wanted me to marry a Chinese. It's only one of the ways they get you, you know.'

'Mitchill,' I said, trying to be patient, 'these people here weren't even in business when you married your wife.'

His face changed. Up to that moment, despite the inconsequential manner of his answers, his expression had remained normal and at least lucid. Now, just for a flash, it had the cunning look of an idiot, and for the first time I realised that he really *was* round the bend.

'Oh, but they were,' he said. 'They started years ago. Long before they got power. They were putting out their agents even then. Look how they filled the Kuomintang forces with them. Look how they persuaded the Americans to back them instead of Chiang Kai-shek after the war. They even refused to bomb the Yangtze crossings to stop them. She was one of them.'

I wasn't getting very far. The poor old bastard would have to be stopped somehow. He was set on what he was going to do, and obsessed by a sick belief that he was being persecuted. I glanced round the room. There wasn't much I could do here, I thought. I couldn't even start getting tough with him, not surrounded by a million Chinese who'd probably take his side if it came to trouble.

'Let's talk about that elsewhere,' I said. 'I can get you back to Hong Kong in a couple of days if you'll come.'

For a fleeting instant I thought of Tsiu Lin and what she'd say if Mitchill vanished with me. Life was tough enough for her as it was and if she found out the truth about me it wouldn't make it any easier. I'd done a lot of talking about truth and honesty and, for all I knew, the fact that she'd not cottoned on to me might well lead to more than suspension for her. It was a bitter feeling but I shoved it to the back of my mind and tried to forget it. After all, I told myself, she was only a girl and I'd met hundreds of them.

Mitchill's face was wearing the shifty look of an old man who was in danger of being cheated out of having his own way.

'Look,' he said, 'I've got it all down here. I've been setting it all down. If only Dwight would take some notice of me.'

He pushed forward the papers that he'd been writing on and I took them from him. He stood beside me, pointing over my shoulder.

'There, see.'

What I am about to do will be misinterpreted by people but I am sure that posterity will understand.

'And here—'

He was behind me now, and I was reading aloud, trying to get him into the right frame of mind.

Though my action may be considered wicked, he'd written, *my motive at least is good. I love life and I love honour.*

I lowered the papers. 'Look, Mitchill—'

I half turned and in the brief instant before it crashed on my forehead, I saw he had the heavy water carafe in his hand.

'Oh, Christ!'—the thought shot through my head immediately—'Fancy being caught by that old one!'

Then I saw a flash of scarlet and silver and pain smashed through my head like a wave flung by a tide across the beach and blackness roared up from below.

VI

When I came round it was almost dark. I was lying half under the bed, as though Mitchill had dragged me out of his way. As soon as I sat up, I realised he'd vanished. The curtain across the corner which he'd used as a wardrobe had been snatched back and was caught over a chair, as though he'd flung it aside in haste, and the hooks behind were empty except for one dirty towel. The case was gone from the bed and the sheet was half on the floor as though it had been pulled off with the case as he'd left. Around my legs were shattered fragments of glass and a pool of water, most of which, by this time, had soaked into the bare boards of the floor. Why I wasn't dead, I couldn't think. That carafe, full, must have weighed several pounds. There was a lump on my forehead as big as an egg and I had a splitting headache.

'You bloody fool!' I said to myself. 'You prize bloody idiot!'

I'd boobed badly. Mitchill's mild oddness had deluded me into imagining that the attack on his wife had been only a brainstorm. I ought to have guessed that any man who'd take a gun to the woman who'd lived with him for over twenty years and borne his children might have been desperate enough to resist any attempts to take him home. I ought to have remembered all that case history of

Dwight's: the Chinese boy Kay, the sergeant, myself, and that grandfather of his who'd died in a mental home.

But it's not every day you deal with an unbalanced mind and you don't expect the unexpected. All the same, I ought to have been wary, if nothing else, because he'd nothing to lose. He'd only a murder charge to go back to.

There was blood on my face from a cut across my eyebrow and the linen suit I was wearing was soaked. I got up unsteadily, holding on to the bed.

I just hoped that Dwight would never get to know about all this. Dabbing a handkerchief in the remains of the water I wiped away the blood and tried to make myself respectable. Then I went cautiously out of the room, closing the door behind me, and groped my way down the dusky staircase.

The clerk was dozing at his desk and he looked up as I appeared.

'Mr. Mitchill,' I said. 'Where is he?'

'Gone,' he said. 'He went out. He said he'd be back tomorrow. He said he had to visit the students' water-conservation project for a night but that he was coming back tomorrow.'

I wondered if he'd been paid, because he wasn't going to see anything more of Mitchill.

He came out from behind the desk and stared at my soaked suit. I guessed that a report would probably be sent to the right quarter as soon as I left, because it wasn't difficult to guess that something odd had happened in Mitchill's room.

'Shall I tell him you asked for him?'

'No, don't bother.'

'Which hotel are you?' he asked. 'In case he wants to find you?'

'Ching Chiang,' I said, hoping to put him off the track a bit.

He nodded. As soon as I'd turned my back he'd send a boy round to police headquarters. Fortunately he didn't know my name and hadn't got my address, but I reckoned I hadn't much time to spare before they caught up with me. It seemed a good idea to prepare some story and get hold of Tsiu Lin as quickly as possible. Perhaps she could help me with a few arrangements to visit the drainage system area at Chengsha.

When I got back to the hotel, I made a telephone call to the Information Section of the Ministry of Foreign Affairs and asked for Tsiu Lin. They kept me waiting for some time, and I sat by the telephone in frustration, watching the seconds tick away on my watch, knowing all the time I ought to change my address before they found me. Although Armour's disguise was good there was no point in testing it unnecessarily.

Eventually the message came back that Tsiu Lin was not available. Angrily I slammed the receiver down, wondering where the hell she was. I suddenly felt lost without her. She'd always been there to answer every question I'd asked and I'd never rung up for her without her being near the telephone. I'd wondered occasionally, in fact, if she were ever off duty.

Two hours later I tried again, and once more they told me she was not available.

'Why not? Where is she?'

'She is not here,' the voice answered.

'Where does she live? I must see her.'

They gave me an address at the other side of the university and, in desperation, I took a cab there. It was a shabby district and the owner of the building was unfriendly. He showed some surprise at my request for Tsiu Lin.

'She should be at the Ministry on duty,' he said.

'She's not there,' I answered. He obviously thought I was all-European and in his angry glance I saw the Chinese hatred for Westerners that was so carefully disguised at the Hsinchiao Hotel. It went back through generations of humiliation to the days when the first self-important white ambassadors to Peking had been announced contemptuously as 'Red barbarians bearing tributes.'

I was shown into the two or three rooms that Tsiu Lin inhabited. They were clean, and furnished in a bare, bleak manner. There was no sign of Tsiu Lin beyond the magazines I'd given her, open at the fashion pages.

'She has not been home since she left this morning,' the proprietor told me.

Suddenly uneasy, I glanced quickly round the room. Nothing was out of place, nothing seemed to indicate that anything was wrong, but I remembered her boy friend, Chung Yen Siang, and wondered if she'd been swept up with him.

I thanked the proprietor and took a pedicab to the Ministry in the Forbidden City, where I was shown to a brightly lit modern office in an old pagoda-style building. A tall thin Cantonese wearing Western clothes, with glasses and slickly parted hair, greeted me.

'Mr. Nolan,' he said warmly. 'My name is Li. We are pleased to see you here. We are ready to answer all your questions.'

'I'm enquiring about the guide you assigned to show me around,' I said, treading warily, anxious not to cause trouble for Tsiu Lin if she were not in trouble already. 'I don't seem to be able to contact her. Perhaps she's ill.'

Li's eyes dropped and his fingers began to trace an idle pattern in the polished surface of his desk. The gesture somehow alarmed me. It was the gesture of a man who is uncertain what to say next.

'Have you tried her rooms?' he asked.

'Yes. She hasn't been there since this morning.'

'I see.' Li thought for a while, then he tapped the desk

sharply with his fingertips. 'We must look into this,' he said briskly. 'Just stay here, Mr. Nolan. I will enquire from Mr. Shu.'

He left me, and I sat smoking and staring round the room. It showed no sign whatsoever of Eastern influence in its decorations or furnishings.

A moment or two later Li came back. 'Mr. Shu will see you,' he said.

I was led into an office further down the corridor, where a small, stout, middle-aged Chinese was sitting behind the desk, beaming a welcome. I didn't smile back. I was alarmed now, quite certain that something had happened to Tsiu Lin, and concerned for my exit route.

Shu indicated a chair opposite him. 'Please sit down, Mr. Nolan,' he said.

I sat down and came straight to the point. 'Where is Han Tsiu Lin?' I demanded.

Shu offered me a cigarette, then he sat back and lit one for himself. He looked up, smiling.

'I regret to say, Mr. Nolan, that Han Tsiu Lin is no longer with us. Her name has been removed from our list of accredited guides. I can offer you another student in her place if you wish.'

I drew a deep breath, wondering how much I was responsible for Tsiu Lin's predicament. The things I'd said to her, though in themselves innocent enough and balanced by the plea I'd put forward of wishing to be honest, had probably been overheard and wrongly construed. What she was suffering now—and I had a shrewd suspicion that it was more than merely removal from the list of accredited guides—was probably because of that.

I found myself wondering what the hell I could do for her. Within the limitations of my job, of course. 'I don't want another guide,' I said slowly. 'I'd got used to Tsiu Lin.'

Shu beamed. 'I can promise that this other student will be just as attractive as Han Tsiu Lin. I'm sure she will be glad to accompany a young man as handsome as you to lunch in exactly the same way.'

I looked up. 'Who told you about that? Tsiu Lin?'

'Yes. It was in her report. There was nothing wrong in it, so long as it was reported.'

'Then why is she no longer with you?'

Shu placed his fingertips together in the form of a steeple. 'She was discovered to be a deviationist.'

I found myself growing hot with anger and my fury must have shown in my face, because Shu held up a placating hand.

'Please don't worry, young man,' he said. 'It is nothing to do with you. You have conducted yourself with complete propriety at all times. We have no complaints about you whatsoever.'

That was a relief at least, and I realised that, whatever they'd done to her, Tsiu Lin had kept quiet about all those dangerous questions I'd put to her. Nevertheless, despite a feeling of gratitude and a knowledge that I was in the clear, I was still far more concerned for Tsiu Lin than I knew I ought to be.

'Why has she been removed then?' I asked. 'Was it because of Chung Yen Siang?'

Shu gave a fat little laugh of delight. 'Ah, so she told you about him? Yes, indeed, it *was* Chung Yen Siang. He was found to be a deviationist, too, and he had clearly influenced the girl.'

'How did you find out?'

'Chung Yen Siang told us.' Shu chuckled. 'He completely recanted all his beliefs when he was confronted and was so ashamed of himself he agreed to give us the names of others he knew who were found to be lacking in true humility towards the State and considered themselves to know more than our Chairman about how our country should be run. The name of Han Tsiu Lin was the first.'

'It would be,' I said bitterly, deciding I wasn't surprised. 'I thought he loved the girl.'

'So he did. But he found he loved his country and the ideals of socialism more.'

'So he betrayed her?'

Shu shrugged. 'I wouldn't call it that.'

'I would. And Chung? Did he go free?'

'Of course. He recanted.'

'I expect he was one of your bloody *hanchous*!'

The words burst out of me unexpectedly. When I'd gone in I'd had no intention of getting worked up over an unknown Chinese girl. I felt like kicking myself.

Shu was frowning, but he recovered quickly and spread his hands, palms upwards. 'The girl was born under British influence,' he said. 'She had to be watched.'

I'd have been glad to wipe that silly smile off his face with my fist, but I had control of myself now. 'Where is she?' I asked more rationally.

'She will be taken to the Chan Tsu Corrective Training Camp.'

'For punishment.'

He gave one of his delighted laughs. 'Young man,' he said, 'I can see you are under the influence of Han Tsiu Lin's pretty face. It has happened more than once. She has been a disruptive influence even in this office.' He laughed again. 'However, you can rest assured we don't chop off heads any more. We merely reshape them. She will be re-educated. For all we know she was an agent of the Kuomintang. She will eventually confess her crimes and see her errors. She will unlearn the decadent bourgeois ideas she inherited from her parents.'

I nodded. I could happily have taken Shu by his fat throat and shaken him.

'Can I see her?' I asked. 'Perhaps talk to her.'

Shu laughed again. 'Of course not, Mr. Nolan. Yours is a bourgeois influence, however much you see our point of view. She might waste time and not recant. It is to her good that she should see no one but her teachers. She will eventually be freed, a cleansed woman.'

For a moment, I had a picture of Tsiu Lin, her pretty, grave face sombre with thoughts of Communism, her slender figure brutalised under a harsh padded suit, her legs hidden, all the normal fragile vivacity damped down to a parrot-like repetition of the ideas that would be pumped into her. Perhaps they even used drugs to change the personality. I'd heard they did. I felt sickened, but horribly aware that there was nothing I could do about it. I couldn't even protest because that would have brought suspicion on me.

'I see,' I said, trying to sound as cheerful as possible. 'I'm sure you're right, of course. Perhaps you'd better let me have another guide, after all. I still have work to do.'

Shu nodded happily. 'It will be Fu Mei Sing, another student. She will be sent to your hotel tomorrow morning.'

'And if it's possible,' I went on, choking over the words as I tried to sound friendly, 'give Tsiu Lin my best regards. She was hoping to arrange for me to visit the Chengsha area, you know, to see the Party Chairman open the new land-drainage system.'

Shu smiled. 'Well, at least, you'll be near each other. The Chan Tsu camp provides labour for the building of the system.'

I stumbled out of the office, trying to look amiable. In the street, I found myself a pedicab and had myself taken back to the Hsinchiao Hotel. I was seething with a frustrated rage that I knew was cock-eyed and wrong and dangerous. The whole thing was repugnant to me, and I boiled inside at the thought of happy, friendly, eager

Tsiu Lin being made into some Communist automaton. It was the first kick at the underpinnings of my confidence.

'Bugger you, Dwight,' I muttered to myself. I was eager to vent my rage on something more personal than the vast Communist system set up by Mao Tse-tung. 'If it weren't for you, I wouldn't be here, and then I wouldn't even have known Tsiu Lin.'

Back at the Hsinchiao I drank a large double brandy and decided to forget Tsiu Lin. I hadn't come to China, I kept trying to remind myself, to work out the problems of a girl. Although she was beautiful and intelligent and young enough to make anyone feel sad at the dew-fresh look she always wore and the way she could make that stupid name that Dwight had invented for me sound like music, she still belonged on the opposite side of the fence.

The brandy warmed me but it didn't help my anger to subside and I had to make an effort to thrust Tsiu Lin from my mind. 'God damn it,' I told myself. 'She's only a little Chink chick. You've never met her before and you'll never meet her again.'

The following morning the new guide, Fu Mei Sing, arrived. I met her in the hall where I'd first met Tsiu Lin. She was pretty, with eyes like jet and a peach-coloured complexion caused by the wind that was blowing. She was dressed in much the same way as Tsiu Lin, in a black suit and white blouse that I noticed was well-filled with bosom, but there was a curious automatic response to all my questions that seemed to indicate that this one had been properly indoctrinated, with no intelligent questioning streak running through her that allowed her to doubt. She never smiled; her small face was always straight and expressionless. In spite of her prettiness she was as sexless as a storm trooper and I guessed she was probably not merely a guide but also a practised informer. After the mistake of Tsiu Lin they weren't likely to allow anyone as clear-thinking near me again.

I didn't mention Tsiu Lin except to indicate that she'd been arranging for me to visit the Chengsha area for the opening of the dams.

'I'd like now,' I said, 'to go a little earlier. To prepare the ground, as you might say. I'd like to talk to the people in the district, to find out something of the team spirit behind this magnificent venture.'

She nodded. 'I will see that you have the necessary documents. When were you thinking of leaving?'

I didn't give myself much longer before the police started enquiring into what had happened in Mitchill's room and came to interview me.

'At once,' I said. 'Today, if possible. That will give me two or three days before the Party Chairman arrives.' Just two or three days to find Mitchill in an area as big as London and as blank as the Sahara.

Fu Mei Sing was busy writing in a little notebook which she shoved into her shoulder bag. I wondered how much of it was the instructions I'd given her and how much information for her superiors.

'I will make the arrangements for tomorrow morning,' she announced expressionlessly. 'It will be impossible earlier.'

I nodded agreement, and when she'd gone I went downstairs to the desk clerk and obtained a Chinese map of the Chengsha area. There were three main townships in the district, none of them large, and I guessed there wouldn't be many hotels. I would have only about forty-eight hours, if they didn't stop me, to unearth Mitchill. With the passes of the Ministry of Information, however, I ought to find it easy to get co-operation.

I returned to my room and began to throw my belongings into the single bag I carried. As I thought of Chengsha, I remembered the Chan Tsu Correction Camp and thought again of Tsiu Lin. The same sense of frustration and fury rose up in me. I hadn't known her long, but with her straightforward honesty she'd made me feel that in spite of the propaganda pumped out at every street corner there was still hope for the country that had bred the fragile, determined little woman who'd married my grandfather; and I realised I missed Tsiu Lin more than I'd expected.

Mei Sing came to visit me that evening. By that time I was hopping with impatience. She brought leaflets on the new drainage system, a specially printed map of the Chengsha district in English, and bus and train time-tables.

'There is plenty of transport about the area,' she explained. 'It is being opened up, and the police have instructions to give all the help they can. There will be other Western journalists there, of course, from France and America and England, who will want to relate the tremendous advances being made in China.'

For their potty little Communist papers, I supposed. They'd all be hand-picked. There certainly wouldn't be any of the opposition there, I knew. Most of them would be not only Left, but Left of Left, from the small, bitter, humourless weeklies run in Italy and France, or from the papers of the new states in Africa, where China was trying to exert her influence. Then there'd be a few left-wing bigwigs from the same areas who were going to produce books on what they'd seen—men such as I was supposed to be myself—men who were already half convinced, the sort of men who could write with heavy authority on a country they'd visited for three whole days.

'I see,' I said. 'Thank you very much.'

'Is there anything else?'

'What about the passes I need?'

'Perhaps you will collect the necessary documents in the morning,' she suggested. 'As late as possible, please. Deputy Director Tai's department has to sign them.'

I had swung away from her, but now, as she spoke, I stopped dead and turned slowly back to face her. My stomach felt knotted.

'Whose department did you say?'

'Deputy Director Tai's. Tai Tso Hua.'

I recovered a little. 'That's what I thought you said.'

'Have you met him?' she asked, watching me shrewdly.

'No,' I lied. 'But I've heard of him. From Tsiu Lin.'

'We think very highly of Deputy Director Tai.'

'I'm sure you do,' I said. And you'd think a lot more of him, I thought, if you knew what his real job is.

'Have you everything you need?' she asked, with an arch look at me. She was quite close and that well-filled blouse was near to my chest. She looked up at me again and her eyelids fluttered. 'I have nothing on this evening.'

I wondered if she meant it literally, because she seemed to be suggesting a roll in the hay, and I bet she'd have joined me like a shot if I'd agreed. A little free-for-all in a hotel bedroom was more than welcome to some people, but I'd been in the game too long to get caught. Eugene Patrick Nolan might not be a very big fish but if he could be put in a compromising situation, even *he* would make a file in the offices of the secret police that might be worth using some time.

Fu Mei Sing looked vaguely disappointed when I said I had all I wanted, as though that wonderful bust of hers had lured more than one man to his doom, and she'd thought it might lure me. When she'd gone, I stood for a moment, deep in thought. Somewhere outside the window the loudspeakers were still blaring away, interspersing martial music by brass bands with Party propaganda and the sweet thoughts of Chairman Mao. 'The American people do not want war. Only the Wall Street monopolists. We must act now or perish. But all reactionaries are paper tigers. In appearance they are frightening but in reality their strength is not great, and we have already overtaken Britain....'

It kept coming at me in a steady stream you couldn't shut your ears to; heavy, ponderous, without tone or inflexion, like the marching of millions of feet.

I was still holding the documents Mei Sing had given me, carefully folded in a little plastic folder, and suddenly, browbeaten, frustrated, defeated and sick at the thought of Tsiu Lin dragging stones or carting soil, I flung the folder at the wall. It struck with a soft whack and the papers fluttered out and fell to the floor.

I stared at them for a while, then I drew a deep breath, trying to get control of myself, knowing I was behaving like a fool. I bent to pick up the papers, and as I did so, I thought of Tai Tso Hua and took out my passport and the other documents Armour had prepared, to give me my identity. I spread them out on the bed, staring at them, looking for flaws.

They looked okay. I hoped to God they were.

VII

In spite of Mei Sing's request to me not to be in a hurry, I was at the Information Section of the Ministry of Foreign Affairs first thing the next morning.

As it happened, I met Mei Sing coming out as I entered and she stopped dead and clapped her hands to her mouth.

'Mr. Nolan!' She gave a little cry. 'You're too early!'

'I'm in a hurry,' I said sharply. 'There's a train at eleven and I want to spend as much of the morning as I can in the city. How about speeding things up for me, Mei Sing?'

She looked doubtful, then put on an arch look of determination. I found myself wishing I still had Tsiu Lin to deal with.

The thought of her managed to give me a nasty jolt and I thrust it out of my mind hurriedly. For God's sake, I told myself, I've come to China to do a job, not get involved with a dame! The last thing people in my line of work had to do was get involved with anyone.

I gave Mei Sing a sour look but she didn't appear to notice.

'I'll insist,' she said gaily. 'I'll make them hurry it through. Just for you, Mr. Nolan.'

I followed her inside, trailing her from office to office as she argued with officials in a shrill, high-pitched voice. No one seemed keen to start work too quickly.

'The daily discussion of unity and criticism is about to begin,' Mei Sing explained. 'At these meetings, we point out the unsocial behaviour of our fellow workers. Everyone must attend.' She gave a little laugh that sounded well and truly false and indicated the arguing clerks. 'In the old days, I'm told, when anyone refused to work he was kicked, expected to be kicked, and got on with it. Nowadays, physical punishment is not given and he has to be remonstrated with. It takes longer.'

At last someone agreed to do something and I was asked for my passport and things started happening.

'Almost deviationists in their attitude to work,' Mei Sing said with another abrasive laugh.

She stood watching, still wearing an artificial look of frustration, as the clerk carried away the documents, then she turned to me, her hands on her hips, that large provocative bust thrust out at my chest.

'It won't take long now. They'll bring it to you here.'

But they didn't. Ten minutes later, a young Chinese

appeared and asked me to follow him.

'Oh, dear, there must be some trouble over accommodation,' Mei Sing said. 'But it'll soon be put right.'

I wasn't so sure it was trouble over accommodation that was holding us up, and there was a distinct tingle of anticipation along my spine as I walked along the corridor.

Shu, the small fat Chinese who had told me of Tsiu Lin's fall from favour, met me, and I noticed at once that he wasn't smiling this time.

'This way,' he said shortly.

The office to which he led me was smaller than his own, and it had a bare ascetic look about it, an astringent look that I associated with dedication, as though the owner, God help him, needed only work to keep him satisfied.

The man behind the desk was small and slightly built with a narrow head and a long high-bridged northern nose. He was wearing glasses now but his face was unlined and youthful—as youthful as it had been when I'd last seen it in Canton four years before. A chair was pushed forward and a cup of green tea was filled for me by a silent woman clerk.

'Mr. Nolan.' The smooth face was devoid of expression, but the black eyes with their curiously opaque appearance never left my face. 'I am Tai Tso Hua.'

Don't I know it, I thought. You careful little bastard, you know me as well as I know you. That damn photograph in my passport didn't disguise me enough, and Tai's sharp eyes hadn't failed to spot the similarity to someone he already knew.

'There are no difficulties, Mr. Nolan,' he was saying. 'But I have always liked to make a habit, since I took over this department, of handing over the necessary documents myself. A personal touch, you understand.'

'Also helps to keep track of people, I reckon, too,' I said cheerfully.

'It also helps to keep track of people, too,' Tai agreed in his soft flat voice, his eyes still on me.

'After all, you must have plenty of enemies in your country.'

'Not as many as there were. But they still exist.'

He turned away towards a desk under the window and picked up a sheaf of coloured slips of paper, all clipped together, and slipped them inside my passport.

'Your permits, Mr. Nolan,' he said. 'Everything is in order. Your internal pass to allow you to move from one province to another. There are two of those. A permit to sleep away from Peking. A permit to travel on the railways. A permit to visit the area of the Chengsha drainage system. A request to the public relations department in the area to see that you have all the information you require. A ticket to attend the opening. A slip with a number on it. That is your seat. You will be among the foreign journalists. You will be very close to our Chairman, with a good view of everything.'

'Quite a bunch of bumf,' I said.

'Bumf?'

'Western joke, Mr. Tai. That's all. Dates from the time of the war, I believe. The one against the Nazis.'

Tai didn't smile. 'I see,' he said.

He handed over the sheaf of papers and held out his hand. 'Good luck, Mr. Nolan. I hope you enjoy your visit. All we ask is that you young writers should be fair to us.'

'Don't worry. I'll be that.'

He opened the door and stood back, a small slight figure in grey trousers and a black jacket buttoned to the throat. He didn't say goodbye, and as I walked back along the corridor towards the street, I was conscious of the expressionless eyes watching me all the way.

The train to the south was already being announced as

I descended from the cab at the station. I had spent a long time moving in and out of shops and swapping cabs and buses, constantly on the move, constantly changing my whereabouts in the hope of throwing off anyone who might be following me. Tai was no fool and I suspected the different hair style and the smart with-it whiskers I wore hadn't fooled him.

Once I thought I spotted someone on my trail. A youngster dressed like a student with a couple of books under his arm turned up twice in the shops and bazaars I visited, and when I went to the park, just to test whether I *was* being followed, I saw him again near the entrance as I left. I threw him off without difficulty.

The gold pagoda clocks over the long front of the station gave me only ten minutes to spare as I went inside. There seemed to be cars and buses everywhere, with well-dressed Chinese mixing with Europeans who were being disgorged under the watchful eyes of Chinese hostesses in neat black skirts and coats. One of the girls was tall and neat-looking and for a moment I thought with a leap of the heart that it was Tsiu Lin, but when she turned, her face lacked the eager vitality I'd expected. My spirits crashed as I thought of her again, by this time a prisoner at Chan Tsu.

I slipped hurriedly between the tall columns of yellow stone and the ornamental shrubs to where the high glass dome echoed the sound of excited voices.

There seemed to be thousands of young people milling about, crowding round the women selling hard-boiled eggs, rice cakes, tomatoes and bananas, and groups of them were standing in solemn squadrons singing Party songs under their scarlet banners. There were so many people, even the *hanchous* couldn't have kept track of everybody. It wasn't hard to hide and I joined one group and tum-tum-ti-tummed my way through a few bars of 'The East Is Glowing Red,' while I looked round to see if I were in the clear.

'You sing well, *Ton Tse,*' a young man with a fistful of books and a little yellow-starred red plastic flag on a stick told me. 'But you should learn the words.'

He looked like a bit of a know-all. 'Yes, I know, *Ton Tse,*' I agreed. 'But even if I don't know the words of the hymn, I know my facts about our great democracy. Uranium is plentiful and the coal output is higher than Britain's, and do you know that in Kiangsi they are hanging electric light bulbs over the paddy fields so that the rice grows all night?'

He obviously didn't, so I was one up on him, and he shoved off quickly.

No one seemed to notice me as I took my place on the train and swung my bag onto the rack. The compartment smelled of antiseptic and even before I'd sat down a woman came along with a spray and a wet mop which she slapped along the floor beside my feet.

The racket in the station, with the shouts of passengers and their relations thin against the iron voice of the loudspeakers was enough to give you a headache. I sat quietly in my corner as the train drew out, ignoring the laughing, cheering students moving in swarms up and down the corridor.

The countryside to the south was flat and sunlit, and full of fields of maize and sorghum. The Chinese peasants hadn't changed much, I noticed, despite the propaganda. Still the same heavy tread, still the same weary, half-starved bodies, though I had to admit that there appeared to be more prosperity than there'd been for other generations. There were new buildings and more tractors and lorries and fewer oxen, and the stations we passed through seemed to be full of youngsters in Sun Yat-sen tunics. I reflected that the régime was banking everything on these kids who couldn't remember the old days.

Sections of the cloudless blue sky reflected on the water

of the paddy fields where the lines of stooping figures laboured as they always had. Once we were well away from Peking, I noticed that the women were more poorly dressed and that the men wore the universal black rags with round cone-shaped hats. The river looked lifeless and still among the rushes where they worked. This was the old China, not the China of the future that was being planned in Peking. There were no propaganda loudspeakers here and life hadn't changed much in a thousand years.

Chengsha was a drab dusty town surrounded by flat plains, yellow with sunlight. It looked, I imagined, much as it always had, although its centre had been torn down for the erection of ugly utilitarian concrete blocks—the new hotels which had become necessary in the area of great reconstruction works. Here were cabs and white-jacketed policemen, and strings of listless red flags and posters and vast pictures of the Party Chairman repeated ad nauseam everywhere on the walls.

The hotel was new but it had a strange look of impermanence and there were already cracks in the plaster as though it had been pushed up too quickly. One end of the entrance hall was taken up with a vast tank of tropical fish and the other with a picture of the Chairman, flanked by red banners. There were also photographs of concrete walls, bulldozers, cement mixers and lorries and tractors of ancient design. A loudspeaker was blaring away outside, of course, and I had to shout to make myself heard at the desk as I signed in.

The room I was given was small and comfortless and looked out over the square. To shut out the noise, I slammed the window to with a bang and flung my jacket on the bed. Almost immediately, there was a knock on the door.

I opened it to find a young man there. He had a military air, and was dressed in a grey tunic with neatly fastened collar and pockets, dark trousers, and a cap set squarely on his head, Chinese fashion.

'Mr. Eugene Patrick Nolan?' he asked, his face splitting into a smile that was patently false.

'That's me.'

'You've come for the opening of the new drainage system?'

'That's correct.'

'May I introduce myself? I am from the information office across the square. My name is Wang Teh.'

I nodded, guessing at once that he'd had instructions from Peking to keep an eye on me.

'There are many like you here in the town,' he went on.

'I'm sure there are.'

'At least thirty-seven foreign journalists anxious to see how China is leaping forward.'

'I'm sure.'

'Several from your own country.' Wang took out a typed list from the briefcase he carried and began to read names that were familiar to me. Many of them belonged on another list that Esmond kept in his files in Hong Kong.

'I expect you know many of them?'

'Yes. Many of them. Is Mr. Mitchill here? He's an old friend of mine.'

The Chinese gave a fluttering gesture, and his eyes flickered momentarily. 'Yes,' he said. 'Mr. Mitchill's here.'

'Where's he staying?'

'Across the square.'

'I'll have to look him up.'

Wang beamed. 'Of course. Is there anything you require?'

'No. Nothing. I'll have a look round first. Later there may be a lot I'd like to know.'

'I am at your service.'

I nodded my head and Wang withdrew silently. Shutting

the door behind him, I put my back to it for a moment, glancing round the room, then I turned and examined the door. It was impossible to lock it, I noticed.

I placed my suitcase in front of it, so that it would jam against the leg of the bed—just long enough to prevent anyone entering unawares. Above the bed was a small ventilator—the sort of place that might hide a camera or a microphone—and I hung my jacket over it. Then I felt carefully all round the washbasin and round the back of the bed and the wardrobe. There appeared to be nothing, but I took the precaution of unplugging the bedside light. There was no telling whether it hid a mike or not.

I washed quickly and changed my shirt, then, taking my jacket, walked down the stairs and out of the hotel. Wang was standing by the desk as I left and immediately the artificial smile flicked on to his face. It disappeared again as I nodded and swung away—so quickly, in fact, it was gone before I had turned my gaze. Careless, I thought. Very careless.

There was a small garden in the square, with a couple of dusty trees and a seat in it. I sat down on the seat and lit a cigarette, my eyes on the hotel opposite. In front of me I could see the square blocks of the new hotels and party offices, and behind me the pagoda roofs of the old town. It was an uninspiring place, and I thought again of Tsiu Lin labouring somewhere just to the south, sweating in the hot sun. My stomach turned at the thought of the months she'd have to spend in the area, probably never allowed to move out of it even when her mental correction was finished. She was doomed to spend her days in this dreary treeless little town of dust and sunshine, condemned to an absence of amusement, Party propaganda and a spiritless procession of days; probably to be forced, eventually, into an unwilling marriage with some official who would give her a few scraps of comfort in exchange for her presence in his bed.

I jumped as the cigarette burned my fingers and I threw it away savagely, aware that once again my mind had been more on Tsiu Lin than on the job in hand. Slowly, forcing myself to concentrate, I lit another cigarette and stretched myself in an attitude of relaxation, like any northerner enjoying the warm sun or the spectacle of the new and growing China.

I sat for a long time, making occasional notes in the notebook I carried in my pocket, and watching the movement across the square. From time to time, Europeans or Africans emerged from the hotel opposite, mostly in groups or with a guide, and I saw taxis appear and disappear.

I had almost decided to go back to my room and watch from there when I saw Mitchill emerge. He was carrying a back pack and walked heavily down the steps as though he were tired. I bent and pretended to be tying a shoelace, my face hidden by my sleeve. He climbed into a taxi and was driven away.

I walked quickly across to the row of taxis and hailed the first one. The driver jabbered at me in Chinese for a while, asking me where I wished to go, but I merely gestured, pretending I didn't understand, and indicated the direction Mitchill had taken.

As we left the town behind, I saw the other taxi in front, and when the driver turned round again to ask my destination, I gestured at it again. The driver nodded and relaxed behind the wheel, following several hundred yards behind Mitchill.

After a while, the road began to rise until it ran on a raised ridge across the plain, with paddy fields on either side, where men and women were working among the rushes. Along the fringes of the road there were more workers, strengthening the banks among the lorries dumping loads of soil. At first, there were only a few, then we began to pass columns of them, thousands of blue-garbed figures, men and women alike, all of them with flat expressionless faces devoid of hope or happiness, all of them carrying mattocks or rakes or shovels.

'From the labour camps,' the driver said, pointing.

There were a few huts among the bamboo clumps, and the curved roof of some rural temple. In front, rows of workers were breaking ground for the new scheme, some in the conical straw hats of peasants, some in boiler suits, their trousers above their knees. For the most part they used antique equipment and I saw the straining docile figures of women creeping forward, human energy alone reclaiming the land.

'It's the same all over China,' the driver said cheerfully. 'Irrigation work, reafforestation, roads, railways, canals, all carried out by reactionaries.' He laughed. 'Very cheap.'

I pretended again not to understand, but I could see here and there across the paddy fields, on a rise in the ground at the end of another raised road, hutted camps surrounded by what appeared to be barbed wire and wooden towers.

'Deviationists,' he said, indicating the thousands of figures, and I began to examine the hopeless faces as they passed, staring at each one intently, until I realised I was looking for Tsiu Lin. Again the weight appeared in my stomach, a solid indigestibility of resentment and bitterness.

'Guards?' I said, waving my hand.

The driver glanced at me, then indicated boys sitting in lorries, and I caught a glimpse of gun barrels.

There weren't many of them and it spoke much for the Chinese mind that these thousands of men and women could be guarded by so few. It had always been so, of course. In the days of my grandmother they had been held in thrall by a few Manchu swordsmen and later by a few companies of marines belonging to one of the European treaty powers. The whole history of the Chinese peasant was one of willing subordination to a few weapons in the hands of strong leaders.

We had passed the labouring thousands now, the men harnessed like horses to heavy wooden carts full of soil, the bent figures of women carrying stones, their heads down, their hair like dusty black wings over their faces as they stooped and lifted, stooped and lifted, stooped and lifted. We were running among trees as the built-up road reached a rise in the ground, and the flat plain below was flooded and empty of anything but rushes. For a while, I conducted an argument in broken Chinese with the driver, enquiring about the means of returning.

'By bus,' he kept saying, faintly irritated as I put on an appearance of failing to understand. 'By bus. From the pumping station.' Gesturing fiercely, he indicated a group of low grey buildings in the distance, surrounded by flags. There appeared to be wooden stands erected nearby and I guessed it was to be the spot where the Party Chairman was to make his speech.

A mile further on, Mitchill's taxi appeared, returning the way it had come, and as it rushed past, I realised it was empty. Somewhere just ahead, Mitchill was on his feet, looking around.

'Here,' I shouted. 'Here! Stop here!'

The driver slammed on the brakes and the car slid to a stop.

'Here?'

'I want to look around. Look around. You understand? See what is being done.'

The driver clearly thought I was mad, and made no attempt to get out and open the door for me. I paid him quickly and watched as he turned the car round. His face was filled with disgust.

As the cab drew away, I stepped into the shadows of the trees. Mitchill couldn't be far away. His cab had been less than a mile ahead of mine, and, allowing for the time it took for the vehicle to turn round and head back again, I knew he must be somewhere within half a mile of me.

I'd already guessed what he was up to. I'd done it myself more than once. He was reconnoitring the ground near the beflagged pumping station, wondering if there was likely to be any escape for him.

I scanned the land around me from the raised ground among the trees. There was no sign of anyone among the rushes. In the distance, by the yellow buildings, the flags stood out brightly against the dusty blue of the sky. I could see a few small figures moving about there, and a straggling column of workers, both men and women, near a group of lorries.

I began to walk along the fringe of the road, keeping as much as possible in the shade of the willow trees and eucalyptus gums. After a while a bus came past, trailing its cloud of dust as it roared towards Chengsha. I stepped back among the trees out of sight and was about to step out again, when I caught a glimpse of Mitchill away on my right. The fool had a high-powered rifle with a telescopic sight. It was the sort that could be dismantled, and he'd obviously had it in the back pack. Where he'd got it, God only knew, but just there, just then, it was as good as a death sentence.

He'd been standing between the trees, as I'd been doing, and he'd probably been invisible because he'd seen the bus approaching before I had and had taken cover sooner. I drew back into the shadow of the trees, stooping slightly to keep behind a clump of bushes, then, as he moved towards the road, I pushed quickly along the side of the rise, dodging between the trees and round the undergrowth. From time to time I caught glimpses of him through the foliage. He was carrying his hat and his balding head looked pink, as though it had caught the sun.

After a while, when I judged I was ahead of him, I began to move up the slope. He was behind me now, and I felt for the automatic. My breath was coming quickly and tension was growing in me. It wasn't because I was afraid. It was because it was Mitchill I was trailing.

Momentarily, I remembered Amy, a hot-blooded, generous girl who'd shown me round Singapore the first time we met. At least, that was what Mitchill had thought she was doing, and I found myself hating the job I'd undertaken.

I stopped dead and straightened up, one hand inside my jacket. Thank God she'd never know the outcome of *this* meeting, *whatever* the outcome was going to be. Because Mitchill had to be stopped—and now.

He was walking slowly, staring over the marshy plain, and he actually had his back to me as I stepped out from behind my tree. As he turned, he almost bumped into me. He stopped dead, and his pink face went grey, and the dark, sunken eyes widened.

Then his brows came down and his thin lips tightened, and for a second, behind the frustration and fury that showed in his face, I saw the empty, cunning look of insanity.

'Hello, Mitchill,' I said softly.

VIII

For a long time, Mitchill said nothing. He was standing stock-still, and I saw his eyes flickering from side to side as his mind worked.

'Why have you followed me?' he said at last. He spoke slowly, his voice curiously thin for such a big man.

'For Christ's sake,' I said, suddenly angry. 'What the hell did you expect? You bloody near killed me with that water jug, you old fool!'

Mitchill frowned. 'I wish I had,' he said.

'It'd have been even worse then. Instead of me, it'd have been the fuzz. The Chinese fuzz.'

'What are you going to do?' he asked.

I indicated the gun in his hand. 'Well,' I said, 'that's quite a tricky-looking little toy you've got there.'

His eyes dropped to the gun. 'Yes,' he agreed, with a trace of humour in his eyes. 'I'm quite good with it, too.'

'I ought to turn you over to the bloody police, you old fool,' I said. 'But I'm not going to. I'm going to try to persuade you to come back. Down towards Hong Kong.'

'No!' The word burst out of him abruptly. 'No! I can't!'

'Why the hell not?'

'They're after me.'

'Who're after you?'

'*They* are.'

'Who's they, for Christ's sake?'

He made a vague gesture. 'They've been after me a long time. My wife was one of them.'

I sighed. 'All right, then. They're after you. But if you come back with me, we can stop them. Dwight's all for you, really,' I lied. 'He just wants you back.'

'He's one of them, too.'

I had to bite back the laughter. 'For God's sake,' I said. 'How can he be? He's spent all his life fighting them. He'd like you to fight them, too.'

'I am fighting them. Here.'

'Look, Mitchill,' I said patiently, 'there's nothing you can do here.'

'I can take one of them with me. A big one.'

I studied him for a moment. 'I could stop you like that,' I said, clicking my fingers. 'I've only got to call the next policeman I see. They wouldn't stop to ask questions.'

'I'd take him with me.'

'Okay, you'd take him with you. But that'd ruin your plan for taking the big one. You'd never get another chance. Much better to come back with me and help Dwight and the rest of us at a distance. You can fight them better that way.'

For the first time, Mitchill looked interested. A sharp look of cunning crossed his face. 'You think so?'

'I'm sure.'

'Suppose I don't want to?'

I took out the Biretta and showed it to him. 'I'd have to persuade you.'

Mitchill considered for a moment, then he nodded. 'Okay,' he said.

I hadn't expected him to surrender so meekly but, since he had, it seemed a good idea to get him back to Chengsha as quickly as possible while he was still in the mood. Once there, I could get him on a train to Peking and arrange for the Embassy to have him picked up and guarded until he could be put aboard an aircraft.

I studied him for a while and put the gun away. 'Let's go,' I said.

'Where are you taking me?'

'Back to Chengsha for a start.'

'And after that?'

'We'll cross that bridge when we come to it. And don't change your mind, cock. No funny business.'

Mitchill shook his head heavily. 'No funny business,' he agreed.

I wondered whether I ought to keep the Biretta in my hand, then I decided that I was already halfway towards persuading him to go home quietly and any suggestion of violence might put him off, so I put it away again. I indicated the rifle.

'And you'd better get rid of that bloody gun, too. Quick! Before anybody sees you with it. It's enough to get us both knocked off.'

He eyed me for a moment. 'Yes. I suppose it is.'

'Better throw it in the lake.'

'Yes. I'll have to get rid of the pack as well.'

'Let's get going then, for Christ's sake!'

Mitchill stooped to pick up the pack. As he scooped the two shoulder straps together and lifted it, I saw the muscles knot under his jacket. I was already stepping back as it brushed my head.

You prize bloody fool, I thought. This was the second time I'd allowed myself to be deceived by him, because of the soft spot in my heart that I knew I ought never to allow, the same soft spot that had set me wondering what was happening to Tsiu Lin. I was going weak in the head. Dwight would have been livid.

As I went to my knees, my mind was working quickly, however. Okay, you old bastard, I decided. Twice is enough for anybody.

As I rolled sideways, I saw the dust spurt up by my head and heard the crack of the gun. Right, I thought, it was a fight, and in my book there were only two kinds of fighting: dirty fighting and dirtier fighting.

Mitchill managed to get off another shot at me as I

jumped up, then I dived for his knees and over we went. I knew he'd lost the rifle and felt a whole lot better for it—that thing would have drilled an oak block like a skewer through steak. We rolled down the bank and I heard the crunch of dried weeds as we reached the water's edge. I managed to slide from under Mitchill's heavy body and came up on the other side, chopping furiously at his neck with the edge of my hand.

He grunted and I realised then that he'd dragged a pistol from his pocket. The old fool had the best part of an armoury on him and I wondered what else he'd got, too. But, as I reached for the Biretta, something halted me, some strange impulse that told me I wasn't fighting an enemy but a man who'd recently been a friend, a man who'd served his country well in peace and war. It still wasn't a killing job in my mind.

I kicked at the gun in Mitchill's hand and it spun from his fingers, but he whirled, incredibly quickly for a man of his size and age, and his fingers grasped my ankle, jerking it upwards so that I landed on my back. As I fell, I rolled over and scrambled to my feet just as Mitchill's great bulk crashed against my shoulders.

Red lights flashed in front of my eyes and all the breath was knocked from my body but I kept on fighting instinctively, bent under his weight and straining my neck muscles against the great forearm that was pressing against my throat, crushing the life out of me. My sight was growing blurred but I remembered to keep my head, and as I struggled to keep my senses, I pressed backwards with all my strength, so that Mitchill had to press forward to keep his balance. When his greater strength was bearing hard against me, I suddenly changed my tactics and bent forward quickly, so that he was carried over my head by his own weight.

As his heavy body hit the dust, his hand was close to his

gun and his fingers tightened over it as I dived for him, gouging at his eyes with my thumbs. He yelled with pain and rolled away, giving me time to make another grab for the gun, forcing it away from me.

We were up against the rocks that lined the lake now and I could feel my muscles cracking under his strength. With the perspiration starting out on my forehead, I was beginning to realise now I'd have to use my own gun in the end and I was wondering if I could take away one of the hands that clawed at Mitchill's wrist to reach for it, when there was a flash in front of my eyes and my nostrils were full of the smell of cordite. The sound of Mitchill's pistol going off seemed only like a pop but suddenly, I realised that the strength had gone from Mitchill's muscles, and I knew I was struggling with a dead man.

Slowly, I relaxed my grip and rolled away. Mitchill was lying on his face, his head in the dust, his feet in the water of the lake.

His face was pushed out of shape by the contour of the earth, his mouth half open and twisted by a stone under his cheek, and blood was pouring out of the hole where his right eye had been.

I got to my feet, brushing the dust from my trousers, and stood for a moment, staring down at him. There was no need to examine him to see if he was dead. The bullet had gone in at his right eye and out at the top of his head.

It didn't require much thought to realise that the first thing I had to do was hide the body and wind up my fact-finding mission at once. I could get back to Chengsha immediately, take the train to Peking, and board an aircraft out of the country. If I moved fast, I could be back in London or Hong Kong and reporting to Dwight before the body was even discovered. In spite of the number of vehicles passing along the road towards the new drainage scheme, in spite of the thousands of workers who were being marched along under their guards, it was unlikely that anyone would discover the body in a hurry, and at least the job for which I'd come to China had been done. Mitchill would not assassinate anybody now.

Quickly, I bent down and, taking hold of his ankles, began to drag him towards the water. The linen jacket he wore rode up to his armpits, and there was a crude smear of blood across the ground like the trail of a slug. At the water's edge, I dragged the jacket down and buttoned it, and began to fill the pockets with stones. There was little else I could do, but it would help to keep the body concealed at least until I was clear of the country.

Finally, I pushed him into the lake among the reeds, shoving him as far as possible into the water until he was hidden, then I threw the heavy pack out as far as I could and watched it sink out of sight.

When I'd finished, I lit a cigarette and stood staring at the water, drawing the smoke into my lungs in deep breaths. After a while, I straightened up and walked slowly up the bank, kicking dust over the smear of blood, then I broke a small branch off one of the willows growing by the water and brushed the dust smooth. I walked back to where the pistol was lying among the rocks and flung it as far as I could into the lake. It splashed and disappeared, and, satisfied, I started to search for the rifle.

I had just found it when, on the road immediately above me, an ancient jeep drew to a stop with a shriek of brakes. I stuffed the rifle back among the bushes just as half a dozen soldiers in the sand-coloured uniform of the People's Liberation Army headed towards me, shouting in Chinese, their rifles out in front of them. I stood stock-still. Then I saw that the man in civilian clothes behind them was Wang Teh, the slight, smiling young man who had appeared at my door as soon as I'd arrived in Chengsha.

'Mr. Wang!' I smiled immediately. 'What are you doing here?'

Wang didn't smile back this time. 'You know what I am doing here,' he said, and one of the soldiers jabbed me in the stomach with the muzzle of his rifle.

I stared at Wang, frowning. 'Tell this bloke of yours to take his gun out of my stomach, or I'll probably break it over his head.'

Wang looked up at me. 'Very funny, Mr. Eugene Patrick Nolan,' he said. 'Very funny indeed. It is good for young men to talk big when they are suffering from a feeling of guilt.'

My eyes narrowed. I knew very well what was in his mind but I had to pretend not to. 'What the hell are you talking about?' I said.

He indicated the men with the rifles. 'Perhaps you had better co-operate, Mr. Nolan,' he suggested. 'My friends here are well known for their impulsiveness. They are ardent patriots and they have no love for imperialistic Westerners.'

He jerked a hand at me and glanced at the soldiers. 'Search him,' he said.

One of the men seized my jacket by the collar and dragged it down over my shoulders, pinioning my arms. Wang's eyes fell at once on the gun I wore in the top of my trousers.

'A very strange weapon for a writer to carry, Mr. Eugene Patrick Nolan,' he snapped.

They had backed me up against the jeep by this time and I stood now with my hands on my head while Wang talked to me.

'Hadn't you better tell us why you had this gun, Mr. Nolan?'

'I kept it for my own protection,' I said.

'There is no need for protection in this country. We have an efficient police force.'

'I didn't know. I haven't been here before.'

There was another babble of excited conversation behind my back and I knew at once they'd found Mitchill's rifle. Wang's voice came quietly, sibilantly. 'We have another gun here,' he said softly. 'A very dangerous one. Why would you require this one?'

'I kept that for shooting the mosquitoes,' I explained, though I wasn't really feeling very confident or funny.

A gun butt jabbed me in the kidneys.

'Let us not be clever, Mr. Imperialist Nolan,' Wang said.

'There are a lot of mosquitoes round here,' I explained. 'I'm a good shot.'

'A fly-spray might not have caused questions to be asked, Mr. Nolan. Two guns do. Why do you have *two* guns?'

'I've told you. To protect myself.'

'Two guns? One a high-powered rifle.'

I shrugged. 'I'm a nervous type,' I said. 'I'm always scared when I'm travelling.'

'Most nervous travellers go in for small automatics. Belgian guns or Czech guns. Quite big enough to stop an intruder. I've seen them. This rifle is a deadly weapon.'

I tried to sound surprised. 'Go on! Is it?'

He paused, then he moved round to face me. 'What are you doing here?' he demanded.

'I told you. I'm a peaceful visitor.'

'I have reason to believe you are up to something. I was tipped off about you by Peking.'

So that's why you were waiting for me, I thought. That's why they'd followed me here. I wondered if they'd noticed Mitchill's absence yet.

'What for? What did they say I was up to?'

Wang moved back slightly so that to see him I had to look

over my shoulder. 'Even the most noble-minded of men are not without enemies,' he said sharply. 'There have been attempts to kill our Party Chairman.'

'Really? I hadn't heard that.'

'Not many people have,' Wang said. 'We keep our troubles to ourselves. But we have to be constantly on our guard against it. Our Chairman has changed China and he has many enemies.'

'Not many in China,' I pointed out. 'He's been careful to get rid of them all.'

Wang swung his arm with all his strength and struck me at the side of the temple with the back of his fist. I staggered against the jeep, straightened up and shook my head.

'That's a bloody fine way to treat a guest,' I said.

'You're no guest,' Wang said.

'Okay, then, if I'm not a guest, what am I?'

Wang glared at me. It's surprising how hatred can change a man's face. He no longer looked young. He didn't even look human.

'I know what you are,' he shouted, losing his temper and lashing out with both hands. 'You are an assassin! That is what you are, Mr. Filthy Eugene Patrick Nolan! An imperialist assassin with the blood of your victims still on your hands.'

IX

I managed to stagger out of Wang's reach at last. What a mess, I thought, my heart sinking to the level of my shoes. I'd stopped Mitchill knocking off the Dearly Beloved only to be accused of attempting to do it myself. This was one for the book all right and it was going to take some sorting out.

For a moment I almost blurted out the truth, but then I knew I couldn't tell them about Mitchill. They'd never believe me. God only knew what they'd think if they found him, but it certainly wouldn't be that he'd been going to knock off a few top Party officials, only that I'd knocked him off instead. It took too much swallowing. And in any case, it was the last thing in the world Dwight wanted.

I wondered how the hell I was going to get out of this one. I knew they'd start being unpleasant before long. What had happened so far was only a taste, and I wasn't the man to take a lot of that sort of nonsense. Don't get involved had been my motto. I'd always sworn that if I were ever in a position where people started beating me up, I'd not stand for it. It had never happened yet but I'd always decided that when it did, there'd be no heroics. I'd tell the truth and let London sort it out.

While I was still trying to think straight and shake off the effect of Wang's blows, he came nearer and stared into my face. I was tempted to spit in his eye and I'd have enjoyed doing it, too, but it didn't seem good policy just then. Not with half a dozen soldiers with guns sticking into my kidneys.

'Who else but an assassin would be prowling round here with a pistol and a sniper's rifle in his possession?' he yelled.

'Look—' I tried, and this time it was one of the other men who struck me. I staggered once more up against the jeep.

'I think you will have to be questioned,' Wang went on in satisfied tones.

'Well, for Christ's sake, let's get on with it! It's no bloody fun standing here with your monkeys knocking me about.'

'No.' Wang nodded. 'Perhaps not. This is no place for that.' He pointed to some barrack-like buildings in the distance across the paddy fields. 'Fortunately, we have a suitable place close at hand. We'll go there.'

By a series of jabs and shoves, I was forced into the jeep,

then two of the men in the sand-coloured uniforms jumped in beside me, holding their rifles so that the muzzles were directed at my chest. A third jumped up behind and sat with the rifle muzzle in the back of my neck. Wang climbed in next to the driver, and the rest hung on wherever they could.

'I suppose you couldn't tell these monkeys of yours that their rifles are dangerous, could you?' I suggested. 'One of 'em might go off.'

'No, I couldn't tell them,' Wang snapped.

'No.' I nodded. 'I thought not.'

The camp on the rise beyond the paddy fields reminded me of the pictures I'd seen of concentration camps. It was surrounded by a high barbed-wire fence, with sentry boxes at every corner, and a guard post at the gate. There seemed to be hundreds of blue-garbed figures but remarkably few armed men.

'What's this place you're taking me to?' I demanded.

'Chan Tsu Camp for Volunteer Workers,' Wang said.

'Volunteers? Is that why you've got armed guards?'

Wang turned. 'It will be as well if you do not make clever remarks at the expense of China,' he said.

I shrugged. 'Okay, but you do rather ask for them, don't you? I heard it was a correction camp.'

I indicated a mixed column of men and women passing us. 'Why don't they simply take control?' I asked. 'There are enough of them.'

'They are volunteers,' Wang insisted.

'You mean you've got the poor bastards so indoctrinated they think they haven't a hope. Who are they—peasants?'

'For the most part.'

'Used to kow-towing, bobbing their heads. First it was to the foreign devils. Now it's to home-grown devils. People like you, Wang, eh?'

'We get no trouble from them,' Wang said smugly.

'You're lucky, sweetheart. You would if I were among them.'

Wang allowed himself a smile. 'You will *not* be among them,' he said.

The gate, a simple wooden frame hinged to the upright and heavily wound round with barbed wire, was opened as the jeep approached. The soldiers on guard seemed to be mere boys, like the ones I'd seen in the lorries, and I guessed that inexperienced or second-line troops were used for the job—boys who were probably still undergoing military training—so that the first-line troops could hold the coast and the mountainous border to the north of India and Nepal and along the Russian frontier.

The jeep drew up outside a low stone building; as far as I could see, the only building not constructed of wood in the whole encampment. Wang signed to me to climb down and I jumped out and was prodded by the guards towards the door.

They led me down a corridor, and, my eyes busy, I saw cell doors with small grilles. At each one there was a face, blank, curious or despairing.

Again there appeared to be a minimum number of guards, a fact that I stored up in my head for future use. There were a few women about, of all ages, from young girls to old bent crones, some of them sweeping the floors, some of them apparently bringing boiled rice to the cells.

The guard commander stopped at the end of the corridor and unlocked a door.

'In!'

I stopped in the entrance and pretended to examine the cell. It looked as clean and antiseptic as a disinfectant bottle. My mind was weighing up chances, but there was a rifle in the small of my back and just then didn't seem the time to try making a break. Brother, I said to myself, this is what comes of Galahading about, succouring dames and halting evil. Jail. You are now up the proverbial creek. Without a paddle.

As I paused, someone gave me a violent shove in the back and I stumbled forward into the cell and flopped down on the string bed opposite the door. The door slammed and Wang's face appeared in the barred opening at the top of it.

'Reactionary capitalist tool!' he said in his soft voice, as though he were making polite conversation.

I looked up. 'I hope you end up paralysed all down one side,' I said as cheerfully as I could.

For a long time, I sat in silence on the bed, my mind busy with thoughts that were by no means as optimistic as my conversations with Wang had indicated. They had me, I decided, not to Nancy it up at all, by the short and curlies.

For a while, I wondered what was the best way out of the jam. Ten to one they'd look into my history and it wouldn't take them long before someone like Tai Tso Hua would decide that I wasn't Eugene Patrick Nolan at all but Harry Dempsey, already a man with a record in China.

I got to my feet and moved slowly round the cell, studying the window, the walls, the floor. But the cement that held the bars was good and solid and I had nothing on me that might be used to work on it. Even the bedframe was of wood. As I passed the door, I saw the face of the corporal of the guard behind the bars. I beamed at him.

'Stop staring,' I advised. 'You look like something washed up on a beach.'

The boy had no idea what I was saying and went on staring, so, unexpectedly, I jumped towards the door and shouted 'Booh!' He fell back, startled, but soon recovered his wits and began to shout abuse at me in a high-pitched childish voice.

I grinned at him. 'Sweetheart,' I said. 'Just let me catch you once on this side of the door without that rifle, and I'll give you such a belt on the ear, it'll make your eyes fall out.'

Uncomprehending, he finally went away; and, chiefly to be a nuisance and to see more of the lie of the land, I began to kick at the door and shout for food.

The little Chinese returned and shouted back at me, but I ignored him and went on yelling. 'I've had nothing to eat all day,' I roared. 'If I'm a prisoner I'm entitled to be fed!'

After a little more shouting, the Chinese stuck the muzzle of the rifle through the grille. Christ, I thought, if I could only get a bit more of it inside the cell. I went on deliberately taunting him. I knew he wouldn't dare shoot me without orders and I jeered and stormed at him until, furious, with the butt of the rifle against his cheek, he pretended to aim it at me. Then, just when he wasn't expecting it, I jumped forward and threw all my weight against the rifle barrel so that the butt, pivoting against the bars of the grille, came round and gave him a smart clip over the ear.

He gave a yelp of pain and shouted at me again. It would probably be all the worse for me later, I knew, but at least it had helped to keep my spirits up.

I'd grown tired of showing what a fine defiant fellow I was by this time and stood against the wall, where the rifle couldn't be brought to bear, and continued to shout; after a while, to my disappointment, the guard disappeared. I shrugged and sat down, then two guards reappeared shepherding in an old woman in a blue boiler suit carrying a bowl of rice and a tin paddle of water.

'That's better,' I said.

The woman put down the rice and the water and backed out, while the guards looked fierce and kept their rifles trained on me as if I were a dangerous wild animal.

I stood up, beaming, and bowed, and the guards retreated, staring at each other, bewildered. In spite of my apparent cheerfulness, I was still far from optimistic. They would be bound before long to put on the high drama of a trial, with all the attendant publicity and photographs and releases to the foreign press, and I had no cause to expect any kind of leniency. The Party wasn't lenient to its own people. I could hardly expect it to be lenient to a foreign devil.

I was beginning to grow depressed by this time, now that the shock had worn off. I'd heard of prison camps where the inmates worked twelve hours a day and then had to endure four hours' political indoctrination, self-criticism and mutual denunciation; where the food was barely enough to keep a dog alive, and where the prisoners slept on planks or the bare floor; where there was no chance of recovering from illness, and the sick were not isolated in epidemics. Dwight had a file on them, with notes on discipline, floggings, tortures and punishments. There were still a few places where they didn't just remonstrate with wrongdoers.

I remembered Dwight's words, too. 'If anything goes wrong, we don't want to know you. You're on your own.' As I'd said at the time, it gave me a great sense of security.

I was still considering my position when the door opened and Wang appeared, followed by the corporal of the guard and two soldiers. He picked up the bowl of rice and weighed it in his hand. 'I hear you are in need of food,' he said.

'Even a prisoner's entitled to eat.'

'Then why haven't you eaten?'

'It didn't look very appetising.'

'In China, we have thousands who are hungry. When people ask for food, we expect them to eat it.'

He made a sign to the guards and they pinioned my hands behind my back.

'Now, Eugene Patrick Nolan,' Wang said, 'let's see you eat.'

Holding the bowl of rice by the underside, he thrust it against my face with all his strength, almost choking me as he ground it against my features.

'Next time you are brought food, eat it. By the time you've been here for a while, you'll probably be glad to.'

He jerked his head and the guards thrust me out of the cell and along the corridor, still spitting out rice and blinking it from my eyelashes. As I was pushed and shoved and jabbed along by the gun butts, faces appeared in the cell grilles and, at the end of the corridor, a young girl carrying a tray with bowls of rice on it cowered as we passed. Wang slammed her back with a thrust of his arm and she flattened against the wall, the rice crashing to the floor behind him.

I was thrust into a small room full of bright lights and pushed on to a stool. Here we go, I thought. The full treatment. The confession.

'Now'—Wang's voice was harsh and metallic—'why were you at Chengsha?'

'I was trying to get material for a book,' I said, brushing the drying rice from my hair and clothes. 'I had permission. I was told I could go there.'

'Not without supervision.'

'They said I could go there when the Party Chairman opened the new drainage system. I had a permit.'

'Why were you on the road where you were found, then? There was no reason to be there. You were not at the drainage system. There is nothing at that point.'

'I wanted to look around,' I said, trying to put on an air of innocence. 'I wanted to see what was going on. When you're writing the sort of book I write, you don't just put down the speeches, you know, and describe the places you're shown. You have to get a bit of background material. Otherwise it sounds like a press handout.'

'I don't believe you.'

'I don't give a damn what you believe,' I said angrily. 'You needn't think you've heard the last of this lot, old cock. I shall protest to my government as soon as I get home.'

'*If* you get home.'

'You can't hold me here.'

Wang sneered. 'The days of gunboats are past,' he said. 'We can do what we please in China.'

'There's still such a thing as international law.'

'It doesn't apply here. Not in Chengsha. What were you doing on the road to the drainage system?'

'I've told you. I was looking for material.'

So it went on. For hours it seemed to continue, with the bright lights glaring into my face all the time, and Wang's persistent questions nagging at me. Just so much, I kept telling myself. I'll take so much, then I'll tell the truth. I'm no bloody hero with a steel-trap jaw. If it starts to hurt too much, I'll tell 'em why I came and let Dwight and the boys in the Foreign Office worry about it. The white-collared layabouts in Whitehall never had to risk *their* precious pink skins away from their office desks, so they could sort this lot out if they had to. If it became too nasty.

'Why were you there?' Wang was saying again.

'I've told you,' I said.

'Why were you carrying guns?'

'I've told you that, too.'

After a couple of hours of it, they let me go, pushing and prodding me back to my cell. The girl with the rice was in the corridor again, this time carrying water, and I saw her eyes flicker towards me in a look of sympathy. The faces at the grilles of the cells, some also sympathetic, some merely curious, were watching as I stumbled back. But I was too tired to care by this time and didn't even try to put on a brave show. I felt defeated, depressed and frightened.

As they thrust me into the cell, I realised it was dark outside and guessed I'd been in the interrogation room for several hours, so I lay down on the bunk, trying to rest. Almost immediately the light was switched on from outside. It was powerful and bright and shone directly on the bed where I was lying.

It was no surprise to me when they came for me again the following morning. Things were pursuing the usual pattern. I'd been briefed on this sort of thing often enough to know what to expect.

My food had been brought by a girl who had shuffled into the cell, not meeting my eyes, and shuffled out again, an object of such despair I'd wanted to say something to her, thank her, try to cheer her up even. But it was impossible in English, and I dared not let them know I spoke Cantonese.

The interrogation followed the pattern of the previous day and went on for most of the morning, with Wang persisting in his questions and me persisting in my answers.

When they came for me in the afternoon, however, I sensed something different in the atmosphere. There were two other men in the room with him this time, men with lists in their hands.

'Where is the man Mitchill?' one of them asked immediately.

'What man Mitchill?'

'Don't try to fool us,' Wang snapped. 'We're too clever for you by a long way. You know the one we mean.'

'Okay,' I said. 'If you say so.'

'Where is he?'

I shrugged. 'How should I know?' I said.

'You were searching for him.'

'Yes. But I didn't find him.'

'You visited his room in Peking.'

'Did I?'

'The Ministry of Information was told by the desk clerk. There is no doubt about it. We have proof.'

'Okay, so I visited him.'

'Why? To plot the assassination of the Party Chairman?'

'Oh, come off it,' I said. 'I know him. That's all. He was a writer, too.'

'He was not only a writer. He had some connection with your imperialist Foreign Office. What was it?'

So they'd been through Mitchill's luggage. Obviously his disappearance had been noticed and they'd searched his room. Doubtless they'd searched mine, too, but at least I knew they'd find nothing there. Mitchill, it seemed, had not been so careful in covering his tracks.

'I don't know what it was,' I said. '*I* didn't know he had any connection with the Foreign Office. As far as I knew he was just an expert on China and he was writing a book on it.'

'Why did you go to see him?'

'Because I was writing a book, too. I didn't want to cover the same ground.'

'Where is he now?'

'I don't know, I tell you.'

'Nolan,' Wang said. 'We have ways here of persuading people to tell the truth.'

'I'm telling the truth!'

Wang's fist came round and there was a flash of pain as it struck me at the side of the face. I picked myself up from the floor slowly.

'I shall report this to my government,' I said.

'Yours is a decadent government,' Wang said coldly. 'Yours is a decadent country. Already we have passed it in the output of steel.'

'Oh, Christ, not that again! I hear it everywhere I go.'

Wang struck me again, but this time I was ready for it and rolled backwards as his fist swung, taking some of the force from it. Nevertheless, I had to pick myself up from the floor.

'Westerners will one day learn to speak respectfully to a Chinese,' Wang said. 'One day it will be the Westerners who do the kow-towing.'

'Okay,' I said. 'When the time comes, I'm willing enough.'

'Where is Mitchill?'

'I don't know.'

'He is hiding here, is he not, waiting to murder our beloved Chairman?'

'I don't know where he is,' I repeated slowly, painstakingly.

'You followed him. Your movements were observed.'

'If you observed my movements, you know all about it. Why ask?'

His fist came round again. Although I managed to avoid the worst of the blow, there was still a lot of power behind it.

For the next three days the pattern was always the same, a sort of mental bombardment or a series of interrogations and prepared conversations lasting hours, in which every word, every comma, every intonation was put under a magnifying glass to soften me up. The bright light was always kept on in the cell at night, to reduce me to weary sleeplessness, then the questioning went on all the next day.

On the fourth day, however, the two men with lists came back, and I noticed one of them was holding my passport. And this time Tai was with them, small and lean and dangerous-looking.

'What is your name?' he asked.

'Eugene Patrick Nolan. You know damn well it is.'

'I know it is not. You and I have met before, haven't we?'

'Sure. In Peking.'

'Before that.'

'Apart from that,' I said, 'I've never seen you in my bloody life before.'

'I last saw you in Canton four years ago. Do you remember?'

'Never been in Canton in my life.'

'There was one of the K.M.T. generals still hiding there. General Ling. A former warlord. We wanted him. You helped him to escape. For that, I suffered a great deal. For a long time the Party did not trust me. But for you, I might now be standing beside our beloved Chairman instead of being a minor official.'

'Rotten luck,' I said. 'But I'm afraid I can't help you.'

Tai frowned. 'I always swore I'd catch the man who caused that.'

'Hope you're lucky. When can I go?'

He stared at me coldly. 'You can't go. It's a long time since I saw you, but I think I still know you. Your name is not Nolan at all. It's Dempsey.'

He'd got me all right. I'd known it from the minute I first saw him.

'You were recently in Saigon,' he said. 'I was there, too, looking for you. I had been looking for you in Sumatra. I followed you to Saigon.'

My heart sank. God, I thought, I hope Dwight's cover-up scheme works. This baby certainly is after me. It was the first I'd heard that I'd been followed in Sumatra. It seemed to be time to transfer my interests to another part of the world. Young as I was, I was probably too old. When you grow old you grow careless.

'You are a special agent of the British government,' Tai said.

'Look,' I shouted. 'I'm a writer! That's all. I don't know your bloody Dempsey.'

'Dark. Tall. Thin nose. I think I'd know you anywhere, Dempsey. You have quite a reputation. According to that dossier, you shot one of our soldiers in the throat in Canton, you murdered a man by the name of Volkov in Korea, and you drowned a man by the name of Slatin in a drainage ditch in Palembang.'

And I got rid of the bastard who was following me in Saigon, too, I thought. But you haven't got on to that one yet.

'No,' I said aloud. 'I'm Eugene Patrick Nolan. I went to King Edward VII School in Sheffield. I worked for a group of North Country newspapers. I wrote a couple of books which were best sellers, so I gave up newspapers and lived off free-lance writing. That's me. I'm here to write a book. I keep telling this bastard here—' I indicated Wang and got a crack on the side of the head for my trouble.

'I told him,' I said more calmly. 'All he does is knock me about. If I had him outside on my own, I'd give him a belt up the bracket he'd remember for the rest of his life.'

'As you did the man in Canton, and the man in Korea, and the man in Palembang.'

'Look, I keep telling you ...'

Tai was staring at me, a reflective look in his eyes. 'You could almost be a deviationist Chinese,' he interrupted.

'So I've been told. More than once. But you're wrong there. What you're looking at came from a Spanish grandmother.'

He gave a little smile. 'If it could be proved that you were a deviationist Chinese,' he said, 'it would go hard with you.'

Don't I know it, I thought. The fact that I wasn't Chinese by nationality wouldn't make much difference if they could just dig up the information about Grandma Dempsey.

'It wouldn't be imprisonment,' he went on cheerfully. 'The punishment for treachery is death.'

It was a jolly thought.

Wang had one of the guard's rifles in his hand by this time, jabbing it towards my throat, threatening me with it, hitting me in the ribs or in the kidneys with the butt as he circled me, shouting abuse and swearing. Then, unexpectedly, he slammed the butt down on my foot with all his force. I crumpled up with a yell, knowing instinctively that something was broken.

As I looked up, cursing him with every foul word I could lay my tongue to, he gestured towards the table and I was dragged to it. My wrists were seized and my right hand placed flat on the top, then Wang brought down the butt of the rifle twice across my finger ends. I cried out with pain and began to curse again.

'The other one!'

As they released me I reeled away and fell to my knees. Immediately, a gun butt struck me on the shoulder and I went full length. Wang's shoe caught me on the cheek.

'Get up!' he shouted. 'Get up at once!'

I remained where I was and the shoe approached again. This time, however, despite the pain in my hands, I grasped the thin ankle and jerked it upwards with all my force.

Wang's breath was jerked out of his body as he fell flat on his back. I experienced a surge of joy, but then the boots and fists and gun butts were going at me again, forcing me to my feet.

Wang's face was a picture of rage as he struck me, first with one fist then the other. At last, however, Tai pushed him aside.

'Peace, *Ton Tse,*' he said. 'We are a patient people and we know how to wait. Let us find out first just who he is.

It would be interesting if he *were* Chinese. It won't be difficult to check up. I'll go to Peking. It'll give him a week or two to recover, then if he is who I think he is, we can investigate his background and you shall have him to experiment on. We might find something unexpected.'

Wang's rage subsided and he smiled at Tai. 'Of course, Comrade Tai,' he said. 'Of course. He should have recovered a little by then. He might be able to endure more.'

They let me go at last and I stumbled back to my cell, my split fingers dripping blood. The dried remains of the rice that Wang had tried to make me eat were still on my clothes, and blood from the previous beatings was on my face and collar. I had had no opportunity to wash or shave, and my eyes and mouth were bruised and puffy where Wang's fists had struck me.

Someone gave me a shove in the back that sent me to my knees and the door slammed behind me. This time, I hadn't the strength to drag myself to my feet, but went on kneeling, staring at my fingers, hardly able to comprehend. Not much longer, I kept saying to myself. It can't go on much longer.

I was as frightened as hell by this time. I'd never been hurt before and regarded most of the things I'd done as though they were about as dangerous as a ratting expedition. In spite of taking chances, I'd always got away with it and I'd never been in pain or very frightened. Now I'd discovered the bitter truth that came some time or other to everybody, that the first shock of pain was enough to take away any man's indifference to danger. I'd found I wasn't as indestructible as I'd thought I was.

After a while I dragged myself to the bed. My foot was throbbing and it took me some time to get the shoe off. It was swollen and, from what I could feel, there was definitely something broken inside it. I sat up and tried to get my handkerchief out to wipe the blood off my face, but my numbed hands would hardly work by now. The fingernails were already blackening and coming off and the flesh was puffed and split.

'The bastards,' I said in a low moan. 'The bloody bastards!'

I was still sitting there, almost weeping with pain and fear and fury, when I heard the guard moving along the corridor shouting, and the cell doors opening and swinging back. I rose and tried to straighten up as the girl came in with the rice.

She moved into the cell, her head down, and placed the rice bowl and the pan of water on the floor, her feet weary, her shoulders stooping. Then something about the curve of her cheek caught my attention and my head came up with a jerk.

In the same moment, she noticed that my shoes and trousers were different from those of the other prisoners, and she stopped and lifted her face to mine. 'No Lan!' she said. 'What have they done to you?'

Two

I

The way Tsiu Lin spoke that damn silly name that Dwight had invented for me still sounded like music in my ears, even though her voice was heavy with weariness and stumbling with surprise. For a moment, I wondered if Wang knew about her and the way she'd shown me round Peking, and had introduced her into the cell as some sort of exquisite private joke. Then I remembered that he couldn't have known and that her presence there was one of those sheer lunatic coincidences that are so hard to believe.

For a second we stared at each other, neither of us able to believe what we saw. Aware of my shabbiness and the dried blood on my face and clothes, and the split awkward fingers held stiffly at my side, I was aware also of the difference in her.

There was a dumb, unprotesting misery about her like that of an overworked beast of burden. Her hair was untidy and unbrushed, and her face, empty of the gaiety I had known, was blank with unhappiness. The shapeless clothes hid her figure and I could see her hands were already scarred and broken by work.

'Tsiu Lin, for God's sake,' I croaked.

In a moment, she was beside me, her arms impulsively round me, her face against my chest, sobbing.

'What have they done to you, No Lan?' she was whispering. 'What have they done to you?'

I could hear the guard following her down the corridor slamming the doors, and I thrust her away quickly.

'For Christ's sake,' I said loudly. 'Rice again? Rice? Rice?

Always bloody rice!'

She backed away, startled and afraid, and I heard the door of the next cell slam and the guard shout.

'Come again, Tsiu Lin,' I begged in a low voice. 'Don't be afraid, and for Jesus' sake, come again!'

There was a momentary flash of understanding in her face, then she was gone. The guard slammed the door, and I suddenly felt tears in my eyes, something I'd never expected to experience in all my life.

For a while I stood staring at the closed door, then I reached for the rice bowl and began to eat, scooping the rice to my mouth with my painful clumsy fingers.

'The bastards,' I said again to myself. 'The bloody bastards!'

When I'd finished eating, I stretched out at full length on the bed, every inch of my body crawling with pain, my arms at my side, my fingers like claws, forcing myself to concentrate on relaxation.

Suddenly, however, there was hope. Tsiu Lin had the look of a whipped dog about her, but her immediate reaction to my misery told me I had an ally outside the cell. My problem now was to decide how best to use her.

I had two or three weeks. No more. By that time, they would have checked my identity and my background. If Dwight's cover story was good enough they'd probably let me go. If it wasn't—and I'd begun by this time to suspect it probably wasn't—well, that was that. I shifted my thoughts hastily and tried to think of something else.

If only I had a weapon, I thought. If only I could get my hands on one of those rifles held by the guards.

I sat up slowly and stared round the cell, wondering if there wasn't something I could use. But I knew there wasn't. I'd already gone over it with a fine tooth comb looking for something that might be shaped into a weapon and had found nothing. Eventually I flopped back on the bed, exhausted by pain and the effort of thinking. I felt abandoned and nauseated by the knowledge of defeat.

When the next meal came and I heard the doors opening along the corridor, my heart leapt with hope at the thought of Tsiu Lin, but this time it was some nameless stooping girl with a blank anonymous face who had offended the régime and meant nothing to me.

Her very humility, however, suddenly made me think. I had noticed long before the number of internees in the camp, and the fact that their humility was a weapon in the hands of the guards. I now began to wonder if that humility couldn't be turned into a weapon in my hands, if I couldn't persuade them to follow *me* instead of the guards. There were enough of them to do a great deal of damage.

Suddenly buoyed up with hope, I ate the rice and lay back on the bed, still thinking. Then, after a while, I struggled to my feet, limped to the door and began to hammer on it. When the guard came, I demanded to see the corporal.

The corporal was uncertain and my noisy attack left him in greater doubt.

'I demand to be allowed exercise,' I shouted. 'I've been in this cell for days now without exercise. I want exercise.'

The corporal didn't understand me and I went on shouting at him in a fury, gesturing with my puffed and clumsy fingers, until he backed away. He returned later with a young lieutenant who spoke English, and I repeated the request.

The officer went away without a word, and I continued to shout and kick at the door with my sound foot until the men in the other cells took up the shout with me.

'Come on, you bastards!' I yelled. 'Come and let me out. You stinking rotten dirty bastards!'

'Bass-tass,' I heard someone yell from the next cell, and

I realised that my protest had roused a spark of anger there, too.

For a while I was silent, crouched against the door, my mind working quickly, then I called out softly.

'Listen—you, Joe!—you speak English?'

There was a long pause, then a quiet voice came back. 'I speak. I speak little. I learn from English sailors.'

'Well done, Joe. What you name? Name? What name?'

'Name?'

'Yes. Me Pat No Lan. You?'

Another pause, then the voice again. 'Wei Fu Man.'

'Wei Fu Man. Good name. Good man. Listen well, Wei Fu Man.' I switched to Cantonese and heard a delighted chuckle from the next cell.

'You speak Chinese, Englishman!'

'I speak good Chinese,' I said. 'But we will speak always in English, except when you do not understand. This way the guards will not hear us. They do not know I speak Chinese, and I do not want to tell them. It is better so.'

'That is good, Englishman. I understand.'

'Good. Now I go back to English. Okay?'

'Okay, Englishman. I listen.'

I drew a deep breath, aware that my heart was suddenly thumping in my chest. 'Why you here?' I asked. 'Why you in prison?'

In halting English the story came out. Wei Fu Man had lived near Hong Kong as a boy but had later moved inland as a fish pedlar and had been reported to his co-operative for complaining about the régime.

'It is bad for people who sell fish,' he said. 'All fishermen must tell *chanpou* when they go out. They are searched. In summer must leave winter clothes on land. Always must sell fish to co-operative, who pay in credit notes which can use only in state shops. Many leave for Hong Kong. Hard to get fish.'

In spite of his protests of loyalty, Wei Fu Man had been sent to Chan Tsu and a further incident had landed him in the cells for corrective treatment.

'Listen, Fu Man,' I said. 'You young?'

'Yes. Fu Man young.'

'Big man? Strong man?'

'Yes. Big man. Strong man.'

'Bigger than guard?'

'Many times bigger.'

'Good. Listen, Fu Man, I get out of here, you help me fight guards?'

There was a long silence.

I tried again, 'Fu Man, you big man. You no kow-tow to little man.'

'No.'

'We get out. You wait. Man in next cell. He want get out?'

There was a silence and I could hear voices talking in low tones in what sounded like a Szechwanese dialect. That was promising, because the Szechwancsc had a reputation for bloody-mindedness and a reluctance to kow-tow to anybody.

Fu Man's voice came again. 'He want,' he said.

'Good. Tell man to find out next man. You savvy "next man"?'

'What we do?' Fu Man asked.

'Tell 'em there are enough of us to get out of here.'

'They afraid to die, No Lan.'

'Tell them if they're clever enough, nobody need die.'

The conversation went on most of the morning, painfully slowly as it was picked up and passed along the cells. In the afternoon, the lieutenant returned with the corporal and two guards.

'The Comrade Commandant of the camp has talked with Comrade Wang,' he said. 'You are to be allowed exercise.

One hour each day. No more.'

'That's not much,' I said, but my heart lifted nevertheless. One hour was better than nothing. 'When?'

'Now.'

'Let's go.'

I'd managed to wrench the top of my shoe open to hold my swollen foot and I limped out of the cell and out of the building. The women were outside washing bowls and pails at a table in the dusty sunshine. As I appeared, they stopped and turned listlessly to watch. Tsiu Lin was among them and as I passed she stared at me with agonised eyes.

I held my head up high as I stumbled painfully across to the dusty patch of ground where I was to exercise. Just to let the lieutenant and the other little bastards see, and to let Tsiu Lin see.

The lieutenant stopped me in a small square of ground in the middle of the camp. 'Here,' he said.

I stared round me, affecting astonishment. 'Here? It's not very big.'

'Here,' snapped the lieutenant.

I shrugged and began to walk crookedly up and down, limping heavily, my injured hands behind my back, apparently solemnly staring at the ground. But all the time, my eyes were busy. Groups of shabby men and women were moving about the compound under guard, and as I watched I saw the gates open and one of the returning columns of workers admitted.

Just inside the camp, I could see the pumping houses of the new drainage system, and outside, in the distance, hundreds of tiny figures working and moving like ants. Quickly, I counted the visible soldiers, and realised once more how incredibly few they were for the numbers they had to guard.

There seemed to be two at each post and no more than half a dozen by the gate. I could see their quarters across the compound, guessing what they were by the boys in shirt-sleeves outside or stooping over pails washing their clothes.

My mind was working fast, drumming the facts into my brain, imprinting details of everything I could see. Suddenly, I was bursting with hope.

I returned to the cell without protesting. Tsiu Lin was still outside the hut, stooping over the pail, a figure of abject humility like the rest, but she lifted her head and for the brief second that I allowed myself to look at her, I saw a new radiance flare in her eyes.

As I passed the cells, I saw that every occupant was watching me, all unspeaking, and all with a new interest in me. At the cell next to my own, I saw a sudden smile appear behind the bars, and noticed with pleasure that Wei Fu Man was no lightweight. He looked young and strong, with a square face tanned by sunshine.

When the guard had gone, the conversation of the morning continued.

'Fu Man! You there?'

'I am here, No Lan.'

'Listen. There are only a few guards in this camp.'

'Few?'

'Not many. Not many guards. Savvy?'

'I savvy. Not many.'

'Good.' I pressed to the grille of the door, keeping my voice low. 'How many people? How many? Like you. Like me. Prisoners.'

He didn't seem able to count beyond a hundred, but in the end I managed to understand that there were over a thousand prisoners and a matter of thirty or so guards and two or three officers.

'That is not many, Fu Man,' I pointed out. 'Yet there are many prisoners. Too many for guards. If we act together, they cannot stop us escaping.'

I was banking on the herd instinct of the Chinese

peasant, that strange humility that allowed him to be driven by anyone strong enough to be a leader, anyone with a mouthful of ideas. It had worked before—for the foreign devils in their gunboats, and for Chiang Kai-shek, who had finally persuaded the solid weight of the masses to ignore the gunboats. Now the Communists, quick to use the resources they had at hand, had driven out Chiang by the same methods and had harnessed that same sheep instinct to their own policies. If they could, I thought, then on a smaller scale, so could I.

Fu Man listened quietly as I talked and when I'd finished he agreed with me.

'It is so,' he said. 'They cannot stop us.'

'Right.' I was growing excited now. 'So, listen. I'm going to get out of here.'

'Get out?'

'Yes. Go. From here. I am going to kill guard. You understand?'

There was a long pause, then Fu Man spoke. 'I understand.'

'I am going. From here. To Hong Kong. You come, too?'

Again there was the uncertain pause.

'For Christ's sake, Fu Man!'

'Yes. I come.'

'Good. We go together. Others come? Other prisoners?'

Again the slow painful conversation went on in low whispers up and down the corridor. At first, out of the twenty or so prisoners in the cell block, there were only three who agreed to help, but by exhausting argument carried on mainly in pidgin English, with only a few words of Cantonese, I got them on my side.

'Only two no come, No Lan,' Fu Man announced.

'Okay. Two no come. We go, *they* come, too. You see.'

'When we go, No Lan?'

'Not yet. Many days. Save rice. Save all rice. Eat little. To eat later.'

'Yes. I save, No Lan.'

'And rest. Plenty rest.'

'I rest.'

When the food was brought that evening, I saw with joy that it was Tsiu Lin again. But the guard stood in the doorway and we were unable to speak. Our eyes met, however, and she seemed to be trying to tell me something.

When the door was closed again, I picked up the rice bowl and found a tiny scrap of paper underneath it.

'Tell me what to do. I want to help,' was written on it in small letters.

I concealed the scrap of paper in my clothes. There was little I could do until she came again, and I had to control my surging impatience.

The next morning, the conversation with Fu Man continued as we began to make some sort of plan.

'Only two guards here at night,' I pointed out.

'Yes. Two guards.'

'We kill. You understand?'

'I understand. When?'

'Soon. I tell. Many days.'

It was hard to make Fu Man understand that we mustn't hurry. It would take at least a fortnight still for Tai to check up on my identity and in the meantime there was a chance my hands might have healed. My foot was improving already, even though I still limped, but the knuckles of two of my fingers would never be straight again, I was certain, and the rest were still split and torn. Within a few days, however, it should be possible to use them again.

I still had no plan beyond escape because escape was enough for the time being. I knew that eventually I would have to think of what came afterwards, but, at present, with the pain in my hands and the difficulty of communicating my ideas to Fu Man and the others, it was exhausting enough just to think of one thing. I knew I would need food and it wasn't difficult to think of saving as much as I could and persuading the others to do the same, but beyond that I wasn't prepared to make plans for eventualities I knew nothing about.

The next morning, the rice was brought in again by Tsiu Lin, and I was able to speak briefly to her while the guard waited outside.

'Bring paper and pencil,' I said softly. 'For messages. Do as I say.'

She nodded and was about to reply when the guard appeared, so she turned away and shuffled out, her shoulders stooped, her head down and humble.

The paper and a stub of pencil came with the next meal, concealed under the rice. The woman who brought it placed it in front of me and disappeared without saying anything. I ate a little of the rice and concealed the rest in my pockets. I began to write painfully on the paper.

Over the next two days the messages continued to arrive with the rice, with nothing to indicate they were there except for a movement of the eyes and a mute appeal to understand. Tsiu Lin had managed now to take over the job of handing out the rice bowls and we were able to say brief sentences to each other. I learned slowly that she had at first been set to work digging, then with a few other women who were not peasants had had her job changed to that of preparing food for the other occupants of the camp. Although the work was not heavy, it was nothing but drudgery. She had been condemned as a reactionary and there was little chance for the future.

'Hope,' I urged her. 'Keep hoping. We'll get out of here.'

In between the bouts of exercise, I spent my time when there was no guard near in writing in the smallest writing

I could manage with my damaged fingers. I passed these messages to Tsiu Lin with the empty food bowls.

'Tell them there are many of *them*,' I wrote. 'Tell them there are only a few guards. Find out where food is kept, and weapons and clothing. Find out everything. Watch for Wang.'

Painfully, slowly, the plan was built up. Every time I went out I watched for a change of duties, and after a few days I had the layout of the camp and the whereabouts of the soldiers and the hours of their shifts firmly in my mind.

All day and every day, the slow conversations went on up and down the line of cells. I passed on everything I knew, wording my information in simple sentences so that Fu Man should make no mistake.

'You know gun? You know how to shoot?'

'All Chinese know shoot.' Fu Man lapsed into Chinese. 'Government teach us. One hand on hoe. One hand on rifle. To drive away our enemies.'

'What enemies?'

'I do not know, No Lan.' He sounded bewildered. 'I have seen no enemies. *My* enemies are guards.'

I laughed and returned to English.

'You read, Fu Man? You read words?'

'I read some words. Not many.'

'Good.'

I returned to the bed and began to draw a crude plan of the camp, marking it in Chinese characters, and when Tsiu Lin next brought the rice, I slipped the paper to her, with another one bearing instructions to copy it out and see that all the prisoners in the other cells were given a copy.

When the rice came the next morning, underneath it there was a slip of paper with the words 'It is done.'

For fourteen days, I put my plan across to the other men in the cells and, through the little scraps of paper, spread it outside to the women, who then passed it on to the other occupants of the camp. Every day I made a mark on the wall behind the bed where it wouldn't be seen so that I should make no mistake.

'We go soon, Fu Man,' I said, when he asked how much longer we must wait. 'One-two days. Soon.'

My hands were improving now and it was possible to hold things again, though they were still painful.

The Chengsha scheme was duly opened. We even had a party of minor officials touring the camp, and daily praise over the loudspeakers of the Great Panjandrum: how fit he'd been, what he'd said, with what delicacy of movement he'd cut the tape or pulled the lever or whatever it was he'd done. I didn't notice much because by this time I was too preoccupied to be interested.

Still the whispered conversations went on and the brief messages went out of the cells. I passed notes through Tsiu Lin to people in the camp she had told me I could trust. I had hesitated at first to involve her but I couldn't afford to have anything go wrong through unexpected panic or misunderstanding, and I was forced to take the men she suggested into my confidence. Other messages went to Tsiu Lin herself, telling her what to do when the time came and where to wait for me.

On the fifteenth evening, it was Tsiu Lin who brought the rice. It had been painful having to see her almost daily yet being unable to encourage her, having to try to instil hope with only the brief messages on the tiny scraps of paper. Though I had seen a change in her face as the despair had disappeared, I saw now there was a look of fear in her eyes.

'Shu is here from Peking,' she whispered. 'He will recognise me. I shall be given other duties. And I heard him tell Wang that Tai is coming soon.'

'Very well,' I whispered back. 'We'll go tonight.'

* * *

There was no sleep in the cell block that night. The word had been passed along the row of cells and Fu Man reported grimly that everyone had now agreed to fall in with the plan.

'They've nothing to lose,' I said in Cantonese. 'It'll be God help 'em either way if we fail.'

For a while I lay in the dark, gently massaging my fingers. The feeling had returned to some of them but at least two were still immovable.

Eventually when the camp was quiet I sat up. 'Fu Man,' I called softly. 'Fu Man!'

'I am ready,' came the answer at once.

'Now is the time. Tell them. Tell them all.'

I heard the muttered words passed along the line of cells, and after a pause the information came back to me that they were all ready. I lay down on my bed and began to shout and groan. After a while, Fu Man also began to shout, and the cries were taken up along the line of cells. Eventually the door at the end of the corridor was opened and I heard the guard appear. I began to groan louder.

'The Englishman,' I heard Fu Man call. 'He is ill.'

I heard the guard's feet outside the door and, crossing my hands on my stomach and entwining my fingers, I pressed forward, holding my breath, until I felt my face reddening at the effort, and the pulse in my temple began to beat. Momentarily I saw the guard's face in the doorway and I flung myself back on the bed and began to drum my heels on the frame, beating with my hands against my sides and groaning. The guard went away and shortly afterwards I heard the key in the lock and muttering voices.

Both of the bastards, I thought. This complicates matters. I lay flat on my back, moaning and holding my stomach. The two guards leaned over me, staring. Gagging and choking as though I couldn't speak, I opened my mouth and pointed to it. It was the first thing that came into my head but it had the effect of making the two men lean forward to see what was wrong. I lifted my hands, the fingers twisted as though in agony; then, as the guards bent closer, talking to each other, I brought my hands together with all my strength. A shaft of pain drove up my arms but the two skulls slammed together with a click like a couple of billiard balls.

I was on my feet in a bound. My sound foot caught one of the men in the groin and, as he bent double with a gasp, I grasped the other man and swung him against the stone wall. There was a crunch as his face hit the stone, then I drew him back and swung him against the opposite wall. Flashes of pain were already crossing my eyes, but the second man was struggling to stand upright by this time, still clutching the pit of his stomach, so I grabbed one of the fallen rifles and clubbed him with it. He fell groaning against the wall.

Bending down, almost passing out with the pain in my hands, I snatched up the keys from where they had fallen and slipped next door to the cell of Fu Man and swung it open. To my joy, Fu Man moved swiftly, not hesitating.

I jerked my thumb, and he nodded and slipped silently into the cell I'd just left, while I went along the line of cubicles, opening the doors.

By the time I'd reached the last one, the prisoners were clustered in the corridor behind me, unspeaking and silent. Fu Man was clutching the two rifles.

He grinned and thrust one of them forward.

I was dizzy now and I had to sit down to recover, but I took the weapon, feeling better as my stiff fingers closed around the stock.

'The guards?' I asked in Cantonese.

Fu Man said nothing but made a movement with his hands to indicate their necks were broken.

The door at the end of the corridor was unlocked and we

slipped through quietly, Fu Man helping me with a hand on my arm.

The corporal of the guard was sleeping on a string bed. Fu Man lifted his eyebrows questioningly and I nodded, making a sign for silence. As I moved on, I heard a grunt and a fluttering sound, like a hen having its neck wrung, then Fu Man appeared beside me.

One of the freed men was carrying the uniforms of the two guards from the cell block, and Fu Man and another man slipped into the jackets and caps. In the growing light they walked towards the guards' shelters at the entrance to the prison block, carrying the rifles. There was no sound, but after a while they returned. From under their smocks they produced two more jackets and caps. The next two men crossed the compound and appeared a moment later with rifles in their hands.

'One hand on the hoe, one hand on the rifle,' one of them said with a chuckle.

We had five rifles now, and pieces of timber had already appeared from nowhere. I indicated the barrack block where the guards slept and we moved silently across to it.

There was a door at each end and outside both I stationed a man with a rifle. Other men were placed along the sides of the hut to keep a lookout.

'The man Wang,' I said. 'I want Wang.'

I had never believed much in love one another or turning the other cheek—not with the Wangs of the world I'd had to handle—and Wang wasn't going to split any more fingers or smash any more feet if I could help it.

Fu Man was nodding and I glanced past him at the other men. Freedom had done something to them. Their eyes were bright and they were longing for a chance to use their muscles. It did my heart good to see them.

'Let's go,' I said.

II

Within half an hour, we were in control of the camp.

I was startled at what I'd stirred up. Clearly, there had been a lot more brutality in the past than anybody had seen or even known about, and there was a great deal of vicious repayment of debts.

Unable to help much because of my smashed hands, I waited outside while Fu Man and the others, even those who had previously doubted, swept through that first hut. Obviously, only fear had held anyone back up to that point. With the feeling that they had everything to gain and very little to lose, they were suddenly prepared to go the whole hog.

Fu Man opened the door gently. In the shadows, I saw the hut was full of sleeping men stretched out on small frame beds. There were no blankets, and in their sleep the soldiers seemed more innocent than their attackers. The brutality and the arrogance had drained from their faces and suddenly I realised how young they were. They looked surprisingly vulnerable, and for a second I almost found myself on the point of telling Fu Man and the others to be gentle.

Then Fu Man indicated the stand of rifles in the centre of the room and I remembered that I lived in a world of an eye for an eye and a tooth for a tooth. It was a case of the weakest going to the wall. There was no room for gentleness. With Tai on the point of producing evidence of my identity, it was either my life or the lives of these boys. There was no mercy in the world, and I didn't hesitate any longer. I indicated the weapons to the unarmed men with me.

The clatter of the first rifle being withdrawn from the stand woke the first of the sleepers, and from that moment there was no longer any point in either mercy or silence. Fu Man drove the butt into the waking boy's face, and in a second the room was a maelstrom of grunting, kicking, stabbing men out of which only one soldier escaped. I tripped him as he leapt through the door and immediately one of the former prisoners was on him, using his bare hands to throttle the life out of him.

Within minutes, the hut was silent. While we were drawing our breath again, I saw a light go on in a hut standing at right angles thirty yards away. I called softly to Fu Man and they swept across to the hut in a silent body, vicious, vengeful and suddenly strong and lustful for blood now that there was a chance of repaying some of the humiliations that had been heaped upon them.

Leaving the killing to Fu Man, I collected three men and padded softly in the shadows towards one of the prison huts. There was a guard on the door, looking bewildered and scared by the noises further across the camp. At that point they sounded like the scufflings of terrified animals in the dark. The butt of a rifle clouted him over the ear and he fell forward, blood pouring from his nose. I grabbed his rifle and smashed the lock. A stink of sweat, urine and disinfectant rushed out at me as we opened the door.

Inside the hut, the prisoners were all awake, but they were too uncertain of what was happening to know how to react. After weeks, months, perhaps years, of bullying, they seemed unable to make their minds up.

'You're free,' I shouted. 'The camp's been taken over. Come on, out!'

Still they didn't move. Only the desperate hard-core prisoners from the interrogation block had had the wits or the courage to act for themselves—which was probably why they had found their way to the interrogation block in the first place. I had to go on shouting at this group. Several of them, obviously thinking they were being moved to another camp, started dumbly packing up their few pitiful belongings, but I knocked them from their hands and kicked and punched and pummelled them into the open air.

When at last they stumbled across the body of the guard, and saw Fu Man and the other hard-core prisoners running from the guard hut, it suddenly dawned on them that they were free. Several of them laughed, then someone yelled, and with a viciousness that appalled me by its suddenness, one of them grabbed the rifle from me and began to pound the dead guard's head to a bloody pulp before I could push him aside.

Almost within a minute, they had changed from a dumb, mute, stupefied throng of prisoners to a mob. Reaching for anything they could find—boards from the hut, pieces of metal, rocks—they began to pour towards Fu Man and the hut that had just been captured.

Finding no one alive, they headed for other huts, splitting up, releasing other prisoners, murdering isolated guards, doing it with a silent viciousness that was curiously shocking. There were no shouts, beyond an occasional muffled scream of terror from a trapped guard; then suddenly it was all over. There were a few muted cries from the guardhouse and a group of bleeding, torn, beaten guards, with broken limbs and bruised faces, were pushed into the crowd; soon they, too, disappeared. Fragments of clothing were flung around, then the mob seemed to thin out and disperse, leaving the bodies in a crumpled circle. No power on earth could have stopped the murders. It was revenge for the humiliations of years.

I had been almost as guilty as the prisoners. I had found Wang in a room in the officers' quarters, and the look on his face as he had turned had given me more pleasure than

I had expected. He had looked startled at first, then shocked, and finally terrified.

'Hello, Wang,' I had said.

'No,' he begged. 'No!'

I was going to break his fingers for him as he'd broken mine and then joyfully shoot him, but when it came to the point I found I couldn't do it. I was getting too involved. There were no personalities in the game I played. Just enemies. You didn't let yourself hate anyone any more than you let yourself grow fond of anyone. In the end, I simply jerked my head at him and went outside, leaving it to Fu Man.

A boy in the faded blue uniform of a prisoner appeared in front of me.

'I am going south,' he announced, beaming. 'I am going to Hong Kong. That was where I was going when they put me in here. Now, nothing will stop me.'

Fu Man grinned at him and he went on excitedly. 'No one will know for hours what has happened. We cut the wires at the guardroom. We killed the captain as he was picking up the telephone.'

'What about the headquarters block?'

'It was empty. Only the clerks were on duty.'

'Did they telephone?'

'They had no time.'

'Right.' The boy seemed intelligent and I decided I had another lieutenant.

'What's your name?' I said.

'Tchao. Tchao So Kai. I am a student. Or I was. There are several of us here.'

'Right, Tchao. You must help us to see that no one leaves the camp. Put a guard on the gate at once.'

Tchao's face fell. 'Aren't we going to leave?'

'Not in ones and twos,' I said, my mind already racing ahead beyond the simple ideas for travel I'd formulated.

'We'll leave when we've eaten and when we're organised. No one knows yet, so we've time. We don't want people streaming into Chengsha, or someone will guess immediately what's happened. There are troops there, and they'll be better troops than there were here. When we go, we all go together and we go with our stomachs full.'

Tchao grinned. 'That is a good idea, Englishman. I have an idea, too.'

'What is it?'

'If we're all going together, why not send some groups towards the soldiers. They'll run, of course, when they're found—who wouldn't—and the soldiers will be so busy rounding them up, they'll not have time to follow the rest of us. We have to make sacrifices.' He grinned. 'And if sacrifices are to be made, then I would rather someone else made them, not me.'

His idea was sound, despite the cynicism behind it, and I was already thinking up refinements to it. Now that we were virtually free, my mind had to rove ahead to what happened next.

'That is good sense,' I said. 'So get that guard on the gate. Nobody is to leave. Then open the women's blocks and find me a prisoner called Han Tsiu Lin. She was in charge of the prisoners' meals in the interrogation block. Send her here.'

Tsiu Lin soon appeared. She still looked drawn and strained but there was an uncertain smile on her face. I said nothing as she approached and she suddenly took a few running steps forward and dropped to her knees to kiss my hands, her head bent in a curiously medieval attitude of supplication. It seemed so completely to acknowledge me as her master, her leader, her lord, it troubled me.

'Get up, Tsiu Lin,' I said sharply but without irritation. 'We have a lot to do.'

She scrambled to her feet, her eyes on my face.

'Do you have any influence with the women?' I asked.

'Not much. A little.'

'It's enough. Go and tell them we want food. We're going to leave this camp only when we've eaten, when we've all got enough in our stomachs to carry our feet forward. I want them to divide up what's left in the store as best they can so that everyone can have a little rice to take with them. Can you do that?'

The camp was full of startled men and women standing around in noisy, chattering groups, bewildered by their sudden freedom, uncertain how to behave. Now that they had taken over the camp, they didn't know what to do with it.

Tsiu Lin brought food on a tray made out of the top of a box. Curiously, though they must have been hungry, no one attempted to take it from her. The crowd parted for her as she walked forward, and watched smiling as she offered us the food.

Fu Man gestured. 'You first, No Lan,' he said. 'It's your privilege.'

He spoke to the watching prisoners, who nodded and grinned, but I handed the first bowl of rice to him and the second to Tchao before handing one to Tsiu Lin and finally taking one for myself. The gesture seemed to please them all. There were more nods of approval, then, as the word got around that there was food for everybody, the crowd dispersed.

As we ate, we worked out some of the routine of the camp and decided we still had several hours before anyone from the town would be likely to arrive from Chengsha for duty.

'We must be clear of here long before then,' I said to Tchao. 'Do you know the country?'

'A little. To the north is Hsuhang.'

'No good. I've got to go south.'

'There are many airfields down there. Many soldiers.'

'East?'

'The river. It's too wide to cross. And there are troops that way.'

'West?'

'The Lo Hun Mountains. They run towards the south.'

'High?'

He shrugged, his thin intelligent face hard, as though he was well aware of the dangers that still existed. 'High enough,' he said. 'But not impossible. They are rugged, though, and it should be possible to hide among them. We might even move a long way south through them. There would not be much food left but perhaps there would be a little in the mountains. There's only Tiengfeng on the other side.'

'We'll make for the mountains,' I said. 'As fast as possible.'

Tsiu Lin looked uneasy. 'What about everyone else?' she asked.

'I'm not responsible for everyone else,' I pointed out.

I wasn't concerned with a thousand other people who'd had the misfortune to find themselves in the Chan Tsu camp at the same time as me. The only thought in my mind was that Tai was on his way back from Peking with a sure knowledge of my identity and I was terrified of being caught where I hadn't a clear retreat. The only thing that worried me was escape and the only concern I still had for the other prisoners was that a few of them—unwillingly or not—were going to draw the guards off my track.

'I'm not responsible for them,' I said again. 'I'm responsible for me. But I want you to come, because you can't stay here. You and Fu Man and Tchao. We ought to be able to help each other.'

She looked uncertain. 'There are many simple people here who need leadership.'

'I'm not the leader type.'

'They know they'll be punished for what has happened.'

'Would they rather stay here and work like cattle for the rest of their days?'

She flushed. 'It isn't that. They're glad of freedom, but they know many of the guards were killed.'

'All the guards were killed,' I said roughly. 'We couldn't afford to have one of them bolting up the road to Chengsha.'

'There were many of them,' she retorted, her voice firmer. 'And they were mostly just boys.'

'They were wearing uniform. That makes them men.'

I was trying to wear my couldn't-care-less look but suddenly I knew I did care. What she said was correct. There were hundreds of people in the camp too old or too stupid to be able to do much for themselves, the people who always need leading, the sheep of society who always need a shepherd. Only a few of them like Fu Man or Tchao were the leaders or the lone wolves who could look after themselves. I tried to brush the thought aside, however. It wasn't my job to look after them. It was my job to get to Hong Kong before anyone found out how much I was responsible for what had happened. I was the pawn in a big game. I was the man Tai wanted for his spectacular—the public trial that would condemn the West. Inevitably, the British government, and doubtless the American government as well, would be linked with any guilt they could pin on me. And Tai would pin it all right. I was not in the game for patriotism, but I knew enough to be aware that that was the one thing I mustn't permit. I believed in looking after myself, but I knew who paid my wages and I didn't intend to incriminate them unless I had to. If I could escape I was going to. And yet . . .

I became aware of Tsiu Lin speaking again. 'Did they *all*

have to be killed?' she asked in a small baffled voice.

She was staring at the bodies scattered by the huts, and I frowned.

'There was no option. It was us or them. You can't ask someone like Fu Man to show mercy. We can't tie them up. We're not playing at cops and robbers.'

'No,' she said quietly. 'No. But they're only children and they're my countrymen, too.'

I looked at her sharply, but there was no suggestion of accusation in her expression, only a sad resignation at the cruelty that existed in the world. I felt faintly depressed. Perhaps I'd expected her to come running across the camp to me, as gay and beautiful and laughing as when I had first known her, open to teasing, a little rueful as she admitted the government's mistakes but willing to laugh at all the stupidity of dogma and pedantry, just as she used to.

But in her short stay at Chan Tsu, she'd probably seen too much suffering at close quarters. Doubtless she'd always known it had existed, but probably she'd never seen any sign of it. Like me, she wasn't old enough to remember the civil war or the beggars that had infested the streets before Communism had cleared them away. At Chan Tsu, she'd come face to face with all the hard facts, and uneasily I suspected that the old Tsiu Lin had gone for ever.

It was time to change the conversation. It was an unhappy dialogue with none of the exhilaration I'd felt there ought to be between two condemned people who'd suddenly found themselves free.

'Is there food enough for everybody?' I asked.

She nodded, her face expressionless. 'More than that. There is plenty of rice.'

'Find us something to put it in. Big enough for plenty. We'll be leaving very shortly.'

III

We had just finished counting the rifles we had captured—thirty-five of them—and I was still making my plans to leave when some fool set fire to the headquarters block.

Already a few enraged men had grabbed sledge hammers and smashed everything they could find in the new pumping station to destroy the drainage that had enslaved them. It would go down well in Peking when they found out, and a few minor officials who weren't clever enough to look after themselves would be kicked upstairs for letting such a thing occur only a week or two after the All Highest himself had opened it.

But that didn't matter much because it wouldn't be noticed for a day or so. The burning headquarters block would. I was arguing with Fu Man and Tchao about the best way to go when we saw the flames. They were only a lick at first, but almost immediately, before it had dawned on us what was happening, great tongues of fire leapt up.

'Put that out,' I shouted. 'They'll see it in Chengsha or one of the other camps. They could be here in an hour. Put it out!'

Tchao was quick to grasp the danger. He jabbered something to Fu Man, and the two of them ran towards the flames, Fu Man cuffing the head of anyone who got in his way. The fire had got a good hold but a bucket chain was organised and, with Fu Man performing prodigies of exertion, we began to get it under control. Then Tchao discovered a fire hose and pump and gradually the flames were beaten down. All I could do myself was shout. Every time I touched anything, shivers of pain still flew up my arms.

When the flames had died away, I made Fu Man get everyone together. They gathered outside the guardhouse, where the lights were brightest, shuffling in the dust so that you could see the motes gleaming in the glare.

'Tell them,' I said to Tchao, 'that we are all leaving together and that no one must head towards Chengsha. I don't care where they go so long as they disperse properly. There must be a good thousand of them here; and any sign of them in Chengsha, any hint that anybody's broken out of camp, and there'll be troops along at once. The officials will be the first to come and they never arrive until ten in the morning; when they do arrive and find what's happened, they'll have to go all the way back again to telephone because the line's been cut. We've still got a few hours of safety.'

Tchao made his little speech.

'Tell them they must head south, north or east,' I went on. 'That way, they'll draw the troops away from us because we're going towards the mountains. And tell them, if they've got any sense they'll not stop until they're a long way from here. If they've got any sense, too, they'll not turn up at their homes, or where they worked, or anywhere they're known.'

While Tchao was explaining this, Tsiu Lin touched my arm. 'What is the point of freedom,' she asked, 'if they can't go home?'

'Freedom's freedom,' I said. 'Wherever you are. So long as you don't have chains on your limbs or on your mind, you're free. Cutting yourself off from home is a small price to pay.'

'For a mother or a father, it's a very heavy one.'

I didn't argue, because she had a very good point there.

Tchao was still telling the crowd to head away from the mountains and disperse, when I realised Tsiu Lin was crying softly beside me. I knew what was in her mind. We'd freed all these people but we hadn't really given them their freedom back. They'd lost all they'd ever possessed. The fact that they'd escaped and killed the guards condemned them more completely than any previous misdemeanours against the régime had. Some of them might eventually have returned to their families and some sort of physical freedom, even if their minds were chained, but now their very appearance among their families would bring the police and the soldiers at once. In the pernicious society they lived in, neighbours eager for advancement in the hierarchy would be more than willing to act as informers for a few crumbs of extra comfort or a little authority.

I thrust the thought from my mind again. I wasn't there to debate the niceties of behaviour. I had to escape and it was my job to get back to Hong Kong, not only to tell them that Mitchill wasn't likely to cause any more trouble but also to make sure I wasn't charged in his place by Tai.

It was still dark as the first people started to move through the camp gate. They set off almost unwillingly, as though they were uncertain which way to go or how to behave now that they had minds of their own once more, but I was pleased to see that most of them seemed to be heading across the plain away from the difficult route west where we could see the black outline of the mountains against the sky. I resisted the impulse to start with them because I wanted them in front of me so that there'd not be too many witnesses to my own chosen route.

It was a sparsely populated country to the west and we were likely to meet only a peasant or two. If we did, I hoped they'd be dim-witted enough not to jump to too many conclusions and guess where we'd come from. The one thing I dreaded was an accidental meeting with an army scout car or a lorry whose crew would realise what had happened and make a bolt for a telephone. We wanted just a few hours to disperse; then, I felt, we could get into the woods and the mountains where our chances would improve at once. I intended encouraging anybody going the same way as we were to turn north so that I could then safely turn south and make my way to the coast in peace.

It was a harsh attitude to take but I had no option.

As we prepared to leave ourselves, Tchao appeared.

'I have good news for you, *Ton Tse,*' he said. 'There has been trouble in the area west of here.'

'What sort of trouble?'

'Riots.' He grinned. 'Over food. There was some shooting and there's no love for the authorities. The people are sullen and they'll be unlikely to help the troops. Telephone wires were torn down to stop them being called during the riots and they haven't been repaired yet.'

'Where did you learn this?'

He jerked his head. 'One of the prisoners. He's from the district. He was brought in here when the troops arrived. He says the people have no love for the soldiers.'

'That's a stroke of luck,' I said. 'It might work well for us.'

The prisoners were still trickling through the gates, carrying rice in little bags or tied up in scraps of cloth or in tins or boxes they had dug out. Then Fu Man appeared with a mule cart. It was a rattletrap affair but I noticed it was well loaded with food—and it wasn't all rice either. There was tinned food from the officers' quarters and even a crate of squawking chickens.

Tchao appeared from behind. 'There was a car,' he said. 'It belonged to the officers. But some fool smashed the ignition with a crowbar. I flattened him.'

I was just going to say 'Good' when I saw the look Tsiu Lin gave him and instead I held my tongue. We could have used the car. We could have got a long way with a car, but the insensate rage which had caused the destruction of the ignition was natural enough in a peasant with no head for planning.

The mule was old and there wasn't much room on the cart with all the things that Fu Man and Tchao had stuffed aboard, but Fu Man tried to insist that I ride. I refused and persuaded Tsiu Lin to climb aboard instead. As I helped her up I stood by the cart gazing at her. She looked tired, a long soft loop of black hair hanging over her eyes, but even in the shabby padded blue suit she was wearing, her hands broken and dirty with work, she still looked beautiful.

I found my heart fill as I looked at her and I swallowed uncomfortably, aware that, whether I wished to be involved or not, I owed her something. Whatever else I did, however important it was to me to escape, I had to make sure that she reached safety, too.

I managed a smile and she smiled back at me, a serene trusting smile, as though she had never doubted that I'd accept responsibility for her. I had to turn away quickly and jerk my head at Fu Man, indicating the gate with my smashed hand.

He jabbed at the mule with a pointed stick and we set off. Along the road we picked up two elderly women who were already finding the march exhausting in their half-starved condition. Tsiu Lin insisted on climbing down from the cart and she persuaded Fu Man to lift the two women up in her place.

I stared at her, furious. I wanted the cart to carry food and eventually to carry us, not old women who meant nothing to me. 'That's for *you*,' I said.

'I can't ride while they walk,' she insisted.

'You'll tire yourself out.'

'They're old.'

'God damn it,' I said angrily. 'We've got to be selfish about this! We've got to think of ourselves. If you're tired, you reduce your chances of reaching safety. You *can't* be unselfish.'

'I can't see old women fall while I ride,' she said simply, and I had to let it go.

Groups had already split off from the main mob, moving south and east. As we had waved them on their way, Tchao had encouraged them with a smiling cynicism, knowing perfectly well they were probably walking into danger. I had said nothing, nauseated by my own feeling of guilt at falling in with his scheme but determined to do nothing to stop them in my own need to get clear.

Once, Tsiu Lin questioned the wisdom of letting them go, and I answered her brusquely.

'It's their own affair,' I said.

'But surely they will be walking into the hands of the soldiers?'

'That's their problem. I don't care where they go so long as they don't know we're heading for the mountains.'

'But couldn't they go into the mountains, too?' she persisted.

'No,' I snapped. 'Leave them be.'

She seemed to guess what I was thinking and she gave me a sad, bewildered look, as though she found it hard to believe such coldbloodedness of me, but I ignored the glance, ashamed that she would think of me in that way but knowing that anything else was wildly impractical. Those people heading east and south had been a weapon I had used to help me escape and now they were my shield from the vengeance of the troops. It was a cruel way to regard them but I could see no alternative. Most of them would inevitably be caught, anyway, I kept reminding myself, because they had never been trained to be self-reliant. I was still able to live with my thoughts, even if I wasn't happy about them.

The people surrounding me were still trudging on,

glancing at me occasionally, smiling at me, plodding dumbly forward, clutching their few possessions and their small bags of rice, their faces blank and anonymous; humble, indifferent and uncomplaining. They seemed less like escaped prisoners than a stream of city dwellers going about their business.

The sun was up by this time and we'd almost reached the first slopes of the mountains at the end of the plain. We were in wooded country now and I was grateful for that because it meant that if anyone had discovered the mass break-out and was searching by air, we might be missed.

So far, though, there had been no planes and no sign of pursuit, and I put it down to the completeness of the take-over of the camp. No guard had survived and no telephone had been left uncut.

I was still uneasy, however. Occasionally, we'd seen peasants trudging by, heavily laden or pulling their huge one-wheeled barrows, or looking up at us with a strange lack of curiosity from the fields where they worked. Migrations of people had become commonplace in China. Millions had been moved at one time or another, due to famine, insurrection or politics, and no one seemed interested in our small group. Sooner or later, though, I knew some self-important youngster, some soldier or official on leave, would wonder why so many people were on the road together, unguarded and unherded, and would put two and two together and telephone to Chengsha. Inevitably the soldiers would be out before long and this time they wouldn't be untrained boys but the tough troops of the People's Liberation Army, well equipped and on wheels.

As the sun rose higher and with the crowd now trailing behind us like a company of soldiers behind its commanders, we passed through a village. The telephone wires, I noticed with satisfaction, were hanging in loops, and there were only a few women around the stalls beside the mud huts. There were signs of damage, too—bullet-pocked walls and smashed doors—and no traffic, and there were only a few sullen people in the dusty main street where an old woman was trying to sell caged singing birds. All the men seemed to be away, probably in the fields or dead or imprisoned after the recent troubles.

No one attempted to touch the food that was displayed on the stalls, and no one asked any questions of us. There was a river at the other side of the village, clear and bright, trickling through a rocky gorge filled with white stones, and Fu Man moved off the road towards it to drink. Tchao followed him, then Tsiu Lin and me. At once, as though at a command, the whole crowd shuffled to a stop, too, and turned towards the river.

I frowned as I watched them, worrying thoughts in my mind. It was clear the group was taking its example from me or Fu Man or Tchao, and I suddenly realised with alarm that it was making no attempt to disperse.

I glanced about me, narrow-eyed and suspicious. A few people smiled at me and the crowd opened out as I returned to the road. Then, as we set off again, they formed up once more and moved off after us.

I stopped dead abruptly, and the crowd stopped dead, too.

I was certain now that they had no intention of breaking up into smaller parties.

'Tchao!' I called the youngster over to me. 'Tell them it's time to start splitting up again. We should be in smaller groups that can't be seen so easily.'

Tchao climbed on to a rock and began to shout. A few men and women shook their heads and began to gesture. When he climbed down from the rock, they surrounded him, talking quickly and noisily.

'They don't want to split up,' Tsiu Lin said quietly to me.

'Why not, for God's sake?'

'They want you to lead them to safety.'

The last thing in the world I wanted was to be trailed by a gang of helpless people for whom I'd have to be responsible. I'd used them to help me only because their numbers, their combined mute strength, had been my one weapon against the guards. I was horrified.

Tchao approached and confirmed what Tsiu Lin had said. 'They say they trust you,' he announced. 'You got them out of the camp. You must get them to safety. They prefer to stay with you.'

I lost my temper. 'God damn it! I can't be responsible for all this lot!'

'You have no option, No Lan.'

I stared at them in fury. Among the moving millions of China, small groups would not be noticed because a man could hide himself like a mote among other motes, like a grain of corn among other grains of corn. But a crowd like this could never hide.

'Tell them that splitting up is their only hope,' I insisted.

Tchao shook his head. 'They don't want to split up, No Lan,' he said. 'They feel there is safety in numbers.'

'They're like a lot of goddam sheep.'

He shrugged. 'They have been sheep too long to behave differently now,' he pointed out. 'It was the foreign nations in China who encouraged them in the belief they were sheep.' His voice was faintly accusing, and I knew that what he said was true.

Tsiu Lin had found another sick old dame by this time and was pushing her on to the cart. I stared angrily at her and at the blank yellow faces watching me, then, without a word, I turned away and began to limp up the hill to where the mountain peaks glowed in the amber sun.

Fu Man jabbed at the ancient mule and it began to plod

after me. Tchao stared at Tsiu Lin for a second, then they, too, began to follow. As though at a signal, I saw from the corners of my eyes that the whole crowd had begun to follow also.

I allowed Tsiu Lin to catch up with me and for a while we walked in silence. After a time we stopped while someone else was helped on to the cart. As it started again, a small sack of rice fell off. Tsiu Lin picked it up and stuffed it back, but it fell off again, and in the end she put it over her shoulder and carried it herself. I longed to help her but with my hands I couldn't even lift it; and all the time I was trying, in spite of wanting to go to her aid, to feel that I had to remain independent. Uninvolved. She didn't complain but simply trudged along silently.

When I increased my pace, I realised that Tsiu Lin was stumbling, gasping and falling behind. I turned and she gave me an apologetic look that was both sad and understanding at the same time.

I stopped dead, and everybody else stopped dead, too, in a curious game of follow-my-leader.

'You are going too fast for me,' Tsiu Lin panted. 'You are going too fast for everybody.'

'We've got to go fast,' I growled. 'We've got to get into the mountains.' My voice was harsh, I knew, but I was frightened and driven by a new anxiety now, by a wretched feeling of responsibility that I didn't want.

'Let me carry that rice,' I said.

'You can't. Your hands won't let you.'

'I can try.'

She shook her head stubbornly. 'I will carry the rice.'

There was a strange sort of humility in her that matched the looks of the people behind, as though all the gaiety that had once been hers had drained away. I found miserably that the look in her face wrenched at my heart.

'I'm all right now,' she said.

I nodded, finding there was a lump in my throat, and set off again. Silently, the crowd followed.

A mile further on, the road narrowed and began to rise, climbing slowly into the mountains. It grew steeper and the crowd began to string out. Without really being aware of it, I realised that the mule cart had dropped behind, and instead of being in the middle of the crowd, we were acting as whippers-in, hurrying everyone on ahead of us; Tchao chivvying, Fu Man bullying in his cheerful noisy way, Tsiu Lin arguing gently in her soft voice, while I watched in a cold frustrated fury as I saw myself sinking into this quagmire of collective help.

We were looking down on the plain, the road beginning to turn among the rocks past a ruined temple, the crowd scattered across the road. Suddenly I heard the sound of a lorry approaching. The air was quiet and I knew it was still a long way away, but as they heard the grind of gears behind them, the last of the trudging people began to move instinctively aside, waving to the others to move over. I shook my head.

'No, no,' I said to Tchao. 'For God's sake! Only the army has lorries. We must stop it.'

Almost before I'd finished speaking, the lorry appeared round the bend and I heard its brakes shriek and saw the dust spurting from locked wheels as it skidded sideways, striking one of the women on the hip and sending her spinning. Fully expecting the road to be empty of everything but a single plodding peasant, it had been going much too fast, driven with the usual arrogance of the army.

As the lorry came to a standstill, I gestured quickly at Fu Man, and, to Tchao's shouts, the men in the crowd surged forward. Soldiers' heads appeared round the canvas cover of the lorry, then rifles, but before they could be used, they were dragged from the hands that held them and the soldiers were on the ground. It was all over within minutes.

There was a twisted, shocked look on Tsiu Lin's face that I didn't want to look at, and I gave orders in a dry rasping voice.

'Hide them,' I said. 'See that their bodies won't be found.'

Men moved forward to do as I suggested, then Tchao and Fu Man approached, with a few other young men holding rifles.

They were looking at me questioningly and I knew they were waiting for me to tell them what to do next. I stared back at them with a sinking heart, daggers of apprehension digging into my mind. It seemed I no longer had any option but to accept responsibility. In escaping from Tai, I had wrecked a whole camp, and probably the Chengsha drainage system as well, and these people, whom I'd made as guilty as myself, expected me to provide them with freedom, as though it were a slice of fish served up on a plate.

I knew I wasn't fitted to do the job but it was something I couldn't put aside. I tried to regard it briskly and efficiently.

'Tchao,' I said, 'how many of us are there?'

He vanished, counting, and came back shortly. 'Two hundred and twenty-three. Perhaps more. Perhaps less. It's hard to count them when they dodge about like chickens with their heads cut off.'

I nodded. 'Other soldiers may come,' I pointed out. 'We've got to be prepared. Find out how many men we have with weapons, and get them together.'

There were a few shouts and a lot of shuffling and muttering and I saw the men with rifles moving to one side. Tchao returned.

'Thirty-five rifles from the camp,' he began, and I swung round on him.

'Thirty-five? Did we keep them *all* with us?'

He grinned. 'I made sure we did.'

He was shrewd and cynical and clearly hadn't many scruples when it came to his own safety. Though I could only applaud his forethought, suddenly I found I didn't like him for it.

'How many in the lorry?' I asked.

'Another seven. And two revolvers. We've also got a few assorted knives and butcher's cleavers.'

He grinned as he spoke, clearly enjoying his own freedom and prepared now to fight for it.

'Ammunition?'

'Nothing but what we carried and the boxes in the lorry. It's for rifles only.'

'Nobody can hit anything with a revolver, anyway,' I said. 'Share it out among the men with the rifles.'

Tchao attended to the instructions and came back, smiling. 'We now have a small army,' he said. 'Together with one lorry, a mule cart and two handcarts.'

'Right,' I said. 'From now on, we'll take no chances. Split the men with rifles into four parties. Send one ahead, and we'll have one on each flank and one behind. We don't want any more lorries running into us.'

Tchao disappeared again, throwing up his hand in a gesture that was almost a salute.

Tsiu Lin was bending over the injured woman. She looked up as I approached, her eyes full of tears. 'She's in great pain,' she said. 'I think it has broken her hip.'

'We'll have to put her in the lorry and carry her up into the mountains where she can be cared for.'

'She'll not live,' Tsiu Lin said. 'She shouldn't be moved.'

'She can't be left here.'

'Why not? Because she will die? Or because she might be found and tell them where we've gone?'

It was the first hint of criticism I'd heard in her voice and it cut me deeply.

'If she's going to die,' I said, 'she might as well die among people who'll look after her. And if we're going to help these people escape, then let's do it efficiently.'

As I finished speaking, I saw that her look had changed to one of hope and pride and warmth—the first I'd seen in her face since we'd left the camp.

'Where are we going?' she asked.

'I don't know.' I wanted to lose my temper, I was so edgy with worry. 'For God's sake, I don't know! I know where I'm going, but I don't know where all the rest of these bloody people are going.'

'They'll follow you.'

Tchao gestured. 'We'll be all right,' he said. 'We have forty-two rifles. In this kind of country, we can stop anything.'

I drew a deep breath. He was so naïve I could have cried. I knew we had to hide. In spite of the forty-two rifles.

'Forty-two rifles aren't much good,' I said. 'They could have a whole battalion against us in no time. Guns, too. Probably planes. We've got to split up. Is there anyone here, Tchao, who knows these mountains? We must find a place to hide. We must have guides.'

Tchao nodded. He was quick and efficient in everything he did. I sat on a rock beside the road. My hands were hurting like hell. Tsiu Lin stood beside me, not speaking, almost like a shadow, as though she had attached herself to me, unemotional, unswervingly loyal, knowing all my faults yet still not put off by them.

Tchao returned. 'We have at least a dozen,' he said. 'Many of the men in the camp were from this area. A lot of them came from the mountains.'

'Tell them to get their heads together. Tell them to decide on a place they all know where it will be safe, where we might find food, some place we can reach by different routes, some place we can hide until the hunt dies down.'

Tchao vanished again and I looked at Tsiu Lin. I saw there was a grateful smile on her lips.

'They seem to want to be organised,' I said bitterly. 'Okay, let's organise 'em. Let's get 'em away from here to safety, then we can send them off to where they want to go. In small groups, properly briefed so they're not detected, so they won't give away where *we* are. Let's find responsible men who can lead them, men with intelligence who won't panic. Let's do the job properly.'

I knew I sounded harsh but she made no comment on it.

'You didn't want this, No Lan, did you?' was all she said.

I shook my head. 'No,' I said. 'I didn't. All I want is to get back to safety.' She took my crushed and broken hands and lifted them to her lips.

'What's that for?' I asked roughly.

'Because you are brave and compassionate and beautiful,' she said.

My eyes pricked. 'Beautiful? Me?'

'To me you are. You would be beautiful if you had a twisted body, because you are brave and kind.'

'I'm not brave,' I said. 'I've never been brave.'

'You are kind. You are helping these people who have forgotten how to help themselves.'

I felt like weeping and this time it was not with fury, because there were also a lot I hadn't helped. 'I'm helping them because I've got no alternative. I don't want the bastards. I just want to go south on my own with you. That's all. I want to get *me* out of this goddam country—and you—and perhaps Fu Man and young Tchao. The rest of them can go to hell, for all I care.'

'You don't really believe that, do you?' she asked softly.

I stared at her for a moment, then I turned away, unable to meet her eyes. 'Yes,' I insisted—but suddenly I wasn't sure any more. When they looked at me like a lot of sheep I knew someone had to get them to some place where they couldn't be stuck back in that God damn compound and half-starved and humiliated. People had rights and one of them was freedom. Another was pride. Perhaps if we hung on to them long enough in the mountains, they'd acquire both.

IV

It took a great deal of time to get the crowd sorted out into eight smaller groups of about twenty people, each group under a guide and each having a party of men with rifles.

We did it from the rear of the lorry. I sat on an ammunition box inside giving instructions, with Tsiu Lin beside me, while Tchao stood on the tailboard shouting in his high pitched voice. There were a variety of dialects among the crowd from Chekiangese and Hunanese to the difficult Szechwanese, and it wasn't easy to get across the idea that the party would be safer if they split up. The guides, all of them suddenly behaving as though they were more important than they'd realised and responding to responsibility with unexpected smiles of pride, had chosen a valley in the hills which, they claimed, had no soldiers and could be reached by half a dozen different routes, all equally difficult.

'It lies alongside the Shih Chi peak,' Tchao explained. 'The Stone Banner, that means. It has a great square slab of granite on the top like a flag in the wind. You can see it a long way away. Beneath it, through the rocks, there are trees and then the valley. Beyond that there is only Tieng-feng.' He shrugged. 'That's what they say. I hope they know.'

'Do you think they do, Tchao?' I asked.

Tchao grinned. 'I expect so,' he said. 'They are only peasants but they seem to know the mountains.' He gestured towards the mule. 'What about that?' he asked.

'Kill it!'

'Kill it?' He seemed startled.

'Yes. Get it off the road somewhere it won't be seen and kill it. And don't let anyone know. We don't want them hacking it up for food and scattering blood or anything that'll give us away. Get rid of the cart, too. And the chickens.'

He nodded. 'Very well. And the lorry?'

'We'll put the injured woman in it. And anyone else who finds difficulty walking.'

'You, No Lan?'

'I can walk.'

'Not well.'

'I can try.'

'You are organising this movement,' he pointed out. 'We need you alert, not exhausted. Organisers are special people. They are more important than the labourers of the world.'

My foot was painful now all the time and I wasn't sorry to be persuaded.

'Get the parties going,' I said. 'Make sure they know their routes. Make sure there are riflemen with each party, and a few intelligent men who can get it across to them that they must be prepared to split up if necessary into still smaller parties. The one thing they mustn't do is ever allow themselves to be seen. Tell them to wait for us under the Stone Banner. How long will it take?'

'Four days, they said. Perhaps less.'

'There must be no stragglers. Nothing.'

'I understand. We must be prepared to kill if necessary.'

I had turned away and now I whirled back to face him. 'Kill who, for God's sake?'

He gestured, as though surprised at the question. 'Even our own people. If necessary we must sacrifice for the good of the whole.'

He was smiling as though he expected praise from me for his ruthlessness and courage. But I didn't feel like that just then. I was already responsible for too many deaths and I knew there would be more when some of those groups we'd sent south and east were picked up. It was something that had never hung heavily on my conscience before because then it had concerned only people in the same line of business who were out to kill me, but this time it concerned humble uninvolved people and there would be many.

'There'll be no killing,' I said.

He frowned. 'We're dealing with people who strangled Catholics in the streets,' he insisted sharply. 'People who dragged innocent men from their beds, beat them, humiliated them and spat on them. They even stirred the peasants up—people like these—to shout "enemy of the people" and "counter-revolutionary lackey" at them. They made honest men dig their own graves, recite a list of crimes on their knees, then, when they'd begged pardon, shot them through the head.'

He seemed angry with me and contemptuous, and he jerked a hand at the watching peasants. 'These are the people who allowed it to happen. They'd do it even to you if someone got to work on them. They wouldn't give mercy. They don't expect it.'

I had no doubt he was right but that didn't make what he wanted to do right, too.

'There'll be no more killing,' I said again.

He gave me an old-fashioned look, as though he felt I was losing my grip.

'Nevertheless,' I said, 'there'll be no one left behind who can be picked up by the soldiers. Even if they have to be carried. They'll have found the camp by now and they'll be picking up the people who went across the plain. Eventually they'll think of the mountains. I don't expect we've got very long. Get them on their way. And tell them they must cover their tracks. There must be nothing dropped or left behind. Not even a rag or a scrap of paper. Nothing that might indicate where we've gone. Make sure that each party understands this and appoint several men to make sure it's done.'

'I'll see to it,' he said. 'We have a few former Red Guards with us. And a few students, too. They have the intelligence. The ones who haven't thought only of going home. They'll be captured.'

The first party set off at once, leaving the road just above the lorry and heading between the rocks. There was no sign of the mule or the chickens, which had been taken off the track and butchered silently. The cart had been dismantled and hidden with the handcarts.

The second party set off immediately afterwards, and then the other parties at short intervals. There was a great deal of arguing but the guides seemed to be well in control.

'Each party has young men with it,' Tchao explained gaily. 'Boys who have had too much to say for themselves. They're intelligent and they're not afraid. They wouldn't have been at Chan Tsu if they had been afraid. They'll see that the guides do the right thing and that everyone knows what to do.'

I nodded. 'It's time the rest of us went now. Tell the guide to take us as near as possible to the track to the Stone Banner but tell him we want a place where we can safely get rid of the lorry without its being found.'

Tchao climbed into the lorry behind the wheel.

'I hope you can drive,' I said.

He grinned. 'Just,' he said.

'Then, for God's sake, go easy.'

Followed by the last group of peasants, we set off jerkily up the hill. Tchao's driving was not as good as his gift for organisation and we crept round corners at a snail's pace. When we came to unexpected hills and rocky surfaces, he had to stop and engage low gear carefully before proceeding. After an hour, however, we were high in the mountains and had left behind all the thick undergrowth. Now the trees were sparser and the countryside was more rocky.

Eventually, Tchao stopped the lorry and came round to the tailboard. 'This is as far as we go. The guide says it's only a short walk from here to the track. There's another path between the rocks on the other side. The guide says there's a fissure below us where we can put the lorry. We can cover the entrance with branches.'

'Are you going to drive it down?'

'I daren't,' he said. 'I'll probably put it over the edge. We'll have to manhandle it.'

They lifted out the injured woman, who was unconscious now, grey-faced, her breathing shallow.

'We shall never get her over the mountains.' Tsiu Lin's voice was soft with compassion.

'We can try,' I said.

'We may have to carry *you,*' she pointed out.

'I'll manage.'

'You may not be able to.'

They helped me out of the back of the lorry and then, with Tchao nervously at the wheel, began to edge the heavy vehicle on to a dusty, stony path through the trees.

I shook my head. 'I'll do it,' I said. 'We can't risk it getting stuck where it'll be seen.'

Unwillingly Tchao climbed down and they helped me into the driver's seat. I started the engine, swearing softly every time I caught the painful tips of my fingers, then I slowly edged the lorry down the path between the trees. The guide ran ahead, waving me on until the path curved and I found myself pushing into a fissure in the side of the hill, half obscured by trees and boulders. It was full of rubbish and there was a large dead bird inside.

I edged the lorry as near to the cliff as I dared, until it brought down a shower of dirt. There was so little clearance, they had almost to lift me through the half-closed door. Then, with Tchao urging them on, trees were cut down and laid across the lorry and boulders dragged across the path. Two men moved up the path with branches, sweeping over the tyre tracks, and headed back down the road towards Chengsha, still flattening the dust.

We waited on the road for them to return. They trotted back, and Tchao gestured to the rocks. 'Up there,' he said.

Above us, I could see heads bobbing among the rocks where two of the earlier parties were climbing. With the guide leading, we began to scramble between the white-faced boulders, struggling over the slopes, our feet slipping on the shingly surface. When we had to reach out to pull ourselves up, I was in agony, catching my fingers every time I slipped, until eventually I had to sit down, panting, the perspiration running down my cheeks, knowing my face was strained and grey from the pain. Tsiu Lin stared at me with concern.

'There's nothing you can do,' I told her roughly. 'At least not until we're clear of this place.'

As I spoke, Tchao came running towards me. He was pointing back down the mountains and I saw two lorries and a scout car heading across the plain towards us, still mere matchboxes far below.

'They're after us,' I said, and Tchao ran among the rocks, shouting and cursing at the peasants, pushing them down out of sight and whacking them over their heads when they insisted on raising them to look.

As I watched, the convoy stopped near the turn-off to the mountains, then one of the lorries and the scout car headed off across the plain. The second lorry swung towards the mountains and began to grind up the slope in low gear.

'Make sure that everyone keeps his head down,' I said. 'If they see nothing they'll decide we headed across the plain.'

Tchao hurried off again, bent double, and I studied the lorry. It was moving faster now, obviously doing a quick run into the mountains to check that no one had chosen that route. Tchao came back and jerked a hand upwards.

'If anyone so much as tries to lift his head,' he said, 'he'll probably get his throat slit. We have them well in hand.'

I peered down between the boulders, watching the lorry as it climbed. It was moving slowly and, as it turned on the twisting road, I saw it was full of men in sand-coloured uniforms. We were not far above the road as it passed beneath us and Tchao raised his rifle and aimed downwards, grinning. Swearing, I pulled him out of sight.

He turned. 'I didn't intend to shoot,' he explained coldly. 'I was just thinking how much damage we could do with our rifles. We could capture the lorry and add to our arms.'

'And do what with them?' I said angrily.

Tchao shrugged. 'Perhaps we could take over the mountains.'

We watched the lorry crawl higher until it finally disappeared from sight, then we turned and began to climb among the boulders again. Half an hour later, we saw the lorry returning down the mountain.

'They've found no one,' Tchao said cheerfully. 'They'll think now we went across the plain with the others.'

Even so, I knew very well that we hadn't seen the end of the soldiers. They'd come back, and next time there'd be more of them.

We climbed until it was too dark to see our feet beneath us. Finally, I fell and rolled backwards, moaning softly with pain, and the guide called a halt. We huddled together among the rocks and ate a handful of rice each. Tchao was almost drunk with elation.

'We should have stopped the soldiers,' he insisted. 'A log across the road on a blind corner and a few rifles among the rocks. It would have been easy.'

'And then what would you have done?' Tsiu Lin demanded sharply.

He grinned. 'Then we would have had not forty-two rifles but perhaps sixty or more.'

'And where do you go from there?' I asked.

'Sixty rifles would have been useful.'

'Not against four hundred, or five hundred, or a thousand. And eventually, there would have been a thousand.'

Tchao smiled, his face friendly. 'We might have started the counter-revolution,' he said. 'Who knows?'

It was cold up in the mountains. A sharp wind was blowing out of the south and we pushed closer to the rocks for shelter. We dared not show lights and several times I peered across the slopes to make sure no fires had been lit by any of the other groups. But there was only darkness and I sank back with relief behind my rock.

'Perhaps we're too timid,' Tchao said, persisting with his theme.

'I've had enough of boldness,' I said quickly. 'I'd rather behave as though I were a coward. I want to be safe. I want to feel safe. Not just for tonight or tomorrow night, but for every night for the rest of my life.'

He peered at me. 'You will go home, No Lan?'

'Of course,' I said. 'And this time I shall stay there.'

'A pity.' Tchao sounded disappointed. 'We could do with a good organiser.'

'To organise what?'

'The fight against tyranny. The country's not as peaceful as they try to pretend. There are many groups in the mountains to the north—the Kuokuntang, the Nationalists, the Democratic Socialists, the Servants of China, the Kansu Movement, the Muslim Movement.'

'I'm not interested. I'm not interested in any fight against tyranny.'

I felt Tsiu Lin's hand in the darkness and I grasped it fiercely, ignoring the pain in my fingers, squeezing it as a child squeezes the hand of its mother. It was safety and security, somehow.

Later I fell asleep, exhausted with the climb, my hands and my foot numb. I was aware of comfort in sleep, and ease and warmth, and when I woke I realised I had slumped sideways against Tsiu Lin, who had cradled me in her arms. I sat up with a jerk, vaguely ashamed to be dependent on her, but she made no comment at my roughness and handed me some rice. She was watching me carefully and I was conscious of being faintly embarrassed under her gaze.

I knew what she was thinking. I'd once learned a piece of poetry and it had always stuck in my mind.

Where thou diest, will I die,
And there will I be buried.
The Lord do so to me, and more also,
If aught but death part thee and me.

She had thrown in her lot with me and as long as I'd have her, she'd follow me wherever I went. After a lifetime of independence and easy-going relations with girls, it alarmed me a little; but when I thought about it, I found that that was how I wanted it. Unknowingly I'd already been leaning on her for some time.

Dwight would laugh like a drain when I turned up in Hong Kong with a Chinese deviationist in tow. He'd stare at me with that cold amused smile and light a cigarette.

'Can't keep away from them, can you, old boy?' he'd say, and suddenly I found myself hating Dwight for all the things I'd previously admired in him—his coolness, his ruthlessness, his efficiency, traits which I'd believed in myself until this moment. It was as though I'd had a light turned on in my mind and I was filled with rage and disgust—at the system and at the people who operated it, and at myself for having been one of them for so long.

The world was already too full of cold, ruthless, efficient people—all living at the top of a pile made up of all the other less cold, less ruthless, less efficient people; all the sad, uncertain, shabby, passionate and compassionate people who covered the earth's surface. The ranks of government were full of leaders; men who liked the sound of their own voices and the look of their own ideas; men who, in their effort to make the world in their own image, had lost sight of the fact that it was filled with an untidy sprawling mass of people who just didn't fit into their precious patterns. Those blank yellow faces with their humble expressions that had watched me as I'd given orders on the road below seemed symbolic of all the world's little people who'd never have the confidence or the skill to look after themselves.

I found my feelings of hatred for men in high places overwhelming, and I had to give myself time to recover from the anger. It was odd, I thought, that I should feel this for the first time, here on this mountain, when I'd never felt it in my life before.

I realised Tsiu Lin was watching me, her eyes on my face.

'You are different,' she said sadly.

'Sure I'm different,' I agreed. 'I became different the day Wang got to work on me.'

'It's not that. You have grown old. You were so young in Peking, so strong and so confident. Now you are old and you are no longer sure.'

She was surprisingly shrewd. I couldn't argue but I was glad that she had noticed.

Humbly, I reached out and touched her cheek and was oddly grateful for the warmth in her expression as she gave me a smile in return.

As we climbed higher and disappeared among the clefts near the summit, Tchao posted men behind us to watch what the soldiers did. We were approaching the Stone Banner now, according to the guide, and we must not be seen.

Shortly after midday, the men we'd left behind caught up with us. They were excited and laughing.

'They say there are more soldiers now, and more lorries.' Tchao grinned. 'But they're all searching in the wrong direction.'

'How far now to the valley?' I asked.

'Perhaps one more day.' Tchao was almost crowing with pleasure. 'When they start counting the ones they've rounded up, they'll wonder how two hundred and twenty-three men and women could disappear from the face of the earth. Perhaps the Party has a point after all. Perhaps people do need to be organised for their own good.'

I stared at him sombrely. I was beginning to suspect that beneath his gaiety Tchao himself was one of the cold, ruthless efficient people I'd suddenly started hating so much. Underneath the smile, perhaps he wasn't far removed himself from the people who'd been oppressing him.

The mountain was in ridges now and we left men behind on each peak to watch for pursuit and follow later. By the second night, we'd begun to descend, and Tchao was laughing with excitement.

'We've made it,' he said.

On the third morning, we passed into the trees again. I was stiff and sore and limping heavily. I was aware that

Tsiu Lin's eyes were on me all the time, full of concern, and whenever the gradient was steep, her shoulder was there for me to lean on and her hand out to steady me.

The woman who'd been injured in the lorry died here. She'd almost made it and we'd carried her all the way on a crude litter made by the guides. The jolting had been too much, though, and she slipped away from us in the way she'd probably lived her life: quietly, humbly, without fuss and without complaint.

We had no means of digging a grave but we scooped out a hollow and laid her in it and placed rocks on top against the rooting wild pig. Then we set off once more, less concerned now with pursuit than we had been and able to make greater speed.

Once or twice we'd seen planes and occasionally helicopters searching for us. But we weren't worried now because the foliage was thicker here and hid us well, and above us we could see the sun on a flat square face of rock against the sky. We had come to the Stone Banner.

The valley, as the guides had promised, was richly wooded and there appeared to be plenty of wild life.

'This could have been a major civilised area,' Tchao said enthusiastically as he stared about him. 'If it had been accessible.'

The trees were full of birds, some of them as big as snipe and partridge, and half a dozen wild pig bolted among the undergrowth.

'Food,' Tchao said. 'The guides say there is plenty of water, too, running off the mountains.'

We were eating the last of the rice when we heard the first of the other groups approaching. Fu Man suddenly burst through the trees, running towards us, laughing with delight. The people with him were ecstatic in praise of his skill and courage and strength.

'Ask if anyone saw them, Tchao,' I instructed.

Tchao chattered noisily for a while, then he swung round. 'No one,' he said. 'Though they saw the soldiers. They say there's another group not far behind. They saw them as they crossed the ridge. No Lan, we've done all we set out to do. We've spirited every man and woman into the mountains. Now all we have to decide is what to do with them.'

I looked at him sharply. 'I know what we're going to do with them,' I said. 'We're going to get them away from here. We're going to get them to safety.'

Tchao grinned. 'What a waste of people that would be,' he said as he turned away.

V

The climb had taken more out of me than I'd realised and I spent the first twenty-four hours in the valley sleeping. When I'd recovered a little, Tsiu Lin insisted on attending to my injuries. There'd been no time up to then, because the most important thing was to get away from Chan Tsu. All else, even injuries, had to wait until we were safe.

Now, however, she boiled water and bathed away all the encrusted dirt and blood that was making septic the wounds on my hands. There wasn't much she or anyone else could do for the broken fingers or the bones in my foot. I should just have to wait for time to heal them, but I knew that I should limp for the rest of my life and that without an operation the fingers of my right hand would remain bent like claws till the day I died.

As I watched her at work over them, I realised that she

had never asked me why I had received such treatment, or why I was in the Chan Tsu camp in the first place, knowing instinctively that I would tell her in my own time. I was aware of an enormous affection for her and was suddenly afraid that the sight of my twisted hands would fill her with revulsion. But she seemed not to notice, her eyes soft and gentle as she looked up at me, her mouth curving in a smile. She'd lost weight and her cheeks had lost the roundness they'd had when I'd first met her; but, if anything, this made her more beautiful than ever. She still wore that hideous blue suit that chafed the soft skin at her throat and made rough marks at her wrists and ankles, but there was a strange inner glow coming from her face, a glow that came from serenity and a sort of mature calm that often made me wonder what went on in her mind and just what she thought of me.

She was enough to stir a bishop with her slim body and that small straight nose and the soft black hair that clung like a cloud round her pale face. I could tell I was getting better, not just because I'd started smiling and teasing her again, but because I was feeling emotions for her that had nothing to do with the tolerance of a strong young man for an inexperienced girl that I'd felt in Peking.

She was suddenly doing catastrophic things to me. Though I'd known for years that men were not fundamentally decent, I'd tried to kid myself that I was when I had to be. Now I wasn't so sure, and the thought of that ugly blue boiler suit chafing at her shapely legs, when I'd seen her briefly in a silk *cheongsam* that clung to her figure as though it were a second skin, stopped me closing my eyes at night.

As the pain went out of my hands and my foot healed, I began to wish to God she were nearer when I tried to sleep and that she'd take me in her arms again as she had on the mountain, when I was too exhausted and in too much pain to appreciate it.

Around us, the group was already adapting itself to the new life in the woods below the Stone Banner. It was a quiet valley and within a few days shelters had sprung up under the capable hands of Fu Man and the peasants, well-camouflaged lean-tos screened by the trees so they couldn't be seen from the air.

The community seemed to have settled down instinctively and quickly. Men took turns as sentries on the ridges above the valleys, and the fires among the trees were masked so that smoke could not be seen.

Tchao was a great help. He kept several of the more active youngsters close to him all the time—boys like himself: Chan Chow, a history student; Chin Kai Kok, an engineer; N'Gai Sang, an agriculturalist. They were all aggressive, forceful personalities, and regarded it their duty to make everyone follow the strict rules we had set up. They were good organisers and believed in socialism, where every skill was used to the best advantage. The best shots were sent off with the rifles to produce game, while the peasants searched out edible plants and roots. Tchao was delighted with the way things were shaping. *I* wasn't.

'They've got to stop,' I said.

I saw Tsiu Lin look at me, startled, and Tchao's surprised glance.

'They'll be planting gardens next,' I went on. 'And you can see a garden from the air. They're starting to behave as though they're going to stay here for ever. And we can't do that. We still have to disperse.'

Tsiu Lin frowned. 'I think some of them don't wish to,' she said.

I felt as though the weight of the world were on my shoulders. 'I don't suppose they do,' I agreed. 'They've no option, though. It's their only hope of safety. No group as big as this can survive for long and eventually someone will think of the valley.'

It was several days before I managed to send off the first group, twenty people with rice and meat and fruit from the woods, heading south over the mountains at the end of the valley. There had been no planes or helicopters for some time and quite a lot of the people round me clearly didn't want to go. They didn't want to give up the security they'd found for the dangers outside, and several of the men and women had teamed up and weren't anxious to return to their former partners.

That was none of my affair, though, and in the end, with Tchao's persuasion and Fu Man's bullying, we made them see sense. There was a small ceremony before the first party left and a great deal of handshaking. They were to head for Tiengfeng, where, once among the turgid mass of people, they could be lost for ever.

They came towards me and bobbed their heads solemnly before leaving, their faces uncertain. One or two at first had even refused to go, complaining that they'd had ideas of planting seed and seeing it grow. Tchao had stood no nonsense, however, and his talk of setting up people's courts among the trees to try objectors had soon settled them. He appointed guides and offered to accompany the first group to see they followed instructions.

'They mustn't straggle,' I said. 'Remember that!'

He grinned. 'I'll remember,' he said.

I was still thinking of my own and Tsiu Lin's safety and knew that stragglers were dangerous. Tchao seemed to know what was running through my mind and I watched him carefully as he left. Outwardly, all the plans we'd made were working properly. Everybody knew what to do and if they did it properly we were all safe. But there was something about Tchao that left me uncertain. He was obviously itching to get out of the valley himself and head south; not, I guessed, because he was eager to return to civilisation but because he suddenly wanted to strike a blow for freedom. He was a born leader with a sharp, incisive manner and a gay personality that brought people to his side; but he was clearly dissatisfied and felt he belonged in a position of power.

'I was head of my student committee,' he had said several times.

I had half expected that once out of the valley he wouldn't come back, and I was surprised when he did. He now had a whole string of new ideas running through his head and seemed eager to put them into effect. They appeared to involve the rifles and he was secretive about them.

He said the group he'd led out of the valley had successfully split up and he brought news of what had happened to the other escapers who'd headed across the plain.

'Rounded up,' he said. 'Nearly every one. We're the only ones who got away. They thought we took that lorry we pinched to the south. They've been looking all the way towards the river.'

'Has the search stopped?' I asked.

He gave me a sidelong glance. 'It's dying down. I don't suppose they expect to find many more now.'

A few days later, another group was sent off and, according to the student who accompanied them, split up successfully like the first. Always the youngsters returned and I noticed suddenly that they had begun to cling together in a clique and that it was they who now handled the rifles. They had obtained them from the peasants with the excuse that the peasants were better fitted to do the manual work while they were concerned with escape.

They were clearly restless and were itching to do more than merely offer passive resistance to the régime in Peking.

As dedicated in their hatred of Communism as their friends had been dedicated to it, they were untouched by all the teachings that had been drummed into their heads. They were an argumentative, prickly lot, uncomfortable to live with, constantly ready for a quarrel and always ready with propaganda against the Party.

'They tell us they've liberated women from the home,' they said. 'So they have—so they can put them to work in the factories. They're clever. They overwork everyone to the point where there are accidents, then they say "Everyone is tired, we must see that they rest," and everybody's grateful because they've already forgotten who it was who overworked them in the first place.'

They seemed to prefer to live apart from the rest of us, and I watched them warily, certain they were planning something stupid that would endanger the lot of us.

My hands were almost healed now but several of my fingers were so stiff I found it difficult to grasp things, and I still limped badly. Tsiu Lin was always at my side, however, as though she'd accepted that that was her place. I could no longer imagine her anywhere else.

I was beginning to make plans for my own escape now. I was growing stronger and, with the pursuit dying down, I felt I had a chance. I was growing bored with the valley and the straitened rations that we endured were beginning to pall.

'Everything here tastes of shellac,' I complained to Tsiu Lin.

We were by one of the numerous streams that drained into the valley. It was a place where willows hung over the water, a quiet spot that had become almost a secret place to us, where we'd been in the habit of going to bathe my hands, a place no one else knew about. The grass was thick and lush and smelled sweet, and the scent of it began to rouse in me all the dormant desires for freedom.

Tsiu Lin smiled. 'You look better,' she said. 'And young again.'

'Not a day over ninety.'

She gave a gurgle of laughter. 'You *are* better, No Lan, you're smiling again.'

'It's the thought of going home. I don't look forward to a winter here.'

She didn't reply and I went on eagerly.

'We'll make for the Pearl River. Perhaps I can bribe a junkmaster to take us down to the coast—to Macao or somewhere like that. Perhaps it'll have to be a fishing boat. Could you endure stinking of rotten fish for a while? We might even have to steal a boat. I don't know. We'll see what turns up.'

I realised her smile had changed to a frown. 'That will be good,' she said.

I'd expected her to be pleased but she seemed worried.

'Doesn't that please you?' I said.

'Of course. I think it is wonderful.' She rose and began to climb up the bank.

'Where are you going?'

'I have things to do. Many things. Particularly if we're leaving.'

I caught up with her and swung her round to face me. As she stared up at me, I bent and kissed her quickly.

Her eyes remained on mine for a while. 'Thank you, No Lan,' she said in a low voice. She turned away and continued up the bank, while I stared after her, perplexed, and as troubled now as she seemed. I decided I'd never understand women.

She remained quiet after that and seemed to keep out of my way, so I said nothing and left her to get over it.

Tchao returned from a trip outside the valley several days later. He was excited and noisy and sought me out eagerly.

'No Lan,' he said, grinning, 'I heard in Tiengfeng that Director Tai is back from Peking. He has sworn to catch you.'

He seemed almost to be gloating over the news and appeared to enjoy the alarm that showed in my eyes.

'Not again,' I said. I'd long since sworn I'd die rather than let Tai have me a second time.

Tchao continued to smile. 'He's worried,' he said, 'because of what they've got just outside the valley. Did you know we are on the edge of a vast secret factory here? It makes explosives—plastic explosives.'

I'd half guessed what was in his mind, and I knew about the factory. I'd known of it before I'd crossed the border.

'I'm not interested,' I said.

His face registered disapproval. 'You should be. In a few years' time it could very much concern your country. You must know that Dr. Tsien brought back the secret of the atom bomb from the United States. China has it now. This is part of the same theme. Destruction.'

'So?'

'We students do not believe in war.'

'And?'

'We propose to destroy the plant.'

'I think you're mad.'

'Not so mad, No Lan. We have explosives of our own.'

I turned quickly. 'Explosives? When did you get them?'

'While I was out of the valley. Some of the other students joined me, and we raided a quarry along the road to Tiengfeng. We found the explosives store and broke in during the night.'

I was listening to him with only half my attention. I wasn't really concerned with his half-baked plans. What he had said about Tai worried me far more.

Tchao seemed to realise my thoughts were elsewhere. 'Aren't you interested?' he asked.

'Yes, of course.'

'We can do a lot with explosives.'

'You wouldn't know how to use them.'

He grinned—a youthful, mischievous grin. 'Wouldn't we? Chin Kai Kok is an engineer. He knows *exactly* what to do with explosives. Chan Chow can help. He is a history student but he has studied chemistry. We also have N'Gai Sang.'

'Being a science student doesn't make you an explosives expert,' I pointed out.

Tchao's eyes narrowed. 'Why? Do you know about explosives?'

'Yes.'

'Then why don't *you* use the explosives and destroy the factory?'

'I'm not interested in destroying factories.'

He stared angrily at me. 'There would be no lives lost, *Ton Tse.*'

'You might be able to convince yourself, Tchao,' I said. 'But you don't convince me. You couldn't clear the factory of people. And the place would go up like a bomb. Many innocent people would die.'

'I wouldn't have thought that would concern you, an enemy of China.'

I was about to argue, then I decided against it. 'There aren't enough of you to do it, in any case,' I said.

Tchao jerked a hand in a gesture of disagreement. 'We have enough men to see the explosives are properly placed.'

'You'd need more than that. It'd turn out to be a pitched battle.'

His face was peaked with anger now. 'We have forty-two rifles, and forty-two men to handle them.'

'No!' I shouted the word. 'This isn't why we got them out of that camp, Tchao!'

He gave me a contemptuous look. 'You got them out of

that camp because it helped *you* to get out.'

What he said was correct. But, having given them back the lives that had been taken from them, I was anxious that no one should persuade them to throw them away again.

'We were going to get them to their homes,' I said. 'The idea of coming here was to give them a chance to rest and gather food before moving on. To make their chances of getting to safety greater. To make *our* chances greater.'

He disagreed. 'It is our sacred duty to destroy all weapons of war,' he said coldly.

I indicated the rifles. 'By destroying men with other weapons of war?'

'It is our duty to undermine the régime in any way we can. Three years of effort, they told us once, and then a thousand years of happiness. Already it's lasted a lifetime. In the old days, wars and floods were an act of God and there were occasionally good years. Now all years are bad.'

'The people are grateful for security,' Tsiu Lin said gently, and faintly I heard an echo of all those grave little homilies she'd given me in Peking about how wonderful China was. 'Though the old people's homes are bare, they're better than most of them ever knew before.'

Tchao turned on her angrily. 'We have become a nation of dupes,' he snapped. 'I notice the leaders don't live in hovels or work with their hands, or allow seventeen-year-old girls to be set over them. It's our duty to overthrow them. When you draw the sword you have to strike quickly and keep on striking.'

'How do you propose to do it?' I asked.

'With a small party of our brave followers. That's all that's needed.'

'You'd need a battalion of trained soldiers. You don't imagine a few men with rifles can get in there, do you?'

'We have a cart,' he said. 'We stole one. We can cover it with sacks and place the rifles underneath them. We can wait near the entrance while the rest of the party arrives in ones and twos; at a given signal, we'll grab the rifles and rush the gate. I can use all the able-bodied men here. They can be marched through the town by a few of us dressed as soldiers. We still have uniforms from Chan Tsu. They'd be at hand to help when the gate was rushed. We'd pick up other heavier weapons from the enemy as we went.'

'And what then?' I demanded. 'When the gate's rushed? Do you know the plan of the place?'

'We shall force one of the officials to tell us.'

'You poor benighted fool,' I snorted. 'I think it's a crazy plan.'

He gestured. 'The men behind me are prepared to die for what they believe.'

I sighed. 'And when you've destroyed the factory? What then? Where would you hide?'

'There'll be no need to hide. We can take over the town. It'll be the signal for the province to rise. There's been a lot of fighting round here lately. Many people are tired of the dictators. It might be the beginning of a counter-revolution.'

'Might! Might! Might! It's all supposition.'

Tchao looked sullen. 'We're willing to try,' he said. 'We intend to steal machine guns and grenades. We'd like you to instruct us in their use.'

'No!'

Tchao frowned. 'You can't escape from here without our help. It wouldn't be difficult to inform someone outside that you're at large in the area and tell them where you are.'

Tsiu Lin's eyes flew to my face and I saw they were full of fear. 'You'd do that?' I said.

'To obtain our ends.'

I considered for a moment, still conscious of Tsiu Lin's

expression. 'Very well,' I said. 'I'll instruct you.'

There was tension in the Stone Banner camp. Suddenly it was split down the centre by disagreement. My idea was still only to reach safety. Tchao's was to be aggressively anti-Party. Soon he withdrew his group to the opposite side of the valley, jeering noisily at the rest as stupid peasants.

Tchao's change of attitude puzzled the easy-going Fu Man. Whatever he was, he had an instinctive command of things, a practical sense of responsibility that was of far more value to us than all the dogmatic theories Tchao liked to put forward. He was an expert at producing food and building shelters, even at a rough peasant medicine. Some time soon there was going to be a clash between him and Tchao that would force me to take sides. And this I didn't want. Fu Man had always been closer to me than Tchao. He was bullheaded but capable and honest, and Tchao I classed with the Dwights of the world, the top-of-the-heap intellectuals who felt their purpose in life was to tell the rest of the community what to do.

Small parties were still leaving the valley but the numbers had dwindled considerably by this time. Only the hard-core resisters remained now. I had a feeling that Tchao's plans had altered and the men were not being directed south but into the town nearby—for the plans he'd formed.

The instinct that came from years of training told me it was time to disappear, and that night I crept to where Tsiu Lin was sleeping.

'It's time we left,' I said. 'If that young fool starts anything, it'll bring the army in here immediately.'

She looked afraid. 'No Lan,' she whispered, 'I'm tired of fighting. I'm tired of hostility and bitterness. I want to live in peace.'

'You shall, Tsiu Lin,' I assured her. 'One day. We've got to get away from here first, though. There aren't many people still to leave the valley and Tchao can handle those.'

A worried frown crossed her brows. 'Tchao isn't sending them south,' she said. 'He's sending them into Tiengfeng with guns. He has been for some time.'

'That's what I thought.'

She looked uneasy and I explained why I was so concerned. It seemed time to reveal myself to her, anyway. 'Tai Tso Hua's down there,' I said, telling her who he was and why he had such an interest in me. 'And if they're caught, Tchao's guerrillas will draw attention to us. We've got to go soon.'

She had listened quietly without comment. Now she gave a small nod of understanding. 'Very well,' she said. 'I'm ready.'

'We'll head out of the mountains south of Tiengfeng to the river. We'll pick up a boat somehow.'

'I'll save food.'

'It'll be as well. We'll slip away when Tchao's next out of the valley. No one'll know. He'll never bother to look for us. He knows we'll never draw attention to them.'

'Do you think he'll really try to destroy the factory?'

I shook my head. 'I don't think he could,' I said. 'The dangers are too great.'

'Perhaps he isn't worried about danger.'

I looked at her quickly.

'Perhaps he doesn't intend to go himself,' she said. 'I think he intends to stay where he can take advantage afterwards of whatever happens.'

'What do you mean?'

She gave me a small twisted smile. 'Tchao considers himself a leader. He sees himself as the head of a new political party based on Tiengfeng.'

VI

There was already a change in the weather. I'd exchanged clothing with the people remaining in the valley, getting rid of everything European that could draw attention to me, and Tsiu Lin had prepared us with disguises as peasants. We spent as much of our time as we could in resting and building up our strength.

'As soon as the next batch leaves,' I warned her. 'The next time Tchao's out of the valley.'

By talking with the peasants, we had made a rough map of our route, with all the major stops marked on it. I proposed to ride where possible, but the first part of the route, past the outskirts of Tiengfeng, would have to be on foot. It was a straightforward plan and I felt that with luck we ought eventually to reach the river and be able to persuade some boatman to take us downstream.

It was obvious that Tchao was still going ahead with his plan. His group seemed to be rehearsing their moves at the other end of the valley. They had recruited a number of young men from the remaining peasants, among them Fu Man.

'What Tchao says is right, No Lan,' he explained carefully. 'I must go with him. Perhaps we shall not succeed but we shall have protested. If no one ever protests, then we must accept the miseries that are forced on us.'

I felt I could understand Fu Man's view better than Tchao's. It was simpler, more honest and completely apolitical.

The planning went on across the valley, growing more secretive all the time, Tchao keeping to himself all that they were doing, although most of their time seemed to be spent in arguing. After a short lull, they began to appear again, all of them silent and Tchao with a smooth, toothy smile on his face.

'I think it's almost time, Tsiu Lin,' I said. 'Are we ready?'

'Everything is ready,' she said.

The following night I couldn't sleep. My foot ached and I walked across the valley to exercise it. As I reached the shelters where Tchao and the students had been living I realised they were empty. I hurried round the other shelters, whispering discreetly with anyone who was awake, and learned that not one of the riflemen was left in the valley.

I hurried back to Tsiu Lin and woke her. She lifted a bare arm and turned over to stare up at me drowsily, her eyes heavy with sleep. As she stirred, I jerked impatiently at her.

'Come on, Tsiu Lin,' I said. 'We must go! Tchao's left the valley. With all the weapons. They must have gone to Tiengfeng. If they fail, the soldiers'll be here looking for us. And this time they'll find us.'

She scrambled to her feet and reached for her clothes. As she pulled the few things we possessed towards her—the spare clothing, the tinned food we'd hoarded and the uncooked rice—she looked at me with a worried frown.

'What about the rest of the people in the valley?' she asked.

My face felt like granite. 'We've got to go alone, Tsiu Lin. If we tell them we're going, they'll go, too. They'll be picked up and so will we. We have to do this on our own.'

She was obviously unhappy about it but she said nothing and followed me down the valley away from the shelters.

By morning we were clear of the valley and two days

later out of the mountains. We moved only after sunset. When the sun came up, we rested in the woods, lying in the grass to recover our energy, building small fires and cooking the rice before moving on again in the late afternoon.

The route took us to the west of Tiengfeng. On the third evening, we could see the lights of the town beginning to appear as we trudged towards the south. The stark outline of the chimneys was black against a bronze evening sky, and we saw occasional workers on cycles passing, ignoring us because they thought we were peasants, like the bent figures in drab black who laboured in the paddies.

'How many days must we walk?' Tsiu Lin asked.

'About three or four from here. Can you do it?'

'If you say I must, I can.'

The darkness increased and there was nothing on the road now except the last peasant carts heading from Tiengfeng to the villages. The sky was lit by the glare from the town and I could see heavy, crimson-tinted smoke.

'I wonder where Tchao is,' Tsiu Lin said, staring towards the town.

'He's either in position now. Or he's failed.'

Even as I spoke I heard the thin spatter of rifle fire over the paddies, and I stopped dead in the dusty road.

'Tchao!' I said. 'I hope to God he isn't rushing into anything. I wanted to be further from Tiengfeng than this before anything happened.'

The faint spatter of firing came again, and then we heard the ripple of a machine gun.

'That's an automatic weapon. He's run up against something.'

'Poor Tchao,' Tsiu Lin said. 'He had such ambition.'

'Too God damn much,' I observed. 'For the sake of those people still up there in the valley, I hope he fails. If he does, they may be safe. For our sake, too, it would be better if he failed.'

The scattered shooting seemed to have stirred something up and we heard the roar of a lorry engine and saw lights aproaching in the distance.

'In the ditch,' I said. We crouched in the long grass, heads down, arms round each other. Tsiu Lin was half hidden underneath my body, and despite the danger, I was aware of her softness. Her foot was hard across my ankle, one shin straight against the muscle of my calf, her thigh against my thigh.

The lights grew and passed us with a roar and a scattering of gravel and we lifted our heads slowly.

'Soldiers,' I said.

Suddenly, to our left, the sky lit up and the ground shook from a colossal explosion.

'The factory!' Tsiu Lin gasped.

The heavens seemed to be full of light that silhouetted buildings and trees, and I saw vast areas of flame and smoke.

'Tchao did it, after all!'

For a while, the earth seemed to tremble as flames rippled along the horizon. It was as though we were looking on a vast eruption. The first tremendous explosion had died now, and, as though thousands of voices were crying out in pain, we could hear the wailing of the city's population. Then more explosions followed, smaller and larger, throwing up sheets of light and flames to the sky. Still crouching in the ditch, we heard little puffs near us, and realised that small missiles, thrown thousands of feet, were descending around us. I dragged Tsiu Lin back into the shelter of the trees. The glare from the town lit her face.

'God damn Tchao,' I said bitterly. 'This'll wake up the whole countryside. They'll put up roadblocks and question everyone. Tsiu Lin, we must get moving. We must get well to the south.'

The din continued in an infernal bellowing that hurt the ears. Dimly, over the racket, I could hear the sounds of bells and sirens and even whistles. I lifted my head.

'Listen!'

Quite distinctly, I could hear the rattle of small-arms fire again.

'My God,' I said. 'The bloody benighted fool! It'll set the whole province by the ears. They'll move in troops and aircraft and tanks. Come on!'

We climbed out of the ditch and began to hurry south again down the dusty road, flinching occasionally at the bangs that came from the direction of Tiengfeng. The uproar seemed to have died down a little now but the sky was still lit up by the glare of burning buildings.

My heart felt turned to stone. 'It must have been like an earthquake,' I said.

Towards morning, we saw headlights approaching down the road and ran for the trees. They belonged to a convoy of three lorries.

'There they are,' I said furiously. 'The first of the reinforcements. They'll be swarming everywhere in a day or two. God damn and blast Tchao and his amateur tacticians!'

The lorries passed, bouncing and swaying over the rutted road, filling our eyes, mouths and nostrils with the dust they threw up.

'More soldiers,' I said. 'They were full of soldiers.'

Instinctively, our stride increased as we plodded along towards the distant river.

We rested that day in a belt of trees and several times, as I lay in the long grass, with Tsiu Lin asleep beside me, I saw several more lorries moving towards Tiengfeng. There was a pall of smoke over the whole area now, darkening the sun and spreading out in a flat haze like a layer of cloud in the still air. Towards evening, the lorries moved back along the road in the direction they'd come. They stopped further along, and the troops spread out on the far side of the road.

'They're looking for someone,' I said.

We pressed deeper into the woods but, as we emerged on the opposite side, sweating and torn by thorns, we saw more soldiers in the fields there.

'We're stuck,' I said. 'We've got to lie low until they move. We can't use the road and we sure as hell can't cut across the fields.'

Tsiu Lin looked scared, but I put my arm round her as we lay in the long warm grass. I was unable to offer her much in the way of consolation. Just when we'd appeared to be working nicely towards the river, Tchao had sent our plans haywire with his crazy attack on the factory.

We woke the following morning, stiff, tired and cold. The soldiers were still scattered in the fields and along the road, so we moved back towards the centre of the wood. I was worried now because our food supplies were running down and I knew we couldn't stay in the wood for ever.

We were just pushing through the bushes, when voices ahead sent us diving for cover again.

'Soldiers!' Tsiu Lin breathed.

Her hand reached out and her thin fingers locked in mine. Her face was pressed deep in the grass and I could see that her eyes were terrified.

I peered through the grass, then I lifted my head.

'Tsiu Lin!' My voice was excited. 'They're not soldiers. They're civilians. Civilians with rifles. Tsiu Lin, it's Tchao!'

I pulled her to her feet and we moved cautiously forward. As we emerged from the bushes, the men ahead of us swung round, their rifles raised.

'Tchao!'

The rifles dropped and Tchao stared haggardly at us. There were about a dozen of them, all students and peasants from Tchao's group at the Stone Banner valley.

'What are you doing here?' I demanded.

Tchao's head turned slowly with a gesture of weariness. 'The same as you, I suspect.' There was still a trace of arrogance in his voice, but it was overlaid now with despair.

'What happened?'

He managed a twisted smile. 'We destroyed the factory.'

He had a bandage round his hand and a bruised and puffy face. Several of the other men with him were bloodstained and injured, and one appeared to be dying.

'It would help,' Tchao said with dignity, 'if instead of staring, you gave us some aid. Have you any food?'

Tsiu Lin made a movement, but I shook my head quickly. What little food we still had I intended to keep. It would go nowhere among the exhausted youngsters, and would only destroy our own chances. Tchao and his friends had brought their plight on themselves and such small help as we could offer would make no difference.

Tsiu Lin moved across to the dying man and began to work over him, lifting his bandages to examine his injuries.

'We need drugs,' Tchao said. 'We shall get them, of course.'

There was a hint of desperation in his voice, as though he were prepared if necessary to head for the mountains and become a bandit.

'They always said the people would rise at the first sign of boldness,' he said heavily. 'But they didn't. They behaved like the sheep they are and waited for deliverance instead of snatching it for themselves.'

'Where are all the others?' I asked.

Tchao shook his head. 'It was harder than we'd thought. Fu Man's party became separated and he had to hide.' He lifted his head defiantly. 'But we destroyed the factory.'

'They'll build another,' I said cruelly. 'In six months probably. Even bombers don't stop output. Labour's cheap and there's material and know-how these days. You've done nothing but destroy lives. How many of you escaped?'

Tchao lifted his head exhaustedly. 'We're all that are left. There are a few with Fu Man but I don't know how many.'

'Did you clear the factory workers first?'

'We hadn't time.'

'You warned no one?'

'We hadn't time, I tell you!' His voice was harsh. 'They were still at work.'

'There must have been hundreds in there!'

Tchao shrugged fatalistically.

'This isn't why we escaped from Chan Tsu,' I said.

Tchao seemed sunk in despair and I was aware of grim taut faces about me and hard eyes staring at him. His failure seemed to have destroyed his authority.

'What about the houses all round?' I asked. 'Did you warn them?'

'Of course not!' The words came out in a shout. 'We had all we could do to keep ourselves alive. They realised what we were up to.'

'What about Chin Kai Kok, the expert? Did he get away?'

Tchao shook his head. 'We sent him into the main store but the explosives went off before he was ready. He never came out. The blast triggered off the other sheds. I was knocked flat by it.'

I breathed deeply. 'What happens now?'

Tchao looked up at me haggardly. 'We must get back into the mountains.'

I jerked an arm. 'The road's swarming with troops.'

'Then we shall have to wait until it's clear. We have no alternative.'

The injured boy died shortly after dark. His body was placed in a narrow ditch that ran through the wood and was covered with branches and stones. They had no spades, so they couldn't dig a grave.

It was only after dark that I permitted Tsiu Lin to bring some of the boiled rice from her pocket and eat a mouthful.

'We must think of ourselves now,' I whispered.

Smoke covered the sky long after the light had gone and we could still hear the sound of shooting. Then, abruptly, we heard several heavy thuds, followed by silence and later by several more thuds.

'Guns,' I said. 'Field guns, at least. They must have brought up artillery.'

The desultory firing went on all night, interspersed with deeper roars that sounded like explosions. Shortly afterwards, we heard the sound of lorries starting up on the road. Lights came on and the vehicles headed towards the town.

The following morning, the soldiers had gone from the main highway. We pushed through the wood, and I saw that the fields were empty also.

'Let's try the road,' I said.

As we moved out, Tchao's men began to follow us. We had just crossed the ditch when a couple of lorries approached from the town and everyone dived for cover again.

But as the lorries approached, I saw the red star on the side had been daubed out and that they were full of civilians. I wondered if they were hostages, then I saw that the civilians carried rifles and that among them were a few soldiers, all shouting and singing. Tchao leapt up abruptly, waving frantically.

'Chan Chow! ' he shouted. 'N'gai Sang! Look—there, in the first lorry! They'll take us to safety.'

The lorry slid to a halt, and the passengers jumped down and ran towards us.

Chan Chow grasped Tchao and embraced him, laughing and shouting.

'Tiengfeng is ours,' he shrieked. 'The people came swarming out of Pu Bien, the working-class district, and overwhelmed the soldiers. They hadn't a chance. We turned their own guns on them. They're all dead or come over to our side. We have the whole town. We're going to Chengsha. We'll bring out the whole province.'

Tchao was grinning with him, but suddenly his expression changed.

'Who brought them out of Pu Bien?' he asked harshly.

N'Gai Sang gestured wildly. 'Fu Man,' he said. 'His party had been hiding in there and when he saw what was happening, he roused everybody up to do something. The soldiers didn't have a chance.'

'Who's in charge of the town, then?'

'Fu Man, of course. He's giving orders as though he's been doing it all his life.'

Tchao frowned. 'What can a fish pedlar know about organisation?' he said contemptuously. 'It's time I was in Tiengfeng. Turn the lorries round.'

'But, *Ton Tse*, we were going to take the word to Chengsha. Fu Man sent us.'

'Chengsha can wait a day. We need to consolidate in Tiengfeng first.'

Reluctantly, the lorries were turned round, the passengers a little subdued now under Tchao's single-mindedness. They had been light-hearted with relief and excitement and his matter-of-factness destroyed their elation.

'You had better come, too, No Lan,' Tchao said, and it was more of an order than an invitation. 'You and the girl.'

Tsiu Lin glanced at me and I nodded, and we were pushed into the back of the leading lorry—not into the cab, I noticed, where Tchao was sitting.

They had just started the engine when someone remembered the body they'd hidden in the ditch at the other side of the wood.

'Better fetch him,' Tchao ordered. 'Send a party to bring him here. He was martyred in our glorious cause of freedom. Let's see that he has a martyr's funeral.'

There was a harsh note of authority in his voice and suddenly no sign of laughter in his face. I felt depressed. Somehow, I seemed to have seen and heard it all before.

VII

Tiengfeng looked as though it had been hit by the cargo of a vast bomber fleet. It had been ravaged by fire and buildings had collapsed in the streets. In the northern part, as we entered, we passed smouldering black walls, charred timbers and twisted girders where the factory had been. The fires seemed to be under control now though, and the streets were running with sooty water and scattered with glass and fluttering paper and hampered by fallen telegraph wires.

Some bodies, like flattened bags devoid of muscle and bones, lay among the debris, and my eyes narrowed as I saw the number.

'There were many casualties,' I said to Chan Chow.

'A great many,' he agreed, with a beam of delight. 'We killed all the soldiers who refused to join us.'

'They're not all soldiers,' I pointed out. 'Many of them are civilians. Some of them are women and children.'

'Great movements demand their victims,' Chan said with the pious solemnity of all revolutionaries growing careless with other people's lives.

'Even peace?' I asked.

But Chan didn't notice the irony in my voice and jerked a hand at the rows of smashed houses and gaping windows. 'There were many casualties here,' he said. 'It was the fault of the authorities.'

'The authorities didn't blow up the factory,' Tsiu Lin protested.

'Of course not. But they built the houses too near to the works.'

The streets were full of people. Most of the older ones who might have had families had a dumb stricken look on their faces, but all the youngsters, many of whom seemed to be armed, were cheering and shouting excitedly as the lorries passed. I was sickened by what I—even indirectly—had started.

'We have the people behind us,' Chan said.

'You have all the younger people.'

He grinned. 'The older people will follow eventually.'

'What happens when the Party authorities wake up to what's happened?' I asked. 'They'll send troops.'

'We'll handle them as we handled the others. We shall send messengers to Chengsha, and Somangtse, and Sukien, and to all the corners of the province. The whole south will rise. The south is the traditional womb of Chinese revolution. All the great revolutions of China started here.'

'That,' I said, 'was before the days of planes and a centralised government who knew where it was going and had the power to see that everyone did as they were told. One province can't hold out against all the other provinces of China.'

Chan smiled. He'd thought out the answer to that one. 'We shall request help from the Americans,' he said.

I snorted. 'I can imagine them wishing to get involved after what happened in Vietnam.'

'The Russians, then,' he said easily. 'They also follow a new enlightened line of thought.'

'They have a long way to go to get round to South China.'

Chan frowned at me. 'You sound like a deviationist, No Lan,' he said sternly.

The lorries stopped at last outside a large square building pock-marked with splinters and with most of the windows destroyed by blast. There had originally been steps in front, but now the entrance was crumbled by a mass of fallen stone and brick and was blackened by burning, as though shells had been fired through the hall.

Fu Man appeared from a small door on the right. He was grinning and his big frame was draped with weapons and ammunition and he had an officer's cap on his bullet head.

He embraced me and then Tsiu Lin, but when he turned to Tchao, I saw that the student managed to avoid his clutch. Fu Man didn't seem to notice.

'We thought it best to send word to the neighbouring cities,' he said.

'Quite right,' Tchao agreed without a smile. 'But it was more important that I was here in Tiengfeng first.'

Fu Man nodded, obviously indifferent.

'The lorries can go again now,' Tchao went on. 'And make sure there are plenty of automatic weapons in them in case there is resistance. If Chengsha and Sukien are going to be brought over to our side, they'll need convincing of the strength we have behind us.'

Fu Man nodded again and Tchao gestured at the blackened building. 'We'll set up a headquarters here,' he said.

'I've done that,' Fu Man said, and I saw Tchao frown. Fu Man was being too efficient.

Without another word, Tchao marched into the building, Fu Man trailing behind him. I noticed that Tchao's own small squad surrounded him and that Chan Chow stood by the lorries shouting orders.

Machine guns were hoisted into the lorries and they roared out of the square, leaving Tsiu Lin standing alone with me, among dozens of mute, blank-faced people who clearly had no idea what was happening. There were a lot of men about, armed with rifles and wearing scraps of uniform, but there seemed little real organisation.

'Tsiu Lin,' I said. 'The first thing we must do is get out of the centre of Tiengfeng before the wrath of God descends on it. Probably they haven't discovered in Peking yet what's happened and they might not for a day or two. By that time, I expect a lot more people will have died in Chengsha and Sukien, and when the reply comes it'll come like a thunderbolt. We've got to get our hands on food and a car before then and move down to the river. In the meantime, we'd better get hold of Fu Man while he's still around.'

Tsiu Lin's eyes flew to mine, full of alarm. I gestured towards the building where Fu Man had disappeared with Tchao.

'This has all the usual look about it,' I said. 'Power's been acquired. Now come the takeover bids. Tchao doesn't like Fu Man running the show.'

'You mean he'll kill him?'

'Let's not be as harsh as that,' I said. 'But he'll certainly get rid of him. I'm as certain of that as I am of the sun rising tomorrow. At the moment, Fu Man's got a lot of authority, because everything that was done here was done by him, while Tchao was hiding in the woods. But in a day or two the politicians will be taking over from the men of action, and then Fu Man might not be able to do the things we want.'

Fu Man was sitting in an office just inside the building, with his feet on the desk, when we found him. He was surrounded by men and weapons and was enjoying himself hugely.

He greeted us warmly and pushed chairs towards us.

'What happens now, Fu Man?' I asked.

He looked blank. 'What happens?'

'The town has to be run. Can you run it?'

'I expect so. We captured it.'

'Running it's different from capturing it. Have you thought about electricity and sewage and all the other services?'

Fu Man looked blank. 'Don't they look after themselves?'

'Not if you've shot all the officials. You'd better look into it.'

He looked puzzled. 'Why? Will it matter?'

'It will if they don't work. The people'll want to know why. There'll be a lot of bitterness and anger, and you can be as sure as tomorrow that there'll be someone who'll be willing to lead them against you.'

Fu Man was no fool and he caught on surprisingly quickly. 'I will send round the town to search out the officials,' he said. 'Do we pay them?'

'If you've got money. You'd better talk to the banks. And you'll be wise to think of your defences. Have you thought what might happen if your people are thrown out of Chengsha?'

He turned quickly in his chair and looked directly at me. 'You think they might be?'

'There's a chance.'

Fu Man nodded. 'I understand you well, No Lan.'

'You'd better get a few trenches dug, too, Fu Man. In case they send planes.'

'Planes?'

'Why not? They can do the job better than infantry these days.'

Fu Man looked worried. 'You're a wise man, No Lan. All this is good advice. We could do with a man like you. We could find you a position, if you'll stay with us.'

I shook my head. 'I'm going home, Fu Man,' I said. 'Too many people in China know about me now. There was a man called Tai. He was in Peking and then in Chan Tsu. He called himself a Deputy Director in charge of travel permits at the Ministry of Foreign Affairs, but he was more than that. He knows me.'

'He was here in Tiengfeng,' Fu Man said. 'They told me he had taken over control when we arrived.'

My heart leapt hopefully. 'Where is he now? Was he among the dead?'

Fu Man shook his head. 'He escaped to Chengsha and then to Tsehseng. For all I know, he's back in Peking now.'

Not he, I thought. Not Tai. He had a long memory and he wasn't far away. Doubtless he'd made his arrangements to hit back, and they'd be well made, too; but he had another job to do as well, which concerned me, and it was my guess he would still be thinking of doing it.

'Listen well, Fu Man,' I said. 'I don't want to meet this Tai.'

'You don't have to,' he said confidently. 'He won't ever come back here.'

I wasn't so sure. 'Nevertheless, I must go. I want to get to the river. Where shall we be able to pick up a ship or get a ride on a junk?'

'Tsochow.' Fu Man rapped out the name without hesitation. 'It's small. I know it well. I bought fish there. There aren't many soldiers. But there are ships and boats of all sizes. It shouldn't be difficult.'

'How far is it from the coast?'

'Two or three days, I don't know.'

'And how far are we here from Tsochow?'

'Many days' walk. How will you get there?'

'By car. I want papers to get us through.'

Fu Man gestured. 'It can be done. I'll see Tchao about it.'

I had no wish for Tchao to know. I didn't trust him any more. 'Never mind Tchao,' I said. 'Can't *you* do it?'

'I don't understand these things.'

I gestured at Tsiu Lin. 'Tsiu Lin does,' I said. 'Give her the run of the place. She'll organise the papers. We need identity cards with stamps and fingerprints. We need passports to move out of the province.'

Fu Man grinned. 'That'll not be any problem. There are plenty around. There are plenty of dead.'

'We need special permission to stay overnight in a hotel, too. And can you arrange a car for us?'

'Of course.'

'We'd better be Party officials of some sort,' I said to Tsiu Lin. 'Or they might query the car. And perhaps we ought to have a spare set of papers describing us as pedlars in case we have to leave it and walk. Party officials don't walk.'

'Very well.' She nodded. 'I know what's wanted.'

'I'd like to leave as soon as we're ready, Fu Man.'

His face fell. 'As soon as that?'

'It'll be better.'

He hoisted his heavy feet to the floor. 'I'll attend to it immediately.' He jerked a hand at one of his men and went to the door, then he turned and looked back at me. 'The office is yours, No Lan. Do what you wish.'

'Thanks, Fu Man,' I said. 'One more thing. Whatever happens, even if things look good, make sure you've got a clear run for the Stone Banner valley.'

He stared at me, and grinned.

'I'll remember, No Lan.'

Food in Tiengfeng was scarce because many of the shops had been destroyed. A few stalls were being erected, however, with oranges, lichees, bananas, plums, tough-looking pears and drab vegetables. There were a few sweets smothered with flies, and rice cakes and meat pies under cellophane covers, all watched by sharp-eyed men and women, some of them still bandaged, on the look-out for looters.

Fu Man sent us to a restaurant with spidery benches and crooked tables where we managed to buy tea in ornamental mugs and a meal of eggs and pork drowned in a flavourless stock. Outside, men were dragging away the remains of a cane roofing mat which had been shredded to ragged straw under the blast of the explosions and was flapping in the gusty breeze. It made a nervous hollow sound all through the meal, slap-slapping against the wall. The market was a ruin, the ground all round littered with trampled wares and broken water jars and rice bowls, and a wall nearby was charred by fire. Booths had been torn to pieces, and bricks and planks were scattered about the streets, with more litter of smashed earthenware and frayed cane matting, drifts of loose straw and dirty fragments of cloth and paper. Collapsed telephone wires clattered in the breeze. The smell was of charcoal, hot metal and steam.

During the afternoon, we went back to Fu Man's headquarters, where we heard shooting beyond the square. One of Fu Man's soldiers told us it was Party officials being shot.

'If we don't shoot them,' he said casually, 'they will certainly shoot us.'

It was my firm belief that they'd be shot anyway before too long had elapsed. The chances of holding Tiengfeng against government troops were too slim even to be considered.

A few hours later, I heard laughing and shouting in the corridor, and Fu Man appeared. He held out the keys of a car.

'There, No Lan,' he said. 'It's yours. Unfortunately there is no petrol. It all disappeared. The tanks were near the factory and went up in the fire. You'll have to search for it.'

He dumped a bag on the floor. 'Rice,' he said. 'Dried meat, tinned meat, chocolate, biscuits. Only soldiers eat those things. If you're careful, they'll last for a long time.'

He fished in his pocket and laid a bundle of dirty notes on the table.

'Money,' he said.

My eyes flew to his face. 'Where did you get that?'

'Found it,' he said, and I guessed it was the property of some luckless Party official. I didn't argue, however, and stuffed it in my pocket.

We slept the night in a small house at Chongsho, a village just beyond the outer suburbs of the town, where the buildings gave way to countryside. There was a stream nearby and willows, and flat fields leading towards the south. Some trick of the blast from the factory had stripped the leaves from the trees and a few wattle fences had been flattened, but the interior was not much damaged, though the garden was littered with scattered tiles. Another family, whose own house, nearer the centre, had been destroyed, occupied the rear rooms.

The owner of the house was a minor civil servant called Ting. He might just as well have been called Wang or Peng or Sung. He was just one of the millions of the ordinary people of China and he was a little bewildered by the events and the uprising in the town. What Fu Man had told the Tings I don't know but they didn't regard me as one of the leaders of the insurrection and seemed to feel I was just a refugee. They appeared to consider me important, though, and were nervous and deferential to me, the mother constantly yanking one of the curious youngsters from under my feet.

To conserve our food, I gave her some of Fu Man's money to prepare us a meal from her own stock, and she produced a sumptuous banquet, which I insisted on the whole family sharing. There was rice wine and a liqueur and we were all warm and mellow when we'd finished.

'That helps,' I said to Tsiu Lin, 'after the rations of the last weeks. While we're here, we'll eat as well as we can.'

When we went to the room they'd given us, I found that Mrs. Ting had laid blankets and cushions on the floor. I protested, but she refused to take them back, insisting they were in part payment for all the food her family had consumed.

I nodded, ill at ease, and she smiled at us and shut the door behind her. Through the open window I could see enormous scatterings of stars like daisies across the sky.

I turned to Tsiu Lin, smiling. 'She thinks you're my wife, Tsiu Lin,' I said. 'She expects us to sleep here together.'

She stared at me with her black eyes. Since leaving the Stone Banner valley she'd seemed silent and troubled, not speaking much, her brows furrowed and her eyes sad. The absence of her smiles touched my heart.

'I am yours if you want me,' she said quietly.

'I do want you!'

Her expression changed subtly but she was still gazing at me sombrely. Curiously, I felt elated. It seemed almost the first time since I'd known her that we'd been alone in surroundings that were anything like comfortable.

Despite the danger, I was enjoying it, and I expected her to enjoy it, too.

'I never see you laugh these days, Tsiu Lin,' I said. 'Never. Not since Peking.'

She managed a small smile. 'I am afraid,' she said.

'You'll be all right.'

'I'm not afraid for myself. I am afraid for you. I shall not cease to be afraid until you are over the frontier among your friends.'

'*Our* friends, Tsiu Lin. My friends will have to be your friends.'

I put my hands on her shoulders and she instinctively tilted her head so that her cheek rested against my wrist. My hand moved up round the back of her head so that my fingers were in the softness of the hair at the nape of her neck.

'Soon we'll be away from here. We'll be in safety. Beyond the borders.'

Her eyes clouded. 'And then?'

I looked at her quickly. 'What do you mean—and then?'

She didn't meet my eyes. 'You will go back to England. You have said you'll go back to England.'

'That's right.'

Her eyes fell and she stared at her hands for a moment. 'Perhaps you know someone in Hong Kong who will give me a post. Perhaps as an interpreter or something like that.'

I stared at her. 'Interpreter? Hong Kong? Tsiu Lin, you're coming with me.'

'To England?'

'To America. To France. To Timbuktu. Where I go, you go.'

Her eyes were fixed on my face. 'You want me to come with you?'

I quoted my piece of poetry at her. I'd been wanting to do it for a long time because it contained all I felt, and I suddenly realised she was doubtful of me.

For a while she remained motionless, her eyes unbelieving, then she gave a sudden sob that shook her whole frame and her arms went around me. As I pulled her close, her eyes were full of tears.

'You didn't think I was going to leave you behind, did you, old dear?' I asked.

'I had no idea what you wished, No Lan,' she whispered. 'You don't tell me much.'

'That's because I don't tell anybody much. I've got into

the habit through the years of keeping my thoughts to myself. I'll try to overcome it.'

She moved her head in a little troubled gesture and tried to explain her feelings. 'I had thought it was not possible for anyone to love me,' she said. 'There have been other men. But they didn't love me. They merely wanted me. And then Yen Siang. He sent me to Chan Tsu. He was prepared to give me up so that he could be free. That isn't love. I thought—'

I took her hands in mine, and her fingers were cold. 'Stop thinking. I love you.'

She gave a deep sigh, but she didn't take her eyes off my face.

'And we shall live together? Always?'

'Sure! Married, if you wish. Is that all right?'

She nodded, her eyes glowing.

'Does that suit your Eastern way of thinking?' I teased her. 'Can you be sufficiently deviationist to put behind you all that pride you had in steel works and drainage systems and fall in love instead with a man?'

She nodded again, smiling with delight now.

'You'll be a lost soul,' I said.

She hugged me. 'I'll become more Western than you,' she insisted breathlessly. 'I shall run your home and you, too. In the best Western tradition.'

'Don't kid yourself it'll be easy,' I said. 'I'm no good to you, really, whichever way you look at me. But there it is, I've put it on the mat now. It's asking a lot of you. I expect I'll give you a hell of a life.'

She was laughing now, light-headedly, and it did me good to see that the anguish was gone from her eyes and that they were ready to light up again at my teasing.

'It's a fool's game,' I said. 'You don't know what you're taking on.'

'I do! I do!' She was like an eager child.

'Then God help us both,' I said.

I looked at her with mock solemnity. 'It's only fair to warn you, though,' I said. 'I'm better now, and since it's all settled between us I doubt whether I can wait until we reach Hong Kong to get ourselves joined in Holy Matrimony.'

Her smile died quickly and I wondered if I'd offended her prim Party sense of rightness. Then she looked up at me shyly.

'The ceremony is unimportant,' she said.

I grinned at her, and she blushed.

'Let's start the honeymoon right now,' I suggested.

As I released her, she waited silently and I touched the breast of the rough garment she wore.

'You look like a peasant, Tsiu Lin,' I said. 'I want you to look what you are. A great lady. One day you will.'

Her hands were by her side, her face tranquil, her spirit calm, her expression full of offer and appeal.

'Oh, for Christ's sake, Tsiu Lin'—the words burst out of me in a croak as I reached out with shaking fingers to the hideous padded suit she wore—'take that God damn ugly thing off!'

She gently put my hands aside and unbuttoned the garment. Then she untied the strings of the shapeless trousers and stood before me, slender and white and devoid of embarrassment.

'I am your wife, No Lan,' she said. 'I have been your wife from the day I first set eyes on you.'

I woke first the following morning. Tsiu Lin was lying in the crook of my arm, her black hair across my shoulder. Her face was peaceful and calm and she seemed to have been purged of all unhappiness.

I lay for a while staring at the ceiling, my eyes wide, my mind busy. I was utterly responsible for her now, not merely because she had helped me to escape, but because, as she said, she was my wife. No church ceremony, no signing of documents could make her more my wife than she was now. In the look she had given me before she had fallen asleep, she had made me her husband.

It was something I had not planned, but I found myself more than satisfied with the situation.

She moved slightly, and I found she was looking up at me, then she turned on her side, her head in the curve of my neck, and I saw she was smiling.

'I am so happy, No Lan,' she said.

'And you'll smile again now?'

'For you I shall always smile. I am your wife.'

I grinned and pulled her to me. 'Very well, wife,' I said, 'although we have work to do, we have a little time first for pleasure.'

VIII

We didn't go near the centre of the town for two days, preferring to be alone, behaving like youngsters in love for the first time. The money Fu Man had provided kept us in food and Mrs. Ting cooked our meals, smiling indulgently on us as she served it.

Ting brought the news. There had been no reaction from the north yet and Tchao had set up an office in the local Party headquarters and was making an effort to clear the centre of the city. But he was finding it difficult, because those of his followers who had survived the attack all had their own ideas about how their new life should be run and they were all eager to have a hand in it. And, because they, not Tchao, had been responsible for capturing the place, they were insisting on having a say.

Nevertheless, now that they owned the town, they seemed unsure what to do with it. News had come in that Chengsha, thirty-seven miles to the east, and Sukien to the north had followed their example and had also risen and taken control. More men had been sent beyond Sukien to Tsehseng and even further to carry the news of the uprising.

'We're all right for a day or two,' I told Tsiu Lin. 'Sukien's where the first retaliation will come. There are no troops between here and the coast and any blow will come from the north and hit the Sukien area first.'

'You think it *will* come?' Tsiu Lin's eyes were worried.

'As sure as tomorrow.'

A small frightened expression crossed her face. 'Shouldn't we be moving on?' she asked.

'Yes. But we need petrol. Mrs. Ting found me some cans and bottles and we can fill the back of the car with them. We can then probably reach the river at Tsochow, stay the night there, and use the rest of Fu Man's money to hire a boat and get away the next night. We could be in Hong Kong within a day or two from there. It's best this way. In the meantime, we're resting. We're making love.'

She smiled at me and I was pleased to see that as hope had returned there was some of the old gaiety back in her eyes.

'We are great lovers,' she said. 'There have been none greater.'

That afternoon, we made our way into the town. Fu Man met us. He looked angry and launched at once into a tirade against Tchao.

'He wishes to control everything,' he said. 'I have taken command of the militia, because I was the one who brought out the men from the Pu Bien district. I am the one who did all the fighting. He simply made mistakes.'

'Be careful of him, Fu Man,' I warned. 'He's ambitious.'

Fu Man shrugged. 'I'm not afraid of Tchao,' he said contemptuously. 'He is only half my size.'

'He understands politics, Fu Man.'

'I'm not afraid of any politician. I have my strength. And I have the guns, No Lan.'

When we asked about news from the north, Fu Man grinned.

'The whole province is rising,' he said. 'Red Guards have been killed in Lingwha, the other side of Chengsha, and Party officials chased out of Nanshai. There is now fighting in Kaikan. The whole province will be ours before long, and then the next province will rise. And then the one next to that. This is the beginning of the counter-revolution.'

'What about the lorries that went to Tsehseng? What's happened there?'

Fu Man looked puzzled. 'They haven't returned yet.'

I wasn't surprised. 'Perhaps they've run into difficulties, Fu Man. Remember what I said: Keep your road to the hills clear.'

Tsiu Lin's face was grave as we left. 'They can never do it,' she said. 'They have no idea of the power of the central government. This is a mere countryside of farmers. There's nothing else.'

I nodded. 'You know that. And I know that. But we shall never convince them of it.'

We called on Tchao. It wasn't easy because outside his office there was a squad of soldiers who insisted on forms being filled in first. I saw more soldiers, all of them young, squatting over their weapons.

Tchao was dressed in fresh clean clothes and was well shaved and groomed. He was worried because people were complaining about the absence of work in the town now that the explosives factory was no longer functioning.

'They're free,' he said bitterly. 'What more do they want?'

It surprised him that anyone should be dissatisfied.

He was nevertheless well established in his office, where he had two girl assistants who had been employed originally in the offices of the explosives works.

'I need assistants,' he pointed out. 'They can look after the details while I give my attention to the bigger things.'

'What about Chan Chow and N'Gai Sang?' I asked. 'Can't they help?'

'Chan Chow has left,' Tchao said.

'Left?'

'He has gone south.'

'A deviationist?'

Tchao frowned. 'You could call him that. He decided he doesn't wish to work for the counter-revolution.'

Perhaps he's realised it's safer not to, I thought. Aloud I said. 'And N'Gai Sang?'

'I have had to have him arrested,' Tchao said.

'Oh! Why?'

'He was trying to undermine my authority here.'

'I suppose he couldn't have felt that he had a right to equal authority after what he did at the beginning of the rising?'

'The people expect *me* to run the town.'

Perhaps, I thought, they'd been given no choice.

'What'll happen to N'Gai?'

'I haven't decided.'

'*You* haven't decided!' I exploded. 'Are you the police, judge and jury?'

'I'm the authority here,' Tchao snapped back. 'And take care, No Lan, that I don't have you arrested.'

'On what charge?'

'There doesn't have to be a charge. You *and* the woman. We expected you to work with us.'

'I'm not even a Chinese national.'

'The woman is. Her loyalty's to us. We could take her away at any time. We have the power.'

'For God's sake, what's she done to you?'

He answered with another question. 'Would you give yourself up to Tai, No Lan?'

'You know I wouldn't.'

He gave me a smile that made me feel cold. 'You might be persuaded to,' he said. 'Through her. I could make a deal with Tai if I had to. They'd make one, you know, for you. Even with me.'

'You're a bastard, Tchao.'

He grinned. 'I'm only joking, of course,' he said. But I knew he wasn't.

He turned away, cheerful again, the harshness gone from his voice. 'The whole of south China's rising,' he went on. 'There is heavy fighting in Lingwha.'

I stared at him, my heart still touched by ice. 'Are there casualties?'

'Of course. You can't build walls without breaking stones.'

'What sort of fighting? Are there Peking troops there?'

'There'll be no troops.' He seemed confident, too confident. 'They'll turn on their masters when they see the situation.'

'I hope you're right, Tchao,' I said. 'What about the rest of the people in the valley below the Stone Banner?'

'They've been sent to their homes. We've looked after them.'

'That's something to your credit.'

Tchao smiled and again there was no warmth in it. 'There might have been some among them who didn't like me,' he observed. 'Enemies in the Stone Banner valley could always be dangerous. I proved this myself and I intend to make sure it's kept empty. I want it for myself in case things go wrong. We have a radio now and can ask for help. And we can get it. Secret societies still grow up in spite of Peking, and Chiang drops parachutes with guns and grenades and ammunition. They also have pamphlets in them. I've seen one. "Your brothers in Formosa have not forgotten you," they say.'

'And will you join Chiang?' I asked.

He sneered. 'That old fool! He was never any good and he's ancient now. No, I'll form my own party and link up where I fancy. I'm not going to end up as some minor official in *his* government. I want some say in things.'

There was still no sign of retaliation from the north, but I wasn't kidding myself that everyone in Peking was sitting on his bottom doing nothing. The whole countryside round Tiengfeng seemed to have turned on the Party, however, and I thought how much Dwight would like it, because while they were looking after their own troubles in Tiengfeng, they'd at least be unable to stir up trouble in Hong Kong or along the borders of India.

I found no pleasure in the thought, though. According to the reports, wherever fighting had occurred the army had resisted strongly and there had been a lot of casualties —many of them people who were not even involved, peasants and workers in whose homes the retreating troops had taken refuge.

I tried to pretend it didn't concern me. Remembering Tchao's thinly veiled threat I was collecting petrol as fast as I could in cans and bottles, trying to say nothing to Tsiu Lin, trying to avoid worrying her. She had no idea what I was thinking and was behaving like a girl on her honeymoon. In her happiness, she seemed almost to have forgotten the danger. Although she was as inexperienced at lovemaking as I might have expected, she was quick to learn. She was sensitive and intelligent, usually modest yet sometimes frankly sensual, never aloof or acquiescent. It was a ridiculous situation that we should make love in this way with the whole of China about to fall on our necks, but it wasn't easy to obtain petrol and we couldn't go without it. Tchao had clamped down hard on transport and he clearly had no intention of letting us go if he could help it. Desite his smile, he had obviously decided I'd make a good hostage if he needed one.

I kept my eyes open, watching events, and began to notice that as the days passed the troops outside Tchao's office increased, while Fu Man grew more worried. I tried to warn him but he was suddenly too busy to listen. One morning I found him outside his headquarters, standing near lorries filled with men with rifles, all of them peasants or working men, all of them pathetically inexperienced. They looked anxious as they listened to him talking.

'What's happened, Fu Man?' I asked.

He turned. 'Trouble,' he said.

'What sort of trouble?'

Fu Man looked angry and bewildered. 'We've just heard from Tsehseng. They were waiting for the lorries we sent. They were captured and everybody in them shot. We've heard they're heading this way.' He managed a ghost of his old grin and slapped my shoulder. 'But don't worry, I'll sort out Tsehseng. I'm sending every man we have.'

'Don't get rid of everyone you can trust, Fu Man,' I said, because I'd noticed that none of the men in the lorries was a follower of Tchao. But he was already too preoccupied to be interested.

He dispatched the lorries and climbed into a car and headed towards Tchao's office for a conference. There was not much I could do, so I spent the rest of the morning in the town and walked back to the Tings' deep in thought. Tsiu Lin and Mrs. Ting met me. Tsiu Lin looked shocked.

'Fu Man's been shot,' she said.

I stared. 'But I've only just seen him.'

'He's been shot all the same.' Mrs. Ting was flushed with excitement. 'The police in the village had a message warning them of the change.'

My eyes sought Tsiu Lin's. 'What change?'

Mrs. Ting's hands fluttered. 'They're putting up notices all over the centre of the town saying he was working against the counter-revolution. The police sergeant said so. Leader Tchao has taken over.'

So it had come at last. I began to load the car with the petrol I had collected and moved it among the trees ready to leave. The day was ominously silent. Every minute I expected to hear soldiers at the door, and I decided to set off as soon as it was dark.

During the evening I went into the garden. The sky was amber and crossed by a flight of duck heading south above the trees. Then, as I stood there, I saw two lorries approaching in the distance. I could see quite clearly that they contained armed men and I knew immediately that they were Tchao's and why they were coming. He had meant every word he'd said and the time had come to pick up his hostages.

I ran into the house shouting for Tsiu Lin.

'Tchao's men are here,' I said. 'He's after us! We've got to leave!'

She reached for our belongings, and I ran outside again towards the car, sick at heart and hoping against hope we'd get clear. But they were nearer now and there was little likelihood of our not being seen. But suddenly there was an iron rolling sound in the sky and I saw that the lorries had come to a halt. To my surprise they turned and started to head wildly back towards the town. It was only then that I became really aware of the sound in the sky. Swinging round, I saw a flight of aircraft approaching and, behind them, a second.

The sky was filled now with the roar of engines, and I realised why Tchao's men had bolted. Tsiu Lin and Mrs. Ting joined me in the garden with the children and we all stared upwards.

There were nine aircraft altogether and the first group passed overhead low, roaring towards Tiengfeng. As they disappeared from sight beyond the trees, we heard the thuds of the first bombs and I saw Tchao's lorries increase speed, swinging off the main road as though trying to make a wide detour round the town.

Mrs. Ting began to cry as the second group of planes wheeled over our heads for their turn over the town. When they had passed, she came to life abruptly and began shooing the children into the house, tears still streaming down her face.

'My husband,' she kept saying. 'He was no revolutionary, No Lan! All he wanted was to live in peace with us!'

The ground shook beneath our feet as the bombs landed and I could see a heavy pall of smoke rising over the town. The lorries had vanished.

'They've decided it's safer to cut off Tchao's little counter-revolution at its source, rather than battle their way down,' I said to Tsiu Lin. 'Bombs are cheap and they'll be enough to stop everything that Tchao started. Two days from now he'll be a fugitive. Thank God they came in time.'

Mrs. Ting was sitting inside the house, watched by the children and the neighbours, rocking from side to side and wailing. We were just leaving when a boy brought a message from Ting. He was safe, it appeared, and had already left the town centre when the raid had started. He was delayed because he was helping the injured.

I had no wish to be held up by any rescue attempt and was itching to be off, but several things stopped me—the fear of being spotted on the road by planes, the need for news, the fact that Ting hadn't yet turned up, Mrs. Ting's misery. They had been so good to us I felt I had to wait, and the day crawled towards evening.

When Ting finally arrived, he was covered in plaster dust and looked frightened.

'The Peking troops have arrived,' he announced. 'They dropped by parachute at Chengsha and commandeered lorries. There was no one to stop them because everyone from Tiengfeng had gone to Tsehseng.'

'What about Tchao?' I asked.

Ting shuddered. 'Director Tai is back,' he said. 'Martial law has been declared. They killed all the counter-revolutionaries they could find. They stripped them naked in the street, made them confess their crimes and then shot them in the back of the head. Even the girls in Tchao's office.'

I wished I'd left. With Tai back, time was running out.

'What about Tchao?' I asked again. 'Where's Tchao? Where's he gone?'

'No one knows. They say he's gone towards Tsehseng but the messages they're getting from there don't mention him. No one knows what to do. All they could find out from the girls before they killed them was that he'd gone into the mountains with his personal guard. They say he's got plenty of arms and he's just waiting for the chance to start another insurrection. They've lost him.'

I went over the car carefully. The tyres were not very good but we had plenty of petrol now and with luck we ought to be able to go a long way. We took two blankets, paying Mrs. Ting twice their value, and placed the sack with the food and rice carefully beside them in the car with the identity papers.

'You are leaving?' Ting asked.

'Tomorrow,' I said.

He sighed. 'It is a bad time for us all just now. There is much suspicion and hatred in the town and there are informers everywhere. They say Director Tai has started a search for a European reactionary spy who has been hiding here in Tiengfeng.'

I hoped my disguise was good but Ting didn't seem to be thinking of me. He'd always assumed I was a Cantonese, a Party official in trouble over some misdemeanour with which he seemed to associate Tsiu Lin. I think he thought that anyone with a woman as beautiful as she was couldn't be entirely sold on Party dogma.

'They have started in the Pu Bien district,' he went on, chattering away. 'They believe he may be sheltering there. Eventually all the town and the surrounding districts will be searched.'

He looked at me again and I wondered if some suspicion had entered his mind.

'I don't want to bring trouble to your home,' I said. 'We must leave as soon as it's light.'

'Perhaps it's as well,' he said, and he seemed relieved because strangers in his home would undoubtedly invite questions. 'They say there'll be much more trouble here soon.'

'If you stay here, you'll be safe,' I told him. 'Don't go into the town, because it's there where the trouble will come. Stay here and say nothing. Pretend to be ill. Don't tell anyone what you think. Keep your thoughts to yourself, then no one can accuse you of having the wrong ones.'

He nodded. 'You are wise, No Lan. I'll do as you say and I'll tell my wife to do the same.'

It was after midnight when I left Tsiu Lin's side. She woke as I slipped from under the blanket, and lifted her eyes to me, startled and afraid.

I put my finger to her lips. 'Don't worry,' I said. 'I have one last thing I must do. Tomorrow we're going.'

Holding the blanket round her, she watched me dress but she didn't ask any questions.

I was going into Tiengfeng partly because I felt I could take Tai's men away from the city and our route south and partly because I felt I owed someone a debt. It had been Fu Man who'd helped me escape from the Chan Tsu camp. Without his strength and willingness, none of us would have left. Without him we'd never have reached the Stone Banner valley. Without him Tchao's plan for the destruction of the factory and the capture of the city would have failed—had failed, in fact, until he'd acted. I felt I owed him a death.

I didn't look forward to being in the city again now that Tai had returned. There would be a description of me in the hands of every soldier in the place. But I felt that Fu Man had to be avenged. My presence had indirectly caused too many deaths, and I was determined that Tchao was going to cause no more.

As I walked towards the city in the dark, I patted my pocket. There was a note there I had written in Chinese characters in a slip of paper I'd taken from a book belonging to one of Ting's children while I'd been pretending to read to her. Beside pictures of Chairman Mao genially patting the heads of uniformed infants, it carried directions to the Stone Banner valley and where to find Tchao.

I felt no conscience as I pushed through the velvety blackness. A wind had got up and I could hear the reeds in the ditch beside the road rustling dryly together. The solitariness suited my mood. I'd long since decided to opt out of the emptiness of my profession. There was suddenly nothing about it that could recommend itself to me. The realisation had come to me several times in the Stone Banner camp, and since then I'd not lifted a finger to destroy anything. So long as Tsiu Lin wasn't threatened, I had no quarrel with anyone. But there was one more thing I had to do—just one thing, because it might be the means of savings dozens, perhaps hundreds, of lives, including hers.

Tiengfeng was dark as I entered the streets. There was a roadblock and a platoon of soldiers across the road but I had no difficulty avoiding them and moved silently among the rubble. There were fires still burning but few lights and no civilians about. The air was full of smoke but clearly a curfew had been ordered so that no one could escape the search for me that was going on even in the darkness. Frightened citizens, waiting for the tramp of feet outside, were out of sight behind their doors, or crouching silently among the wreckage of their homes. Occasionally I saw groups of soldiers standing together.

I waited in the black shelter of a ruined building as soldiers came and went in the glimmer from the lights of their lorries and the glow from the fires. A sentry, his rifle slung on his shoulder, strolled up and down near the vehicles. After a while the other troops went inside, except for two or three men sitting in the lorries. But it was cold and I could see they had the windows closed and that they were steamed up with their breathing.

I went on waiting. After a good half hour, the strolling sentry stopped near me and began to unbutton his trousers to relieve himself. I picked up a house brick silently and weighed it in my hands. Then, as he faced the wall, I drew my arm back and the brick hit him just behind the ear.

I held him as he crumpled. His rifle clattered against the wall but I caught it and silently lowered him to the ground. I glanced towards the lorries but no one had moved. They obviously hadn't heard anything.

I felt for the boy's heart and was glad to find that he wasn't dead—though he'd have a hell of a headache the following morning. Then I stuck the sheet of paper I'd stolen from Ting's daughter through one of his buttonholes so he couldn't possibly miss it when he came round. Beyond that, there seemed to be nothing more I could do and I slipped away over the rubble and found the road out of town.

IX

The following morning we shook hands solemnly with the Tings and all the children. They didn't ask where we were going. I'd felt it would be safer for them not to know, in case they were ever questioned, but Ting seemed to guess we were heading for the coast and gave me the address of his cousin Sha Nai Su at Tsochow.

Neither I nor Tsiu Lin had mentioned Tsochow and I wondered if it were the beginning of an escape route that many people in the district knew about. I didn't ask questions, however, but thanked him for the address and promised to use it if I could, then I turned the car and headed for the sun.

We were no longer dressed as peasants but wore fresh blue boiler suits and caps like officials.

'No one should stop us, Tsiu Lin,' I said as we rattled over the badly made road towards the south.

She turned her head to look at me. 'Suppose we have to leave the car?' she asked. 'We'll look strange, won't we, two people in smart suits walking along a country road?'

'I've thought of that. That's why we've brought the old clothes as well. If we have to abandon the car in the country, we can become peasants again and carry these suits in our blankets to wear when we reach Tsochow. It might be easier dressed as an official to acquire a boat down-river.'

She nodded and touched my hand.

'Are you afraid?' I asked.

'Not when I'm with you.'

I hoped her faith in me was justified because *I* wasn't feeling very happy. Although the reports we'd heard indicated no movement of troops to the south, as soon as Tchao's bid for power was seen to be failing there'd be officious people eager to gain promotion by showing their loyalty to the regime. They'd be watching for fugitives from Tiengfeng and they wouldn't hesitate to report us.

Planes flew over us all day from the north. When the petrol tank of the car was empty, I filled it up again from the cans and bottles in the back, and replenished the water in the radiator from a stream. We stopped under the trees a little further on and ate.

Tsiu Lin was silent and preoccupied, but small warm glances in my direction indicated how closely she had bound herself to me.

I insisted that we rest for an hour, and we lay in each other's arms in the warm sunshine before we set off again. There were no towns of any size on the route we'd chosen, and no one in the villages we passed through—mere huddles of mud houses that would keep out neither the rats nor the winter rains—seemed to concern themselves with us.

At one bridge, however, there was a squad of soldiers with a lorry who demanded to see our papers. They were P.L.A. troops, tough and intelligent, but Tsiu Lin's work had been good. She had somehow managed to make use of a number of different stamps so that the documents didn't appear to have been issued at Tiengfeng. We could easily have come from Tahking or Watnam, and we were waved on without difficulty. The sergeant was even apologetic.

'We have to do it, *Ton Tse*,' he explained. 'There's a big search on for some Western reactionary they're after.'

He glanced at me but my disguise was sound and my

papers were in order. For all he knew, I really was Chen Ho Hok, a Party official on my way south on Party business.

'Have you heard news from Tiengfeng?' I asked as I started the car again. 'We heard bombing.'

The sergeant grinned. 'Flattened, *Ton Tse*. That little lot was soon over. Troop carriers have been landing at the airfield at Tsehseng. They'll be reinforcing the place already.'

I thanked him and drove away, grateful that we were already so far south.

We stopped the night at a small hotel, posing as man and wife. No one queried our papers. The hotel was small and as uninteresting as a house brick, like the one in Chengsha where I'd stayed before my arrest. There were the usual listless red banners, and loudspeakers blurting out Party dogma and the thoughts of Mao Tse-tung. We told the manager we were tired and wished to sleep, and lay on the bed in our room, feeling it would be safer if we didn't get into conversation with anyone. After dark, the dogma changed to news and we learned that troops were already entering Tiengfeng from the north.

'The traitor, Tchao, has been arrested and shot,' the announcer said. 'He had escaped into the mountains but information as to his whereabouts was handed in by a courageous patriot acting unselfishly in the interests of the nation, and he and his men were mopped up.'

I felt Tsiu Lin move closer to me, but I thought of Fu Man and didn't feel a twinge of conscience.

We rose early the next morning and headed south again. The countryside was flat and dusty all the way to the hills.

'We must be getting near to the coast,' Tsiu Lin said.

We ran out of petrol late in the afternoon in the hills outside Tsochow, so we opened all the windows and pushed the car down the bank of a small river and watched it sink out of sight. Then we changed among the reeds into the rough peasant clothes in which we'd escaped from the Stone Banner valley, and stuffed the blue boiler suits into the sacks.

It had suddenly grown colder and it was almost evening now. Rain started to fall and we had to try to find somewhere to shelter for the night. We could hardly march into Tsochow looking like a couple of drowned rats, and we began to walk more quickly, our eyes alert for shelter.

The road was surrounded by rocks of all sizes, piled one on another in strange shapes and interspersed here and there with clumps of thorn and small stunted trees. There was no traffic but we decided to move into the rocks for safety. The path we took grew rapidly steeper until the only growing things about us were stunted trees and small flowering shrubs and sparse grass, with an occasional flat-topped pine.

We began to feel safer. After a while, we found a cave in the hillside, where the entrance was hidden by fallen rocks. After the lash of the rain and the beat of the rising wind, it was surprisingly warm inside. It was filled with small broken sticks and rubbish and leaves; but we realised that they'd make a soft bed to lie on and pushed them all together and trod them flat before putting down the blankets.

The cave was well hidden from the road. We were unlikely to be seen there, so we decided to build a fire to dry ourselves off. While Tsiu Lin prepared food, I began to hunt among the stunted trees for broken branches. They were wet with the rain and smoked and steamed when I first lit them; but gradually, as they dried out, they filled the cave with light and warmth.

Full of food and glowing with the effects of some of the Chinese brandy I'd taken the precaution of buying in Tiengfeng, I looked at Tsiu Lin. She was watching me with shining eyes, a smile on her lips. Then she shyly lowered her gaze as if encouraging boldness.

'I don't think anyone will find us here,' I said, reaching out for her.

When we woke the next morning, it was still pouring with a rain that was changing now to sleet, coming in an icy deluge from the north. The sky seemed to be hanging on to the pale shadow of the hills and there was an aching coldness in the air as the rain lashed across the valleys in long sweeping veils, filling our ears with the sound of water and sending streams rattling in torrents down between the boulders outside. There was no point in trying to move on, so we remained in the blankets and clutched each other for warmth.

We stayed where we were until midday, when we reluctantly sat up and warmed food on the remains of the fire. The sky was still heavy and the storm showed no sign of stopping.

'It seems as though we're holed up here for the winter,' I said with a grin. 'However, until the food runs out, I'm not complaining. The only one who'll object will be Dwight.'

She stared at me, her eyes troubled. 'Who is this Dwight?' she asked. 'Is he a friend of yours?'

'Not so you'd notice,' I said. 'He was a sort of official. My superior.'

'You have to go back to him to report?'

'I suppose so. But that's all. Dwight and I are finished. I know it and it won't take him long to realise. He's a pretty intelligent man.'

It was three days before we moved on again, but we were both well rested and well satisfied with each other as we began to descend the hillside.

The night before had been bitterly cold and full of

brilliant moonlight which had illuminated the rocky hills in a way that took the breath away. Now the sun had reappeared as suddenly as it had gone and the mud was already drying and cracking in wide zigzag shapes like the 'crackled ice' pattern which is the most poetic of Chinese designs that you see on everything from cheap ginger jars to old porcelain.

We were still dressed as peasants, intending to change back to the boiler suits when we saw how the land lay in Tsochow. We stopped just before we reached the outskirts, staring at the town and the river from the dusty road. The sky was like a blue rag flecked with cloud and the town lay in the sunshine in a huddle of dun shapes, the tiles of its roofs and the curves of a drab pagoda dimmed by dust. Even the trees, washed clean by the recent rain, had already collected their load of dust once more and stood tawdry and yellow-looking under the sun. It had an empty look about it, but I could see figures moving about and the shapes of junks gliding past beyond the houses.

In Chinese *chow* means large town but there was nothing very imposing about Tsochow. It was a drab, dreary little place, but just then it looked like a gateway to freedom.

It seemed to be full of soldiers, however, when we entered it, and a few enquiries round the marketplace soon made it clear they were Tai's men and they were there to keep a look-out for refugees from Tiengfeng.

The information unnerved me a little but the most sensible thing seemed to be to behave as peasants would. I answered questions slowly and stupidly as though I didn't understand, fishing into my rags to produce the spare set of papers we'd prepared, to prove we were what we said we were—itinerant pedlars heading for the rice fields in the hope of picking up a little business among the workers there.

They let us go without taking much trouble to check on what we said and we arrived at the river after dark, to stare longingly at the nests of sampans and junks that lined the banks. Thousands of lamps twinkled in the shadows and I could hear jingling Chinese music coming from some of the boats and the spicy smell of cooking. Soldiers were embarking on junks and passing upriver towards Tiengfeng.

Nobody moved very fast, however, because this was Chinese China, not the cosmopolis of the future thought up by Party officials. There were no speeches here because no one was prepared to exchange the city for this drab little town where life hadn't changed much in a thousand years. To the people of Tsochow reality was not Communism but the fickle river that destroyed their crops and killed their sons. This was the eternal, tragic China and this the river of sorrow, flowing all the way down to the sea.

We decided that in view of the number of troops in the town and the reason for their presence, it would be safer not to use a hotel, so we found a hovel near the marketplace where no one would ask questions. There were dozens of itinerant pedlars there who traded with the people from the junks, and dozens of boatmen who slept overnight on their trips up and down the river. We shared a small room with several other people, but since we looked like peasants, no one even bothered to look at us.

Tsiu Lin sat near me, her head bent most of the time, preparing rice in a bowl over a small flame, her hair loose and over her face, so that her delicate features could not be seen, and I was big enough for no one to wish to argue with me. She kept carefully close to me, deferential as any Chinese peasant's wife would be, huddled in her rags by my side. For most of the time, I affected to ignore her, as a peasant would, and we slept crouched together until the first signs of dawn began to rouse the other people, and the place came alive for the new day.

The following morning, we headed for the river again, searching for Sha Nai Su, the cousin Ting had told us about.

We found him in an open-fronted store he owned and cautiously told him who had sent us. His eyes flickered and he signed to us to follow him into a room at the rear of the store, where he gave us tea to drink with small sweet cakes. I asked him about boats downriver.

'Why do you want a boat?' he asked warily.

'We wish to reach the coast.'

He looked at me with unblinking eyes. 'Are you fugitives from Tiengfeng?' he demanded. He was a lot brighter than his cousin.

For a moment I hesitated, but there seemed little point in denying it. Sha knew I was a fugitive, because otherwise I wouldn't have been asking for help to reach the coast.

'Yes,' I admitted. 'We're from Tiengfeng.'

'Did you cause all that trouble there?'

'No. That wasn't me. I wasn't even in the city.'

For a moment, I wondered whether he would try to raise the alarm and if I were going to have to murder him, but at last he nodded. 'I believe you,' he said. 'Ting Kai Li would not have sent you if you were an enemy of my country. I have a friend who has junks moving down every day to the coast. I will go and see him. Come back here this evening.'

Worried, we wandered among the ropes and shackles and the rubbish of the riverside all day, then cautiously returned to the shop. We had debated the whole time whether it was wise and whether Sha would have soldiers waiting, but in the end we decided we had to take a chance.

Sha directed us into the room at the back of the shop

again, and showed no sign of enmity or suspicion. 'We will go at midnight,' he said. 'There is a junk leaving in the early hours. They are arranging somewhere for you to hide. In forty-eight hours' time you will be past all the military stations. The junk is due to pass Canton in daylight tomorrow and will stop at Shojien to unload about midday. You will stay on board until dark, when you will be provided with a sampan which you must row yourself. It will be a long row.'

I looked at my broken hands for a moment. 'I shall row,' I said.

'I can help, No Lan,' Tsiu Lin said.

Sha indicated the room. 'You must wait here until midnight,' he said. 'By this time the day after tomorrow you should be safe.'

The two hours till midnight seemed to have leaden feet and I was in a constant sweat of fear in case Sha was bluffing us. But he seemed honest enough and even provided us with a meal of chop suey and gave us rice wine to drink.

He took the boiler suits from us. 'It's as well you wear old clothes,' he said. 'In case you are seen on the river. You must look like people of the river. They say Tai's agents are everywhere.'

He took half of the money we had left from what Fu Man had given us to provide 'squeeze' on the man who owned the junk. 'Save the rest for the junkmaster,' he said. 'He will provide the sampan for you from it.'

At midnight he led us down to the river. The lights were dim now, as people settled to sleep, and the music and the cooking smells were gone. By the river, Sha found a sampan whose owner was prepared to take us out to a junk moored just offshore, and ten minutes later we were clambering aboard.

Sha spoke quietly to the junkmaster, who looked at us quickly. Then I heard Tai's name mentioned, but the junkmaster didn't seem to be arguing. He merely shook hands solemnly with Sha, who bowed to us and disappeared into the darkness.

The light from a lantern indicated an open hatch and a ladder, and we climbed down with the junkmaster. He seemed to be the only person on board. In one of the corners of the hold, there was a crate large enough to sit in, and it was clear people had sat in it before. It stank abominably. There were sacks, an earthenware pot and two tin plates in it. From one corner, a metal stovepipe was attached, I noticed, to the base of a ventilator.

'Many people use,' the junkmaster said. 'You have food?'

I nodded and he seemed satisfied.

Dubiously we climbed inside and sat down, and the junkmaster replaced the side and began piling hides on top of it. The stench became appalling now but there was plenty of air coming down the ventilator. After a while, there were sufficient hides on top of us to deaden most sounds, and we were in complete darkness.

I had a torch and we switched it on long enough to settle ourselves, then we huddled down on the sacks to sleep.

'Forty-eight hours, Tsiu Lin,' I said softly. 'We have forty-eight hours with nothing else to do but hold each other.'

We waited in the darkness, deciding to reserve the torch for emergencies. We were both growing sickeningly aware that if Tai's soldiers decided to search the junk, there would be no means of escape for us. There was also the possibility that the junkmaster, having got us safely into our dark prison, might even at that moment be sending a sampan ashore to summon soldiers.

The thought of Tai still terrified me, because now I was responsible not only for myself but for Tsiu Lin. The fear of her in the hands of such a man sickened me, and the idea of her slender body being beaten as I'd been beaten made me feel physically ill. I had to fight to avoid retching.

Later we heard feet on the deck and in my wretchedness I decided at once that it was Tai's soldiers. But nothing happened, and I realised that after all it was only the crew coming aboard the junk. There was a great deal of clattering, muffled by the hides that had been placed round the crate, then we heard the steady beat of steps backwards and forwards above us and I guessed that the junk was being loaded. The coolies were marching up the gangplank carrying their sacks and bales of hides, singing in the high-pitched two-noted song that accompanied all working coolies in the East; a sad resigned song like the humming of insects, rising and falling, the two notes never ceasing as the men jogged up and down the gangplank with their loads.

Occasionally, dimly, we heard the deep booming note of a ship's siren as a steamer slid past, and from time to time the slap of water against the sides of the junk and the lurch as the vessel moved in another ship's wake. Pungent smells made their way down the ventilator into the crate, and in the darkness it required all my dwindling courage to keep Tsiu Lin from sickness and terror.

Yet we were obviously safe for the moment. We could breathe, we had food, and we had enough room to move a little.

After a while—I judged it several hours—we heard a series of thuds and clanks, all of them muffled by the cargo round the crate, then we heard the thump of the motor and sensed that the junk was moving. It was still pitch dark and I switched on the torch to reassure Tsiu Lin.

She stared at me with wide frightened eyes, her lips parted, and as the light came on, she grabbed at once for my hand. I put my arm round her and drew her to me.

'Be brave, Tsiu Lin,' I urged. 'Be brave.'

The next thirty-six hours seemed like a nightmare. I was afraid all the time that the junkmaster might have spoken with Tai's men and would decide to give us up. Besides the steady drip-drip of fear, draining away courage as if it were a leaking tap, we were also miserably stiff. We had thought at first that we were comfortable, but soon we began to realise that the crate wasn't really big enough to stretch out properly, and eventually we were both constantly shifting restlessly from cramp.

Once I heard Tsiu Lin crying quietly, but when I switched on the torch, she had wiped her eyes and managed to smile at me, though I could see moisture still on her lashes.

'I am all right, No Lan,' she said. 'Don't worry.'

It grew surprisingly hot inside the crate and I began to wonder if we were likely to suffocate. Then I felt Tsiu Lin's body sag slowly against me with the heaviness of exhaustion, and soon afterwards I must have fallen asleep myself.

When I woke, I realised that the junk's motor had stopped and the vessel was motionless again. I heard clanking somewhere, and reverberating thuds that ran through the timbers of the ship and even into the crate.

I switched on the torch. Tsiu Lin was crouched inside the curve of my arm, and I could read the strain on her face.

'I think we've stopped,' I said. 'Perhaps we're there.'

She didn't answer and all my old nightmares returned. Perhaps Tai had stopped the ship and was making a search. My heart was cold inside me and I hardly dared think about it.

We waited, half in dread of Tai's men, half impatiently in case we really had arrived and someone was coming to let us out. Soon we heard the steady beat of feet again on the deck, then the thumpings again from forward. The motor started and we felt the junk in motion once more. I didn't know whether to be overjoyed that the halt had not been caused by Tai's searching soldiers or whether to cry out with misery, because we hadn't yet arrived, and all I could do was try to keep Tsiu Lin's spirits up with a few feeble jokes and a great deal of optimism I didn't feel.

She huddled against me. I pulled her closer, and felt her lips on my cheek. Her mouth sought mine, urgently, desperately, as though she drew strength and courage from the embrace. Then she took my hand and held it against her cheek for a while, before placing it on her breast. I heard her give a deep sigh that seemed to tear her apart.

She didn't complain, however, and how she felt I couldn't know. But I was on the point myself of screaming with fear, misery, frustration and cramp when we heard the thumps again forward and realised the motion of the junk had stopped once more. Again we heard the thud of feet above us, then silence again, and we waited in anguish for relief or discovery. For a long time nothing happened and I wanted to weep with rage. Then we heard voices and realised that the hides were being moved from around the crate.

At last we felt fresh cool air rush in on us. The hold was empty except for the junkmaster. The crew seemed to have gone ashore and he had clearly done the last of the unloading himself. The hides were stacked on each side of the crate so that there was only a small opening to crawl through.

He gestured to us to follow him, but it was dark and difficult. We kept falling over the hides until, eventually, our eyes growing accustomed to the dim light, I saw the hatchway of the hold. I could feel the tension in the junkmaster. I'd been aware of it even in Tsochow, but here it was almost like a battened-down hysteria. He moved jerkily, urging us all the time with signs to hurry, forcing us in front of him with little panic-stricken pushes.

We followed him up a ladder and felt the cool touch of rain on our faces. It seemed bitterly cold up on deck after the stuffiness of the crate, and we were both limping and bowed with stiffness. The junkmaster pointed over the side of the ship and I saw the sampan moored alongside. It was old and smelled of fish.

'Fellah no stop to Kowloon Light.'

I could have told him that myself. I knew the Pearl River at that point as well as he did.

I gave him the rest of the money and helped Tsiu Lin into the sampan. Then, with a wave, the junkmaster unfastened the bow rope and we drifted stern-first away from the ship, pushing ourselves off from the towering sides and slipping under the square high poop.

As we broke free, I felt the wind for the first time. It was coming from the northeast and was bitterly cold. It was helping us south, though, and in addition, it seemed to me that the tide was falling, carrying us with it to the sea. All I had to do was keep the sampan in the middle of the river and out of the way of any traffic.

The swirl of the tide grew swifter with every minute and eventually we were whirling madly downstream. The river was already enormously wide but it was dark enough to be unable to see far. Once I had to work on the stern oar like a madman as we found ourselves being swept down on a huge steamer that was moored in midstream and on another occasion I saw what looked like a small gunboat ahead and had to drag at the oar to carry us away from her. We nearly fouled her anchor chain, but she seemed dead and dark and no one challenged us.

We had almost broken clear and were staring backwards when we came hard up against a buoy. We hit it broadside on and the sampan was almost overturned. Tsiu Lin gave a little scream and clutched at the side as water slopped over her legs. The sampan was old and leaked and I kicked a tin along the bottom boards towards her.

'Bail,' I said roughly, and she picked up the tin and

frantically began to lift the water over the side.

'Slowly,' I advised. 'Don't rush it. Take it easy. You last longer that way and we've a long way to go.'

As we swirled south, I tried to judge where we were by working out the curve of the river, but it was almost impossible in the dark. By this time the tide had grown fierce and was carrying us so swiftly that there was little I could do to give us direction. We were being swept closer and closer to the shore. Dimly, through the growing light, I could see hills, high hills, and began to recognise them as part of the New Territories.

I knew there was bound to be some sort of boom across the river near here and looked out for it. After a while, through the darkness, I made out three naval-type buoy-laying vessels lying in line with what appeared to be a small tug and guessed that this was it. Fortunately, we had a shallow draught, so I steered as best I could for the centre of the gap between the two most widely spaced vessels, believing that there the boom chains would have sagged well below the surface of the water.

As we surged towards them, however, I realised I had misjudged the strength of the tide and we were being carried nearer to the tug than I'd intended. I heard the scrape as the sampan passed over the top of the chains, close by a winking red light. It sounded thunderous in the silence and immediately a door opened on the ship and in the light behind it I saw men's heads. I heard running feet on the decks and a shout, then a beam of light probed the darkness and I guessed it was from something small like an aldis lamp being used as a hand-held searchlight.

Another light, much bigger this time came on, and I heard a shot. It was so unexpected I couldn't believe my ears. Then a machine gun opened up and I saw the spurts of water all round the boat.

'Over the side, Tsiu Lin!' I shouted.

As she half rose, I flung myself at her and we splashed into the water just as bullets began to chip splinters from the stern. We came up on the far side, Tsiu Lin spluttering and gasping in the cold water as she clung to me, and I held on to the side of the drifting sampan in the bitter water until at last the bursts of firing stopped. For a while I heard the men on the ship talking as we moved further away from them. They seemed to think they'd killed us and I heard them laugh. At last, thankfully, the lights went out.

We'd been swept close to the shore now but when I tried to climb back into the boat, I realised that the last few days and the cold had taken away my strength.

'Oh, God!' The words came out in a groan as my muscles failed to work.

I managed to lay my hand on the bow rope and passed it under Tsiu Lin's armpits to hold her secure, then I fought to climb back into the sampan. I managed it at last and struggled to get her back into the boat with me. She had become a dead weight with exhaustion, and gave little whimpering cries as at last I dragged her roughly over the side and we flopped down on the bottom boards, frozen by the biting wind and unable to move. I knew that along the border the Chinese kept fierce dogs against the passage of refugees and I could only hope that the tide would carry us ashore where it was safe.

How long we lay in the bottom of the sampan, soaked and frozen, I don't know, but when I came to, I realised we were motionless alongside a stretch of rocky shore, the boat's prow between a couple of large boulders. The tide had long since turned and was tugging gently at the sampan, swinging it round.

'Tsiu Lin!'

I reached out and shook her, but she seemed to be unconscious. I knew that if I left it long enough, the tide would catch the boat again and carry us right back where we'd come from. I must do something at once. I lifted Tsiu Lin in my arms, and she opened her eyes briefly, the lids fluttering with exhaustion. Then, even as I reached for the oar, I felt the boat lurch free and knew that there wasn't sufficient strength left in my muscles to do anything to stop it being carried out into the river again. I did the only thing I could think of. Staggering to my feet, holding Tsiu Lin to me, I deliberately fell with her over the side into the water.

The shock of the cold river took my breath away and for a moment I lost my grip on her, but as I came to the surface, I felt her struggling feebly beside me and grabbed at her, fighting to keep her head above water. Up to my chest in the water, Tsiu Lin's hair plastered across my face, I fought my way towards the shore, falling again and again as I stumbled on the rocky bed of the river. At last, half-drowned, I managed to grasp the jutting overhang of a bank and drag myself into the shallows, one arm still supporting Tsiu Lin. Desperately slowly, fighting for breath and with the last ounce of my strength, I heaved her on to a little shingle beach where, beyond the reeds, grass and bushes sloped upwards. Gasping, panting, swearing, I dragged her among them.

I fell beside her on the grass; grass that was wet with dew and bitterly cold, but grass that covered dry solid land. Then, with the first light from the east, I saw towers to the north of me, high wooden constructions with roofs that I knew housed searchlights and machine guns. For a moment, the breath catching at my throat, I stared, my teeth chattering with the cold, trying to orientate myself, trying to identify the contours of the land. Then I saw roofs and radar masts and a three-tiered passenger vessel trudging like a beetle across the water in the distance.

I lay on my face, breathing deeply, knowing we were free, knowing that the grass under my broken fingers was free grass that pushed up free blades towards a free sun. Then I heard Tsiu Lin murmuring that ridiculous name Dwight had given me, a name which by this time I accepted as my own.

'No Lan, I think we must be safe.'

I put my arm round her in the growing light, feeling her slender body through the saturated clothes and brushing the wet hair from her eyes. She was crying, deeply, heavily, and with a terrible relief. Then she lifted her head and took my face in her cold trembling hands and covered it with frantic, fluttering, joyous kisses.

X

Within a week of our reaching Hong Kong, the telephone rang in the hotel room where we were staying. It was Esmond.

'Heard you were back,' he said.

My eyes flew across the room to where Tsiu Lin was standing. She was still pale and her eyes looked tired. The first thing I had done when I recovered in the hospital at Rennie's Hill was to draw money from my bank and go to the shops. I'd brought back dresses and underwear that had made her gasp with pleasure as she had sat up in bed.

There had been nothing wrong with either of us except exhaustion and hunger and cold, and when we had recovered a little on the bank where we'd scrambled from the river, we had cleaned ourselves in sea water and begun to climb. There was no path and the undergrowth had been thick, but gradually we had broken into a run, in a kind of panic to make sure we were safe, until we'd been covered with scratches and our clothes had been torn on the thorn bushes. Tired and hungry, we'd come at last to a road, where we'd thumbed a lift to Kowloon. There we caught a bus with several other refugees who'd made it after fifteen hours among the fish in the hold of a fishing vessel and still stank of the cargo.

After two or three days in the hospital where they'd sent us for a checkup, I took her to the Castle Peak Hotel, thinking it was probably the safest I could find and that we could hide there in peace until we could leave the colony. I hadn't expected them to find me so quickly.

My eyes rested on Tsiu Lin as she watched me anxiously. She was wearing a close-fitting high-necked *cheongsam* of fine silk that showed every line of her body, its high neck accentuating her lovely throat. She'd done her hair in a high bun on the top of her head and her pallor was enhanced by the make-up she wore. My heart stopped as I looked at her, as it had done every time, I realised now, since I'd first seen her in Peking. Western aids had made her breathtakingly lovely.

As I stared at her, I became aware of Esmond's voice in my ear.

'You still there?' he was saying irritably.

I started to life. 'Yes,' I said shortly. 'I'm still here.'

'As I was saying, I heard you were back.'

I was still staring at Tsiu Lin. The two or three days we'd had alone had been achingly beautiful and nobody, not Esmond, not Armour, not even Dwight was going to take them away from me. Tsiu Lin was looking at me with a small worried frown, and I smiled reassuringly at her. I was full of confidence.

'Yes,' I said slowly into the telephone. 'I'm back. How did you find out?'

'Various sources.' Esmond sounded smug.

I decided it must be the bank or one of the shops we'd been in. Doubtless he had his contacts everywhere. I hadn't bothered to think about them, preferring to spend the days with Tsiu Lin, watching her delight at the clothes I bought her, and self-satisfied with the pleasure she seemed to find in me.

At first, she'd found it difficult to realise she was free to do as she pleased, free to think what she liked, say what she liked, wear what she liked, make love when she liked.

I'd introduced her to the dog and she'd laughed as the little blighter had tried to lick her face. But it was the bed that had pleased her most. I don't think she'd seen one as big ever before. I'd made them show me all the rooms in the hotel they had free, and had picked the most lavish. Over the last three or four days, the bed had become a sort of talisman of freedom to her, and we used it well to catch up on a lot of sleep and a lot of lovemaking.

Esmond was growing irritated on the other end of the telephone again. 'Hello?' he said fretfully.

'Yes,' I said. 'I'm still here.'

'Thought you'd gone to sleep.' He paused, then his voice came eagerly. 'Dwight's back in Hong Kong.'

'Is he?'

'Bit of luck he happened to be here when you arrived, isn't it?'

'Yes, isn't it?'

'How about coming round?'

'I'll be round,' I said. 'All in good time.'

'Fine.' Esmond sounded pleased. 'No hurry, old boy. Always here.'

I put the telephone down and turned towards Tsiu Lin.

'Is it trouble?' she asked.

I shook my head. 'No. Not trouble. There'll be no more trouble of that sort again—ever. I have to report, that's all. Tomorrow will do. I've a lot of things to take care of before then. I have cables to send. Things like that. If there's to be no more trouble, I must make sure of it.'

She nodded and mixed me a drink. She had already become surprisingly adept at it. I placed it beside me on the table, wondering if she'd really taken to the dog and if the dog would really take to her. They seemed to be doing all right so far and I was determined to have the little blighter back. This time he wouldn't have to live in a flat, either, but somewhere he could run in freedom across the fields and through the flowers. He had endured my absences often enough.

'Come here, Tsiu Lin,' I said.

She came towards me meekly and stood in front of me.

'Look at me.'

She lifted her eyes to my face. There was still a hint of doubt and disbelief behind the happiness. I had to conquer it.

'Not just with your eyes, Tsiu Lin,' I said. 'With your head. Always with your head. It's a beautiful head.'

Her head lifted higher.

'That's it,' I said. 'I'm proud of you, Tsiu Lin, and you can hold it high. Now I want to see you smile. You must learn to smile again, because you're beautiful. You're the most beautiful woman I've ever known and I need your smile.'

The small smile which had started on her lips had spread and widened until it was full of warmth and love.

'But you must never smile like that at other men,' I said gravely. 'A small smile, perhaps. But *that* one is for me—and preferably alone, in bed.'

She stared at me for a second, still smiling, then the smile died abruptly and tears came into her eyes and she flung herself into my arms, her head on my chest, her body racked with sobs.

'There'll never be any other man, No Lan,' she said. 'You are my man and I am your woman.'

I kissed her gently. 'Tomorrow afternoon,' I said, 'we fly

to India. And from India to England. From there—well, anywhere perhaps. Tomorrow morning, there are certain legalities to go through, including one in church with you. Tonight, there's nothing but you and me. Except dinner, and we'll make it a royal performance. Dressed like that, they'll wonder who the hell I'm with. And then we'll come back here for coffee'—I smiled—'and whatever else might transpire.'

She lifted her head again. She'd stopped crying.

'You are pleased with me?' she asked.

'I'm pleased with you,' I said. 'I'm so pleased, my heart feels like cracking and I can't draw sufficient breath. I don't think I shall ever properly understand my luck.'

Dwight was as smooth as ever when I called on him. It was late in the afternoon but, in spite of the heat, his clothes were as immaculate as usual. He held out his hand, smiling, then drew it back quickly.

'What happened to your hand?'

'Small payment for what I did,' I said. 'You've probably never realised it, but people like me get paid twice. We draw money from you, but from the other side we get our payment in small shocks to the system. Over the years they take their toll. Courage is an expendable thing and these are the leakages.'

Dwight looked at me curiously. He offered me a chair without saying anything and I sat down as he took his place on the other side of the desk and rang a bell. Esmond came in, beaming, and held out his hand. Like Dwight, he stared at my fingers.

'What happened?' he asked.

'He's just been telling me about it,' Dwight said smoothly. 'A little homily, in fact. What did they do it with?'

'A rifle butt.'

'And Mitchill?'

'Mitchill will give you no more trouble,' I said. 'I did the job. I've simply come for my money.'

Dwight reached into the drawer and took out an envelope, which he tossed across the desk towards me. He never worried about the salaries he paid. He seemed to regard money with some contempt. I suppose it came from having plenty himself.

'The cheque's inside,' he said. 'It's substantial. There should be quite a bit in that account of yours now.'

'There is. I've made sure there is.'

Dwight smiled. 'I like to hear that sort of talk,' he said. 'Makes for security ... and trustworthiness. There'll be a little something in the Honours List, too. Of course, it'll be for political services or something vague like that, but you'll know what it's for and so will we. It'll go with the other one you got.'

'And everyone will think I was secretary to some bloody politician, I suppose?' I said.

Dwight shrugged. 'Can't do any better, I'm afraid. After all, we can hardly admit what you've been up to, can we? What did you get up to, anyway? When you didn't turn up, we decided we'd lost you, but as the Great Panjandrum seemed to remain hale and hearty and we heard nothing of Mitchill being put on trial, we came to the conclusion you'd done the job and waited for you to reappear. When you didn't we decided you were in trouble, or dead. Then, bingo, out of the blue, we get news from the police that there's a chap called Nolan in hospital here, accompanied, we were told, by a damsel of more than fair proportions.'

'Keep your hands off her, Dwight,' I said quietly.

He said nothing, but I saw his eyebrows lift.

'Hadn't you better tell us all about it?' he said.

'I got a little involved in a counter-revolution in the Tiengfeng-Chengsha-Sukien area.'

Dwight's jaw dropped. 'Did you start that?'

'Not exactly. Not directly. But I was mixed up in it. You needn't worry, though. You're not involved.'

Dwight looked relieved. 'Who's the girl you're staying with at the Castle Peak?' he asked. 'One of Mao's deviationists?'

'Yes,' I said, and Dwight looked startled.

'Didn't know they bred 'em as beautiful as that,' he observed. 'I saw you in the restaurant.'

'You would.'

I rose to my feet. 'I'm leaving now. I'm flying to England.'

Dwight coughed. 'Er, there's just one thing.'

I stopped by the door. I knew what was coming.

'There's something just come up,' he said. 'Not much. Saigon again.'

I smiled. 'Too late, Dwight. I'm leaving for England.'

'With the girl?'

'With the girl.'

He stared at me, his eyes suddenly as cold as little flints of ice. 'You can't just bring someone out of China like that. She'll have to be screened. We'll have to come and see her.'

'I've got a gun in my luggage,' I said. 'One that you gave me some time ago. If anyone comes near that girl or tries any nonsense I'll shoot him. As sure as God I'll shoot him, Dwight.'

'Don't talk rot, old boy.'

'Do I normally talk rot?'

'No. Not as a rule.'

'You've got to take my word for her,' I insisted. 'If you want to make enquiries, make 'em, but don't bother her. Is that understood?'

He nodded. He looked a little puzzled. 'Something's happened to you, Dempsey. You're different. You've grown up suddenly. Is it this girl?'

'I married her this morning,' I said. 'She's waiting outside now in a taxi with the dog and a few of my possessions. Since you sold most of 'em there weren't many except what Esmond was keeping. He's still got them. I've arranged for all my business here to be handled by a lawyer.'

Dwight stared at me, a faint suggestion of contempt on his face, as though I'd done something despicable.

'You can't really bow out as easily as all that.'

I smiled and fished in my wallet. Taking a slip of paper from it, I laid it in front of him. 'You'd better read that,' I said. 'You've no longer got any claim on me. If you look at it you'll see it says "Dempsey, Harry Graham. Following a motor accident. No flowers." It's from *The Times*. You put it in. I can't see how you can have a claim on a dead man, Dwight.'

Dwight was still quite sure of himself. 'Chap called Nolan's been on our payroll for a while, though,' he said. 'In fact, you'll find that cheque's made out to Eugene Patrick Nolan. With the Saigon thing coming up, I thought it might be as well.'

I placed two sheets of buff paper in front of him. 'These are two cables,' I said. 'One's an instruction to my bankers in London to pay a bill for an insertion in *The Times*. The other's for another death notice. It'll have gone in this morning. Doubtless you'll be seeing it in time. It says "In China, three weeks ago, Eugene Patrick Nolan." Or words to that effect. He's dead, Dwight.'

I was enjoying myself now, and I forestalled any reply by going on quickly. 'And if you try to stop this cheque, on the grounds that Nolan's dead, too, I shall take pleasure in informing the Chinese just how much you *were* involved in that little insurrection that started in Tiengfeng. I know the exact details, remember, and they'd believe me. It finally spread across the whole of the province and, unhappily, there were a great many deaths, not only among its sympathisers, but also among the comrades. An explosives factory was destroyed and a whole town laid waste. They'd be glad to lay the blame for it at your door. I'm sure they're looking for a reason to say it was started by capitalist reactionary tools from the West. This time, instead of you having *me* by the short hairs, Dwight, I've got you. I'm going home. I shall probably open a fish-and-chip shop or a whelk stall, but it'll be as far from London as I can make it. It might even be Switzerland. A lot of people like to say rude things about the Swiss, and they probably deserve 'em, but they've got no race problems and no decaying remains of an empire. They haven't even got leather jackets and rioting students. They have got peace, though, and that's what I'm looking for. My luck's run out. I'm finished.'

Dwight looked startled and angry. He started to say something, but I didn't listen. I got up and slammed the door in his face.

As I left, he crossed to the window. Esmond followed him. Later, in a letter he told me what had happened.

They saw me enter an open car in the street below. Tsiu Lin was waiting in the front seat, and when I appeared her face changed at once. From anxiety, it became radiant as I climbed in beside her, and they saw her hand touch mine, as though reassuring herself that I was real. For a second, my fingers closed over hers.

'My God,' Esmond said enviously. 'Where did he pick *her* up?'

'One of Mao's deviationists,' Dwight said.

'No wonder he's anxious to settle down.'

Dwight gestured as the car drew away from the curb. 'He'll be back,' he said.

But it was more to save his face than because he believed it, Esmond said. He'd seen the look that had passed between me and Tsiu Lin and he was only indulging in wishful thinking.

By the time Esmond left, he'd taken out a file bearing my name and was beginning to set the papers in it on fire with his cigarette lighter. He dropped them, still burning, into a metal waste-paper basket.

'You writing him off?' Esmond asked.

Dwight lifted his head, he said, and gave him that cold stare that we'd all experienced at some time or other.

'He was written off,' he said, 'the minute he met that girl. People with girls who look like that are no good to us, Esmond.' He dropped the last of the papers into the basket and stirred the ashes with a ruler, so that the office was filled with acrid grey smoke.

'Finis,' he said. 'End. Who have we got who can take his place?'